Credits:

Edited by Linda Ingmanson

Cover Design by Deranged Doctor Design

Trident
Rescue

ENEMY
hold

ALEX LIDELL

Young Adult Fantasy Novels

TIDES

FIRST COMMAND (Audiobook available)

AIR AND ASH (Audiobook available)

WAR AND WIND (Audiobook available)

SEA AND SAND (Audiobook available)

SCOUT

TRACING SHADOWS (Audiobook available)

UNRAVELING DARKNESS (Audiobook available)

TILDOR

THE CADET OF TILDOR

SIGN UP FOR NEW RELEASE NOTIFICATIONS at https://links.
alexlidell.com/News

JAZ

Grit pressed into Jaz Keasley's fingers as she worked more of her hand into the groove of the granite cliff she hung from. The cool breeze kissed her face, considerately clearing her forehead of the few loose wisps of hair that had managed to escape her high ponytail. Jaz drew a deep breath before pressing her hips toward the stone as her left foot skimmed the surface in search of a foothold. This part of the climb was the trickiest. After too many attempts and a near tumble, the rubber edge of her climbing shoe finally caught a small edge of rock—but that was all she needed. With a powerful shove of her muscles, Jaz hauled herself up and over.

"Show-off," Sebastian called from the ledge below as he took up the slack in the belay line.

Jaz put an anchor into the stone and clipped her rope through it, then added an extra one to make things easier for Sebastian. Even though her climbing partner had more strength and several inches on her in height and reach, Jaz was the better climber—and Almagre Run was all technique.

At twenty-five Jaz led the US women's division in competitive rock climbing and had no piece of gear that wasn't provided by a sponsor. Now she was training for Clash of the Titans, an exhibition event that would, in all likelihood, define the next stage of her career—if she had one. Her chest constricted at the thought, the anxiety not unlike that of a division one football star balancing on that precipice between an NFL draft and end of play.

"I'm coming down to do it again," Jaz called and rechalked her hands from the pouch hanging off her harness.

"You're a masochist."

She snorted and made her way back, landing softly beside Sebastian. "You want to try? Just keep your hips close to the rock and watch out for the lighter-color holds. They aren't nearly as stable as they look."

"Easy for the Vector Ascent poster girl to say." Sebastian stretched his back and looked wearily up the mountain. They'd been at it for over six hours, and tracks of dirt and sweat marked his too-pretty face. With his glittering green eyes, athletic build, and just enough freckles, Sebastian was attractive enough to have several modeling agencies vying for his attention.

Too bad he didn't play for her team.

If he had, Jaz could imagine setting up an arrangement with him. They had enough trust between them to literally put their lives into each other's hands every training day, and Sebastian's lean, lithe muscles would certainly make for a delightful time.

Oh, well—perhaps it was for the best after all. Sebastian went through men like kids went through Easter candy.

"You spend too much time doing this," Sebastian said, interrupting Jaz's thoughts.

"Doing what?"

He started tying in with a retraced figure-eight knot. "Hauling your ass all over various mountain ranges."

"So do you," she shot back.

"True, but I also spend time doing activities that don't require life-saving equipment to be attached to my person. Condoms notwithstanding."

That was the thing about Sebastian. He said what he thought, and he referred to sex as casually as he referred to eating, walking, or chewing gum. He also knew when to keep his mouth shut, which made him privy to a great deal more of Jaz's life than anyone else in Denton Valley.

She wiggled her brows. "Are you offering?"

Sebastian rolled his eyes. "I mean it, Jaz. You've made your life about the upcoming Clash of the Titans, and it's not healthy. Being consumed with winning is fine short-term but you do it to the exclusion of all else for months on end. There's always another event you're training for in the wings. You never let yourself enjoy any of the other facets of life available to you. What about recreational time? What about having fun?"

Jaz waved her hand at the Colorado mountain range stretching before them. "This *is* fun."

"Sure," he conceded. "But it's not naked fun. Nothing beats naked fun."

"You're nuts."

"No. I *like* nuts. Of all varieties, shapes, and sizes."

"Good for you." Jaz played with the nylon edge of one of her neon-orange ropes. She couldn't remember the last time she'd been out on a good date. Or even a decent one. But things were complicated just now. "What are you really getting at, Bastian?"

"What I'm saying…" He gave her an individual nudge for each of those three specific words. "Is that you have no extracurricular social life apart from a few girlfriends and myself. And that, my dear Jaz, is not the healthiest approach to having a rich and fulfilled existence."

"You know what else isn't healthy for a fulfilled existence? Defaulting on my student loans, losing my apartment, and telling my financial genius brother and A-list acting parents that I'm broke —which is exactly what's going to happen if I fall flat in the Clash of the Titans and Vector Ascent drops me like Arc'teryx did." Aside from Jaz's attorney, Sebastian was the only one who knew the full extent of her situation, so she felt no need to mince words. "Less talk, more climbing."

"Fine, but leave Friday next week free. I see I need to take your boy situation into my own hands."

3

"Very funny."

"I'm serious. I've been making a list, actually. We'll start with Devante—he showed up at one of our climbing happy hours that She Who Must Train All the Time missed and started drooling when I mentioned I know Vector Ascent's poster girl."

"And what else do you know about Devante?"

"His measurements."

Jaz rolled her eyes.

"Let's not confuse bedroom gymnastics with matrimony. Different qualifications."

"Whatever." Waving her hand at him, Jaz checked her harness and stepped back up to the stone. "On belay."

After finishing up for the day, Jaz and Sebastian hiked back to the car, their cell phones waking with insistent beeps the instant they crossed into a reception zone.

"Let me guess. You've missed a call from a modeling agency, the evening's date, and..." Jaz squinted in mock thought. "And a message from another date that you forgot about. You double-booked."

Sebastian grinned. "I never double-book—at least not by accident." He took out his phone and scrolled through the messages. "No dice today. Just a reminder from my dentist's office. My turn. I bet you have messages from—"

A credit card billing office, an upset landlord, and a line of credit declination, Jaz thought.

"A lawn-care salesman, Steven Spielberg, and—"

"Kyan."

"Spielberg is more likely."

"No, I mean Kyan really did call. *And* text." Jaz flashed the phone screen to Sebastian as proof. Kyan, Jaz's older brother, was notoriously bad about reaching out to her. In fact, the last time she remembered him calling and texting was to announce his son's healthy birth—and that was probably his wife, Ivy, using the phone. This time, the message was significantly more ominous.

My place. Now. Mom and Dad are here.

A thousand scenarios rushed through her at once, each

4

shredding her soul with shards of terror. Her finger hovered over the Call button, but for the first time in her life, Jaz couldn't bring herself to press it. But then the phone rang again, Kyan's name flashing on the screen.

"What's going on?" Jaz demanded.

"I'll tell you when you come." Kyan had slipped into what Jaz thought of as his *careful* voice.

"And you won't tell me over the phone?"

"I'd really rather not." A sigh. "Just get your ass over here."

Jaz didn't remember getting into the car or the drive itself, didn't remember whatever it was Sebastian had said after she read the text aloud. One moment, she was standing in the glorious expanse of the Colorado mountains, and the next, she was pounding her fist against the front door of Kyan's split level.

Kyan opened the door, his broad shoulders filling the frame. Six years older, he was Jaz's perfect opposite. Where Jaz was petite, Kyan was physically imposing. Where she was fiercely independent, he was a disciplined Navy SEAL. Where Kyan had a preternatural understanding of financial markets that let him make money from money, Jaz apparently had an equally great knack for investing in just the wrong thing. At the moment, however, none of that mattered.

"What's going on?" Jaz demanded, taking in Kyan's tense face. "Is someone sick? Is it cancer? Did the baby—"

"Everyone is all right."

She shoved him. Hard. Right in his muscled chest. "Do you have any idea the terror your little text put me through?"

The asshole didn't even rock back on his heels from the impact. "Hopefully enough to make you reasonable for a few minutes."

Kyan bladed his body to let Jaz into the house—and right into their mother's welcoming arms.

"Jazzie." Lola Keasley placed her hand on Jaz's cheek. "It is so good to see you, honey. How is school?"

"It's great," she lied, throwing Kyan a hard glance in a reminder to keep his mouth shut. She hadn't told her parents she was taking a year off, and this wasn't the time—though not even Kyan knew

5

about her financial destitution. She hugged her mother back tightly, then wrapped her arms around her father, who'd also come up to crowd the doorway. "Are you guys all right?" she asked into his shoulder. "Kyan scared the hell out of me."

"Good," said a low male voice from inside the living room. As her parents stepped away, Jaz's gaze came to rest on the last person in the universe she wanted to see.

Liam Rowen, one of her older brother's best friends and the most chauvinistic, patronizing man in the universe, filled the threshold between the living area and kitchen. Dressed in a black silk shirt that fell over chiseled muscle, Liam managed to radiate the kind of arrogance that would make Hollywood proud. Except, unlike the actors who starred in her father's movies, the former SEAL had the experience to back up his silent claims of leashed violence.

And not just in actual combat theater.

Liam's preference for being a *dominating* partner was the best-known secret in Denton Valley, with gorgeous women literally dropping to their knees for a chance at his attention. Typically, Jaz had nothing but encouragement for whatever ways consenting adults found their mutual pleasure—but with Liam, it wasn't a fair playing field. His strong jaw, panther-fluid body, and all-seeing hazel eyes created an aura of intensity that melted most people's common sense. Add in his legendary military history, successful private security business, and popular night club, and it was no wonder that Liam Rowen always got his way.

"What is *he* doing here?" Jaz asked her brother as they walked into the living room. When she passed the stairs, cooing sounds trickled from the second-floor nursery where Ivy was probably putting down the baby.

"Why don't we all sit down?" Lola sat on the overstuffed brown couch and crossed her long legs. Model turned actress and now a head of her own agency, Lola was never anything less than perfect. Or less than dramatic. Pulling Jaz to sit beside her, she gave her a tight smile. "I'm afraid our support for Girls Aflame has been gaining quite a bit of media attention."

"The nonprofit working to expand girls' education?" Jaz frowned. Lola's modeling agency had always made significant donations to Girls Aflame, and Jaz helped raise awareness by talking up the organization in interviews. "Wasn't media attention the whole point?"

"Yes, but—"

"But that very success has drawn the opposition's attention," Liam said, bullying his way into the conversation. All right, maybe he wasn't bullying, but he hadn't been invited either.

Striding over to the coffee table, Liam tossed a page with cut-out newspaper print on the faux-aged wood. "This came to your parents' house."

TELL YOUR SLUT DAUGHTER TO STOP DOING A MAN'S JOB. IT'S FOR HER OWN SAFETY. GIRLS AFLAME = GIRLS IN FLAMES.

Jaz pushed the paper back at Liam. "I'm the only female climber in the Clash of the Titans, and Robillard—the climber I replaced—was a fan favorite. Half the climbing gossip on the internet has claimed for years that I've slept my way to the top. The other half is too busy criticizing everything from my technique to my favorite color.

"This isn't just a complaint. It's a threat," Lola said.

"Have you received anything similar?" Liam asked.

Jaz shrugged. "I've been getting hate mail for years. Find a sin, and I've been accused of it. When I signed with Vector, we agreed they'd screen the mail for me."

"So you don't even *know* whether someone is after you?" Her mother threw up her hands. "You've been playing an ostrich. Head in the sand. Good God!"

And this is exactly why I don't tell you things. "Hate mail comes with the job, Mom. Don't tell me it's any different in Hollywood."

"Don't you go turning things around on me, Jazmine. You have no idea what I do."

"Point being, with all this rock-climbing business, you've become more and more prominent in the public eye, Jazmine," her father put in, his tone judgmental. Hugh Keasley had never approved of her propensity to hang off cliffs. Ironic since he'd been just fine with her being in front of a television camera as a kid. Also, no matter what, he insisted on calling her by the Disney character name they'd christened her after. "And with you taking up the Girls Aflame torch this year, we're worried for your safety."

"If this note has you so worried, have you spoken with the police?" Jaz asked.

"They're useless," Hugh replied automatically. "As usual."

"Or maybe they just recognize bullshit better than you do."

Liam raised his hand, breaking into the argument. "For the police to be in a position to act, the threat has to be both credible and specific. The fact that this isn't actionable for the police force doesn't make it false."

"That's what I said." Hugh stood behind Lola and put his hands on her shoulders. "We'd like for you to bow out of the Clash of the Titans. Take a year off. Get out of the public eye. Focus on your degree."

No wonder Kyan wouldn't say anything over the phone—he'd known Jaz wouldn't have shown up if she knew the intended direction of the coming train wreck. "You want me to bow out of a career-defining event because some mental case mailed you a mean note?" she asked patiently.

"Don't make light of this," Hugh shot back. "You're getting too old for this flippancy."

Lola reached up to take her husband's hand, her voice softer than Hugh's. "If we didn't think this situation was worrisome, we wouldn't have flown out here. If you won't do it for yourself, do it for us."

Jaz's blood pounded through her, but she made herself keep her tone in check. "So you're shutting down production of *Her Dream*?" she asked, though of course she knew the answer. Hugh's upcoming blockbuster was well into production, with shooting set to start the following month and Lola cast in a prominent role.

"That's different." Hugh's voice went from calm to furious in a matter of heartbeats, proving his reputation as one of Hollywood's most short-tempered producers. "We have security and a major contract. You have a goddamned hobby that you should have grown out of a decade ago." He glared at Kyan. "I told you she wouldn't be reasonable."

At least Kyan had the decency to look uncomfortable. He was a hero for joining the SEALs and purposely putting himself into harm's way. She was an irrational brat for following an athletic dream. For two people who'd made their careers on female empowerment films, her parents' irony would be hysterical if it wasn't so hurtful.

Kyan raised a brow. Despite the mortar round scars that marked one side of his face and disappeared into the collar of his shirt, he still had a model's body. After marrying Ivy and having baby Bar, he'd come out of his cocoon of personal misery and back into the public eye, working with the Wounded Warriors and other programs aimed at helping veterans. "More accurately, I told you that asking Jaz to walk away from climbing was a fool's errand."

For a second, Jaz thought that Kyan was actually on her side. But then he kept speaking.

"Liam will put a security detail on her. It'll be fine, Dad."

Jaz spun on him. It was one thing to hear Hugh's typical chauvinistic tirade, but it was another thing altogether to let Kyan get away with it.

"This family meeting is over," she said. "Kyan, Liam, run along and let the grandparents coo over the baby."

"Not entirely your call." Liam, who'd been blissfully quiet, now crossed his arms over his chest, which made his shirt stretch over his biceps. "If your parents contract Trident Security for a protection detail, I don't need your consent to have my men keep an eye on you. Of course, if you hold the contract instead, the security detail can integrate better with your lifestyle preference."

"My preference is for you to go to hell."

"I said better integrate, not forge a new reality."

"And here I thought you only bullied willing victims."

"Keep thinking. It will get easier with practice."

Kyan snorted back a laugh, then turned to Jaz. "Listen, this *thing* is happening. You know Girls Aflame in general has been drawing attention, and Dad isn't going to back down until things settle. It will make your life a great deal simpler if you just contract with Liam's guys. They'll do the job either way, but I guarantee you'll find it less intrusive to be their boss instead of their target."

Heat and fury filled Jaz's blood. She didn't have the money to hire Liam's company even if she was inclined to, which she wasn't. Not to appease her overprotective father's latest whim. But if this Liam-Hugh-Kyan combo thought she was going to make tailing her easy, they were in for a rude awakening.

2

LIAM

"So how much should I be worried?" Kyan asked Liam as they slid into their regular booth at the back of the North Vault seating area. Around them, the aromas of freshly sliced citrus fruits commingled with the tang of rum, tequila, and other liquors. With its subtle indirect lighting and blue-on-blue color scheme, the Vault managed to be upscale and sexy at the same time. Liam had designed every part of the club to create a sense of a world within a world. An escape for people needing it. The drinks were quality, the sound system the best Denton Valley had to offer, and the booths both roomy and private.

"About the threatening letter? I'd call it a low-risk, high-impact scenario at this point. But Jaz has had an incredible year. She's public and she's vocal. Hell, Vector Ascent just put up billboards of her modeling the latest gear." The one on the local freeway made Liam's body tighten each time he passed it. "She underestimates the amount of unwanted attention that level of notoriety attracts. Whoever authored that particular note might not come calling, but drunk idiots certainly will."

Liam didn't add that for all her athletic prowess, Jaz Keasley was small. She might be able to handle herself on a mountain face, but cornered in an alley with a few drunks was an entirely different matter. Liam had seen the effects of large opponents against smaller prey enough times for it to stay seared into his memory. Though he tried to stay cool and rational about the whole thing with Jaz, he was naturally protective when it came to women. Especially his best friend's younger sister.

The younger sister who'd somehow grown from a scrawny annoyance into a lithe, strikingly gorgeous woman with her large dark eyes, suntanned skin, and a sprite's mischievous gaze that turned heads. Headstrong, petite, and reckless, Jaz wasn't at all Liam's type. She also hated Liam's guts. Which all made his cock's tendency to awaken when Jaz was around absolutely infuriating. Not that Kyan needed to ever, *ever* know that.

"Why didn't she take ownership of the contract for herself?" Liam asked, more harshly than he'd intended. He'd been certain she would. It had been her logically best option. Hire the security team, then promptly order them to go to hell. They wouldn't have, but Liam was prepared to deal with that problem once his people were in place.

As it was, Jaz simply walked out on the lot of them.

"Jaz is competitive." Kyan shifted a large shoulder. "Maybe acquiring anything felt like losing."

Great. More pride than sense. "I'll have a team together by tonight, but I'm not charging your parents. Or Jaz, for that matter, if she ever sees reason."

"Trust me, her family can afford it." Unlike Liam, who'd grown up dirt poor, Kyan's family had always had money.

"So can I."

"I know, but paying for something gives a sense of control. That's a great deal more important than a few thousand dollars." Kyan's tense face said he was dead serious. "I'd consider it a personal favor if you charged them."

Liam understood the need for control, though he still hated taking money from his best friend's family. After the whole thing blew over, he'd donate whatever they paid him to Girls Aflame.

"Incoming, five o'clock." Kyan motioned almost imperceptibly behind Liam.

In the reflection from the window, Liam saw a tall blonde woman with long legs, a generous bust, and a sashay that would make a catwalk proud. While he couldn't make out the woman's face, he had a good idea who it probably was—though he hoped he was wrong.

"Liam," Sandy's melodic voice called. So much for being wrong.

Kyan raised a brow as if to say, *Called it, didn't I?* To Kyan's credit, Sandy was exactly Liam's type—tall enough that she could almost look him in the eye, jaw-droppingly gorgeous, and, given the right atmosphere, generously submissive.

Kyan put a palm on the table, signaling his intent to leave Liam to his guest.

Liam slid his fingers across the edge, an answering request for Kyan to stay put. Great as everything about Sandy was, Liam just couldn't bring himself to be interested. He smiled and stood to kiss Sandy's cheek. "Good evening, Sandy. Can I get you a drink?"

Sandy's smile faltered. She knew Liam well enough to know that if any sexual play was in the cards for the evening, he'd never be offering her alcohol. It was a hard-and-fast rule he never compromised on.

"There's a get-together at Gordon's this weekend," she said, clearly switching tactics. "You've been missed."

Gordon lived at the edge of Denton Valley and hosted kink-based parties about once a month. Liam had stopped going over six months ago, a few months after he'd stopped hosting his own on special evenings at the North Vault. He was tired of playing—which frustrated him more than anyone else. Yet for some godforsaken reason, perfectly gorgeous women like Sandy, who genuinely enjoyed his taking charge, no longer aroused any interest from his mind or body.

"I'd love to, but unfortunately, work is keeping me here," he told Sandy, who hung around for a few more moments before making her way back to the expansive dance floor. As she was leaving, Liam signaled the bartender for a Grey Goose vodka straight up and left the drink at the edge of the table, where everyone could see. If Kyan noticed the move, he gave no sign of it.

That was one of the reasons Liam loved him.

WHEN LIAM LEFT North Vault to take the monthly family Zoom call his mother insisted on, he wished he'd drunk more of the Goose. But it wouldn't really have helped. Nothing helped. Resigning himself to the inevitable, Liam dropped into a leather wingback chair beside his bedroom window and powered up his laptop, his gaze lingering on the outside. This room faced out on the Denton Valley park, so a section of meadows and trees ringed by businesses appeared like an illusion from his twelfth-story view. Add in the crown of the Colorado Mountains as a backdrop and the place was the perfect mix of nature and civilization.

"Liam, good evening." A familiar middle-aged face filled the screen, tugging at Liam's attention. Before he could answer, Patti Rowen turned away and yelled into the background. "Liam's on Zoom, Lisa."

This was how the call typically went. His mother coming online first, then demanding his sister jump on too. He suspected Patti thought he and Lisa would never speak otherwise. And she was probably right. Much of the distance between Liam and his family had been put there by choice.

First by their choice, when Patti and Lisa sent him away to military school. And now that he was grown, his.

"I'm on, Ma." Lisa appeared on the screen, splitting the Zoom session. Despite living with their mother, she was connecting from her own room.

A beat of uncomfortable silence passed. Then his mother forced a smile. "How is everything in Denton? I see you've started to expand internationally?"

Apparently, Patti was keeping up with Trident Security's website. She didn't need to have bothered. A parent either cared about her kid, or she didn't—and she'd made herself clear when Liam was twelve.

"It's all fine," he told her.

"Are you sure it's not too early for the international angle while you're still adjusting to incorporating the search and rescue into Trident Security? I still don't see why you took on that project. The Rescue was just fine the way it was."

"The Rescue needs more people," Liam said with exaggerated patience. "And having people, requires infrastructure." When Cullen Hunt had originally set up the Rescue, he, Eli, Kyan, and Liam had all taken a couple of shifts a week to keep up their skills. Now, with the guys starting families, they could no longer dedicate the kind of time a consistent search-and-rescue outfit required. Not that he wanted to get into the details of that with Patti. "How are you?" he asked instead. "Are you going to do the Charlevoix this year, Leece?"

The Charlevoix Marathon was a ten-kilometer course that tracked along Lake Michigan. His sister had been competing in it over the past three years, and while she'd finished, she'd never won any of the top prizes. She lacked the drive.

A familiar pang of guilt raked through Liam's chest—getting assaulted at fifteen did that to a person. Worse still, he was there when it happened and could do nothing to stop it.

"Fine." Lisa's voice was polite but tight. It was a subtle thing. Something others might find difficult to detect but Liam picked up anytime he spoke to her.

"Ann Arbor is beautiful in the spring. You should come see it." This was his mother's latest refrain. He'd been raised in poverty within the confines of Flint, Michigan, but paid to move Patti and Lisa to the much more desirable Ann Arbor as his first major undertaking once his business took off. The mortgage and utility bills went directly to his credit card. "We could hike together. You still like hiking, don't you?"

"We may all be hiking soon," said Lisa. "The car needs new tires."

"We'll replace the tires, dear," Patti assured her.

Lisa snorted. "With what money?"

Liam kept his face impassive. He sent his mother and sister a monthly stipend, but Lisa had never seen a dollar that she didn't immediately spend.

"The car is fine," Patti said soothingly. "We can take care of—"

"She means we can leave it as is," Lisa cut in. "Do you want your mother driving with dangerous tires?"

Liam sighed. "Send me the bill. I'll take care of it."

"You just had to make us beg, didn't you?"

Liam ignored that. His mother did too. In fact, she pretended that everything was wonderful and launched into a general monologue of some sort. Maybe because he'd already used his patience quotient up with Jaz or maybe because dealing with these two was perpetually stressful, but Liam muted the sound and stared out the window for a few heartbeats. His family was a complicated thing. Liam's father had walked out on Patti when Liam had been a toddler. As a single mom, Patti worked two jobs to keep Liam and Lisa fed, and the three of them had been close until that time when Liam was eleven and Lisa fifteen. When he'd been unable to stop the drunken rich kid who'd barged into their house thinking Lisa owed him something.

The kid's parents threw money at Patti. She took it. Told Lisa and Liam to shut up about what happened. Lisa did. Liam didn't. So at twelve, he got sent off to military school, with the rich kid's parents covering the tuition. So long as he didn't come back. Not even for vacation.

Though he'd found his calling in the SEALs, the bitter taste of an eleven-year-old's failure and a twelve-year-old's betrayal always returned to sour his tongue during these weekly calls. Letting out a lengthy exhale, Liam clicked the sound back on to catch his mother's clumsy rambling midway through.

"…such a pretty little thing. Having grandchildren to dote on is such a gift, you know."

Ah, the mention of grandkids. The older he became, the more frequently she mentioned this. Patti never came right out and asked if he was dating or serious about anyone. Instead, she dropped lines about the joy of babies in a continuation of the Rowen line. As if a squalling infant could fix anything.

As if he were a fit partner for any woman—at least his unsuitability for a relationship was the one thing he and Lisa agreed on.

He peered at his watch, assured himself that a respectable amount of time had passed, and barged in with a work excuse the next time Patti paused for breath.

~

THE TIMER BUZZED JUST as Liam blocked Aiden's roundhouse and extended a spinning back kick into his abdomen. Aiden grunted as he stepped back, and Liam shook out his forearm, which still ached from connecting with Aiden's shin. Aiden, who'd joined Trident Security Group a year ago, was proving to be as damn good in hand-to-hand combat as he was with a firearm.

"Yer in a mood." Aiden's Scottish burr sounded musical despite the fatigue. With the man's seemingly easygoing disposition, people often underestimated the steel beneath. In truth, the former member of the Scottish Black Watch could take—and dole out—more punishment than most humans could imagine. Though lately, more and more of that punishment seemed to be quietly directed at himself. Liam suspected PTSD. Not that Aiden was willing to admit it. At least not yet.

Liam braced his elbows against the ropes, sweat dripping down the groove of his back. "You're out of shape."

Aiden was no such thing, but Liam felt the need to give him a hard time about missing two practices this week. Something about actually doing the work Liam was paying him to do. Plus, he *was* in a mood. Instead of receding, the irritation he felt at Jaz had only grown since yesterday's confrontation. She hadn't come around to accepting a security detail, though the danger she was courting was clear to everyone except her.

"I need a team to babysit Jazmine Keasley. Who do we have?"

"Who do you want?"

"Someone…" Female. He wanted someone female. Except Trident Security didn't have female operatives. "Someone she won't be able to wrap around her finger. And don't underestimate her ability to do it."

"Want me to take a run at her?" Aiden asked.

That was the last thing Liam wanted. Aiden hadn't met a woman he didn't want to take to bed, and no one was going to be taking Kyan's little sister there. "If you're too busy to come to practice, you're too busy to take on the sprite." They both knew Liam was bullshitting, but that was one of the benefits of being the boss. "But see if you can't find a competent pair that won't put up with a rich brat's shenanigans. And have someone go to her place today to set up a security system. If she protests, tell the guys to lock her in the bathroom."

The buzzer went off again, and Liam pushed himself away from the ropes. Settling into a fighting stance, he shifted his weight between the balls of his feet, taunting the Highlander into dropping his guard. Liam really needed to hit someone today—and if Aiden gave him half a chance to whale on him, he wouldn't hold back.

JAZ

"What exactly are we doing here?" Sebastian asked over the blaring music that pulsated through the aptly named Pulse—Denton Valley's premier gay club. "Not that I'm complaining or anything."

"Wagging my tail." Jaz surreptitiously inclined her head to the pair of men in dark slacks and ironed button-downs who'd followed them into Pulse. She'd met the two men, Harkness and Percey, when they attempted to invite themselves into her apartment last night. After telling them exactly where they could stick their cameras, Jaz closed the door in their faces—but not before informing them that their next attempt at breaking and entering would be reported to the police.

By this morning, Trident Rescue and Security had rented the apartment across the hall from hers and moved the pair in.

While Harkness took a post near the door and Percey settled himself on a barstool with a clear view of Jaz's table, she filled Sebastian in on the details. His eyes widened, then narrowed suspiciously. "Jaz, hon, if there is a jihad with your name on it, maybe this isn't the wisest decision."

She smoothed the fabric of her pink Cache top, the tastefully open slit over her abdomen revealing just the right amount of skin. This wasn't the kind of place men would look at her sexually, but it was one where style would be appreciated—and evaluated—and Jaz was enjoying taking the outfit for a test drive. "There isn't—not beyond general rhetoric. I did my research, and Sky is doing some for me as well." Sky was an investigative journalist with a knack for uncovering reality. "It's an excuse for my father to clamp down on my climbing, which he's hated for years. He knows I do this for freedom, so anything to take that freedom away is alluring."

Sebastian looked unconvinced. "And Kyan?"

"Kyan is overprotective by nature. And after what he went through in Afghanistan, he isn't exactly rational when it comes to anyone mentioning explosives." Jaz ran her finger over her wineglass, a rare bit of vulnerability seeping through her facade. "I've worked so hard to get out from under their shadow, Bastian. There's this ball of fear inside me that if I don't do this now, I never will. The Clash of the Titans has to come on my terms, not anyone else's."

It took Sebastian only a heartbeat to think before he nodded in collusion. "Tell me what you need."

Jaz smiled wickedly. "Can you have one of your friends buy a drink for my two brave guards at the bar? I'm heading to the restroom and out the window—it's only one floor up, and the wall outside is child's play for bouldering."

Returning to her apartment, Jaz hung a smiley face outside her door and headed off to bed. Harkness and Percey didn't know it yet, but they were all going for a run the following morning, and Jaz wanted some sleep. A few days of this—a week at most—and Liam would have so many complaints from his employees that he'd do the work on unnegotiating the arrangement on Jaz's behalf.

IF HARKNESS and Percey were less than excited about a 4:00 a.m. run—which they did in their boots—they let none of the distress show in their faces. Instead, they kept pace with Jaz's sprints and recoveries without complaint, which was disappointing. Jaz kept them outside and moving until she was certain that their lack of running shoes had gifted them blisters.

Well, if nothing else, busting her security detail's balls was going to help keep her in shape.

Jaz's shadows proved themselves quick studies, however. By the third day, they'd figured out Jaz's habit of taking punishing runs at any time of day, and started carrying workout clothes and water in their rucksacks as they followed her about. Which meant it was time to up the stakes.

On Friday evening, Jaz zipped up an oversized jacket over her clothes before going into the hallway. Sitting openly in front of the security camera, she began tying her pink running shoes. A moment later, Percey was out in the hall with her, his own running shoes in hand.

He eyed her warily.

"You've caught on to the game," Jaz said with a shrug, the first words she'd uttered to the shadow directly since throwing him and his partner out of her apartment on the first day. "I don't see the value of keeping my runs from you. I'm not about to hand you a typed agenda, but yes"—she waved toward the camera—"I'm going for a run, and I know you know. So you might as well be comfortable."

"We appreciate that," Percey said, his voice hesitant, as if waiting for the other shoe to drop. Like Harkness, he was in his early twenties—a few years younger than Jaz's twenty-five—and his quiet determination to do a good job almost made Jaz feel guilty about her evening plans.

"It's our job to meld into your lifestyle, ma'am," he said, motioning to Harkness through the camera. "The more you share with us, the better—and more unobtrusively—we can execute our mission."

"Technically, your mission is called stalking."

"We aren't breaking any laws, ma'am."

This was debatable, but Jaz didn't press the point. The shadows probably were doing their best to be both efficient and courteous, but their stoicism was proving inconvenient. They'd either not complained to Liam about the assignment or did and were told to suck it up. She needed to address this at the source.

Waiting courteously until both men had their running shoes laced up, Jaz started her familiar routine of jogging down the three flights of stairs, out the back door of her apartment complex, and into the running path in the woods below. She kept the pace light, slowing as she needed to keep from working up a sweat in the cool evening air. A mile into the run, she shifted her direction back to the well-lit Denton street, following a similar route she'd taken—on purpose—several times that week.

This time, however, instead of looping back toward her apartment, she detoured to one of the nicest hotels in Denton's downtown, Kinship Resort and Club. Entering the marble-floored lobby, Jaz slipped off her jacket as she walked, revealing a skintight cocktail dress that was custom cut to emphasize what curves she had. She'd never be able to afford such a garment now, but fortunately, her closet hadn't disappeared with her bank account.

She pushed down the bottom part of the dress to cover her hips, pulling off her running shorts in the same motion. The little move, which she'd learned from YouTube, had taken days of practice but the impressed gaze of the concierge made the quick wardrobe change worth it. As her final act, Jaz pulled a pair of delicate red sandals from her jacket pocket and deposited her sneakers and sports gear into an ultrapackable sack.

"I'm here for the Special Needs Charity Gala." She gave the concierge a dazzling smile and extended her bag. "Could you store this for me until the end of the evening?"

The men's jaws were set tight as they joined Jaz in the mirrored elevator a few moments later, their running gear and athletic shoes drawing disapproving glances from the staff. Jaz took a twirl, her fingers teasing her hair—which she'd blow-dried and put carefully into a bun before leaving the house—into a sensual frame around her face. The light from the crystal lights bounced against the subtle ruby necklace hanging around her neck and, just before the elevator dinged its arrival at the top floor, she slipped on a matching set of earrings.

Harkness and Percey, dogging her steps, looked ready to lose their lunch.

"It's nothing personal," she said, patting Percey's muscled arm.

"No, of course not," he said tightly.

"Well then, enjoy the evening." She smiled as the elevator doors opened and strode out into the black-tie event—Trident Security employees making an utter fool of Liam's company before Colorado's elite movers and shakers as they followed behind her.

4

LIAM

*L*iam Rowen had never gotten comfortable wearing a tux, but sometime in the last few years as his security business had taken off, he found himself wearing one too often. At least he wasn't alone at the evening's charity gala. Cullen, Eli, and Kyan, his best friends from their time at the Trident Military Academy and later comrades inside the SEALs, were also in attendance—though they all came from wealthy enough backgrounds to have had tuxes hanging in their closets from childhood.

"How is Dani's practice?" Liam asked Eli, whose psychologist wife was switching over from doing executive evaluations to focusing on helping abuse and PTSD victims.

"Too well," Eli said glumly. "Unfortunately, there isn't a lack of clients around. Especially with more former military types finding their way to Denton."

"What's the latest on Trident Rescue and Security?" Cullen asked, taking a glass of champagne from a server's tray with one hand while snaking the other around his wife's waist. Liam knew Sky was trying to get pregnant, and a bit of hope rose inside him when she didn't take a flute for herself. "Or is that a bit of a loaded question after I just dumped that search and rescue onto your lap?"

Liam tugged his French cuffs straight. Absorbing the medical wilderness-response outfit into Trident Security did come with a management headache Liam had not been prepared for. With the new medics and rescue personnel he'd hired, the outpost was becoming a bit of the Wild West. If he told his friends—his family—as much, they'd trip over themselves to help in some way. But that wasn't fair. They were all recently married and starting families.

"The Rescue is fine," Liam said. "I wish I could go out on more calls, though."

"The inherent downside of running a multimillion-dollar corporation," Cullen said with understanding. "It can make you feel like an overpaid desk jockey. If you need to get into the field—go. The place will hold itself together better than you think."

"I'm making a play to expand Trident Security into the international theater," said Liam. "Protection for traveling dignitaries. Hostage negotiation and rescue. Think Obsidian Ops with morals. It's a bit of a project, but talk about good field experience when it's done."

Kyan, whose brush with Obsidian Ops last year nearly cost him his life, crossed his arms over his chest. "O2 isn't going to just let you encroach on its turf—especially since you both pull from the special forces crowd. It's not that big a world."

Before Liam could shoot back a remark about Kyan, of all people, lecturing him on risk, Eli raised a quelling finger.

"Before you focus on those international markets, you might want to rethink your domestic image, mate," the Brit said, focusing on something over Liam's shoulder. "Aren't those your associates making fools of themselves over there?"

Liam turned slowly, following the direction of Eli's gaze. He saw Jaz first, her understated cocktail dress stunning as she mingled with guests beneath the three massive crystal chandeliers. Instinctively, his attention slipped from her to the gold-wallpapered wall in search of the two men he'd assigned to her detail—and felt himself go ice cold with rage.

What in the ever-loving hell?

In tight leggings and lime-green running shoes, Percey drew more attention than the human-sized penguin ice statue in the middle of the goddamned ballroom. The second man, Harkness, was little better off with shorts, tank top, and a mulish expression. At least the pair hadn't ventured much past the front door, but even that was more than enough.

Unsurprisingly, a determined-looking manager was already making her way to Liam.

"I apologize for intruding on your evening," the young woman said with polite deference that in no way hid her disapproval, "but I understand you have a security team on duty at the gala today. They are more than welcome to attend, but this is a black-tie event, and I'm afraid their choice of attire is somewhat casual for the occasion."

Liam was extra careful in setting down his champagne flute, lest he shatter the crystal into bits. "You have my sincere apologies, Marla." He inclined his head at the manager, his voice tight. "And you will have theirs too, if they are still able to put syllables together by the time I'm done with them. Excuse me."

Harkness and Percey needed no more than a glance from Liam to know to follow him out into the hallway, tension crackling around the pair with enough force to make the air prickle. The men were nervous. They were fucking right to be nervous. They'd be right to be terrified. As it was, it took all Liam's self-control to wait until they turned a corner into a relatively private corridor before he wheeled on them. Murder flashed in his eyes. He knew it did.

The men stiffened, their military training causing them to stand at attention despite the civilian environment, their faces schooled in preparation for the tsunami they fully knew they deserved.

"Explain." Liam addressed Percey, who was supposed to be in charge.

"We thought Ms. Keasley was going for a run. By the time we realized she had alternative plans, it was too late to adjust." The young man didn't meet Liam's gaze.

"The dress didn't tip you off?"

"She, err, hid it under running clothes."

"So let me get this straight," Liam enunciated every word, heat filling his blood. "Your goddamn job was to watch the environment for unusual behavior and stop potential trouble before it started. And with all those fucking powers of observation, you missed an evening dress and bright red sandals? How the hell are you going to mark a suicide vest on a hostile you get a glimpse of when you can't see that the five-foot woman you have cameras trained on is dressed for a black-tie event?"

Silence.

"Those weren't rhetorical questions," Liam barked. "Answer me."

"Stop bullying them." A light soprano voice that Liam really, really didn't want to hear just injected itself into the conversation. High heels ticked against the polished wood floor until Jaz Keasley herself parked that tight cocktail dress that hugged her body right at Liam's shoulder. The rubies in her ears underscored her already beautiful eyes, and her small breasts perked up visibly under the silk in the hotel's air-conditioning.

It made Liam want to throw a blanket over her.

Crossing her arms under her breasts, Jaz leveled him with a glare, though it required tipping her head back. "I've made my feelings on a security team clear to you. Percey and Harkness are guilty of nothing but having the poor judgment to work for an asshole."

"This has nothing to do with you or your feelings, Jazmine. Go back to the party."

"Nothing to do with me? What universe did you get beamed up from?" Jaz scoffed.

This was insane. *She* was insane. Liam's jaw tightened, but he checked his body and voice to the kind of self-control civilization expected from humans. "I am disciplining my men. I would appreciate it if you get the hell out of my sight just now."

"And let you take your temper out on two people who can do nothing to defend themselves? Like hell."

The defenseless special forces men shifted their weight uncomfortably.

Jaz raised her chin. "I've been tormenting your team all week to make a point. But since these two proved to be more stoic and honorable than you deserve to have your employees be, I needed to take my message to the root. This is my doing, Liam. Mine. And in case you're still having trouble reading the writing on the wall, let me spell it out for you: You don't get to force something on me. Not you, not my parents, not my brother. So long as you keep sending teams to stalk me, I'll keep making Trident Security look like a loony bin."

Despite her small stature, Jaz's presence filled the whole corridor, and Liam was starting to wish that the tongue-tying discomfort that seemed to afflict most women who talked to him had some effect on Kyan's younger sister.

It didn't.

"This evening was the opening volley, Liam. You keep going toe to toe with me, and the next time I show you up, I'll make sure there are cameras around. I'll turn this detail into a PR nightmare worthy of a Hollywood blockbuster. Am I clear? That's not a rhetorical question."

5

JAZ

*J*az kept her gaze locked on Liam's as he made a motion to dismiss Percy and Harkness. Hearing their sneakers whisper softly against the floor, she made a thick mark on the internal scoreboard that had been ticking inside her heart all evening. She wasn't so naive as to think Liam would concede the whole bout, declare her victor, and go away—but he did have the next move.

She just wished she had some inkling of what the man was thinking as he tugged his gold cuff links inside their crispy slots. Liam looked good in a tuxedo. Hell, he looked good in anything, which was a large part of the problem. Liam had always been glorious, the kind of perfect-bodied man that turned heads whenever he walked down the street. All her brother's friends were fit, but something about Liam's slight curl of hair at the nape and piercing hazel eyes had captured Jaz since she was little. Just a pesky younger sister of the popular older brother.

Unlike the others, and especially Kyan, who'd never had the time of day for Jaz's presence, Liam had talked to her. Acknowledged her existence. He hadn't gotten along with his family, and one year when Jaz was twelve, he'd spent the summer bouncing

ALEX LIDELL

between his friends' houses. Which was when little Jaz had written her deepest heartfelt thoughts into a letter and delivered it to Liam. The expression of her feelings had culminated in a suggestion that the two of them meet in private in the middle of the night. She'd had an image of lying with him in an open field and watching the stars. Of feeling his lips on hers.

Her heart had raced as she gave him the note. Watched him open it. Watched his face turn an angry kind of red that was not at all what she'd expected. Instead of letting her go gently, Liam had marched both her and the letter right to Kyan and then to their parents.

She hadn't just been humiliated, but to add insult to injury, her parents had grounded her for trying to make plans to sneak out with a boy with no one knowing.

The hurt feelings of a tween were long gone, but that incident had opened her eyes to Liam's controlling nature. He'd had a notion of what was and wasn't appropriate for Jaz, and he used any means he had at his disposal to enforce it. As they'd gotten older, she saw that scenario play out over and over in many ways. In the orders he'd issued to his girlfriends. In his high-handed manner. She wasn't surprised when Liam discovered his more sensual preferences lay in power-exchange relationships.

What she never understood was why Liam's attitude toward her had gotten increasingly hostile as they got older, until the two could barely stand being in the same room with one another. The most likely scenario was Jaz's insistence on independence and the point she made to support organizations like Girls Aflame. Liam liked to be in charge and in control, especially of women, and Jaz didn't fit into his picture of the world.

Now, however, their little strife was spilling over onto other people, and Jaz couldn't allow that. "I mean it, Liam. Stay the hell away from me. And understand also, that if you punish Harkness and Percey, I'll find a way to skin you alive." Jaz tapped a slender finger against his triceps, wishing not for the first time that she'd gotten some of her father's genes when it came to height.

Finally, Liam spoke. "You're truly against Percey and Harkness being disciplined for failing at their job?"

"You set them up for failure when you assigned them to an unwilling target. It wasn't fair play."

"Their job doesn't rely on a target's willingness. In our line of work, we don't play fair. We play to win."

"That explains so much." Jaz played to win fairly.

Liam sighed, his hands sliding into the pockets of his tuxedo. Beneath the jacket, his cummerbund hugged his middle tightly, defining a tough, muscular abdomen. "We seem to be at an impasse. We both have things that the other wants."

Jaz smiled at him, showing her teeth. "I'd say what we have is me wanting you to go to hell, and you stubbornly refusing to get your ass there."

Liam pretended she hadn't spoken. "As I said, we both have things the other wants. I want to do my job, which you are making difficult. I also would like to discipline my employees, which you appear to be against. You, I presume, would like your parents to remain ignorant of the fact that you aren't, in fact, currently enrolled in grad school—a confusion that I could easily clarify for them."

Jaz's stomach clenched. Liam *would* tell on her. He'd proven that much in the past. "Talk about playing dirty."

"You're the one playing, Jazmine. I'm trying to be a damn adult and have a reasonable discussion."

Jaz let out a small growl of exasperation. "All right. Reasonable discussion. Let's presume for a heartbeat that you're capable of that. So, in that spirit, please explain to me what it is exactly that you want, Liam. Don't tell me you're so strapped for jobs you need this contract. Or that you think a few unspecific notes that even the police won't do anything about are a good reason to stand up this whole circus? I checked in with my Vector rep. There have been only two other messages that match this MO. It's just some disturbed person."

Liam inclined his head as if acknowledging her point. "I agree that the author of these specific notes is more likely than not a mentally unstable individual with no capability to create havoc. But the sticking point with mentally unstable people—they are *unstable.* Unpredictable. As I've told Kyan, your sudden movement into a highly public position does make you a general target. It doesn't matter whether it's this guy or some other idiot—there's a safety concern here. So in answer to your question—what do I want—I want to keep the promise I made to your brother to keep you safe."

Swallowing a retort that would tell Liam exactly where he and his promises to her brother could go, Jaz forced herself to speak in calmer tones. Neither of them was going to walk out of this hallway with everything they wanted, so perhaps it was time to treat this like a business negotiation.

"How about a compromise, then?" Jaz said matter-of-factly, imagining herself across a conference room table. "You want me safe. I want me free. To this end, I propose a one-week threat-assessment period. During this week, I will fully cooperate with your people following me around and checking every rabbit and squirrel that looks my way funny. At the end, come up with a *real* assessment —not a hypothetical one based on hype. If—and only if—you identify specific areas of danger, I will cooperate with whatever mitigation strategy we need, all the way up to a security detail if warranted. If you find nothing of real actionable note, you back off no matter what my parents or Kyan or Santa Claus want."

Liam's brows tightened as he appeared to consider the offer. "Two weeks, not one."

"Fine."

"I do the assessment personally, and you *actually* cooperate. As in, you do what I tell you."

Jaz's jaw tightened. "You promise Harkness and Percey won't be punished and that you do nothing to interfere with my training for the Clash of the Titans. There is no *tell Jaz to stop climbing* loophole."

"Agreed. Your team gets let off with a warning, and I will work my assessment around your training needs. Needs, not *wants.*" Liam raised one finger. "One final condition. You spend the two-week assessment period living in a spare room in my condo."

"What?" Heat rose to Jaz's face. So much for thinking they could have a reasonable discussion. "Absolutely not. No chance."

Instead of stepping away, Liam spread his shoulders and took a step toward her. "I'm being a realist, not an asshole. I'm one man. I can't spend twenty-four hours a day watching cameras to see if you haven't snuck out on me. I need to control the environment."

"And I said I'll cooperate. My word isn't good enough?"

"No."

"Fuck you." Jaz's hand curled into a fist.

Liam's gaze flickered down to it, then returned to her with cool impassivity.

Reaching into the inside of his jacket pocket, Liam pulled out a phone. "I'm about to make a call," he said with nerve-grating calm. "It will either be to Trident HR to fire Percey and Harkness, or to our logistics department to move the essentials from your apartment over to my condo. Who should I dial?"

6

LIAM

*S*tanding with his back against the kitchen island, Liam braced his elbows on the quartz countertop and watched a pair of men carry in the last of Jaz's things. By his count, there was one bag of clothes and toiletries, a laptop case, and enough climbing equipment to outfit a small battalion. And there was pink. A lot of fucking pink. He didn't think anyone beyond fifth grade had pink as a favorite color—but either Jaz did, or she'd taken the time to sort her possessions to bring only the most irritating along with her.

Seeing another set of ropes being carried in, Liam waved toward the elevator outside the penthouse door. "My building does have an elevator, you know. You won't have to rappel down to get a cup of coffee."

"I just like having my gear at hand," Jaz called out while directing the movers to place each piece of equipment just so. Her tone was conversational, nothing like a military commander's, yet each instruction was so well thought out and precise that the men obeyed instantly. "Plus, it's not like you don't have the space. This place is nearly the size of Kyan's house." As she spoke, Jaz picked one of the ropes that had come slightly undone in the move and began to re-coil it into a neat bundle.

She was right about him having the space. With his apartment taking up the entire top floor of The Overview at Bear Creek, Liam had nearly three thousand square feet to work with—which wasn't something he could say for Jaz's place. In fact, when he'd stepped foot in her place earlier in the day, the studio's claustrophobic feel took him by surprise. If not for the designer items and high-end sporting gear, Jaz's apartment was the kind someone from his family's background would live in—not the daughter of Hollywood's top producer.

Liam looked around his living room, noticing a Kindle—in a pink leather cover—now clashing with his minimalist emerald-green design, while her coconut scent seeped through the apartment. He hoped to hell he wasn't getting himself into more of a problem than he could handle. At least Liam's ferns had survived the invasion intact. The plants, such as they were, suited him perfectly. Like his friends who had everything from kids to German shepherds in their homes, Liam craved having something living around him—and had settled on several potted fern plants and spread their leaves generously.

Except now he was going to have ferns *and* Jazmine Keasley.

Somewhere behind him, Liam heard Jaz thanking the men who'd helped move her things and closing the door behind them with a click. "So, where is the red room of pain?"

Liam turned away from the window, where downtown Denton Valley sprawled against the backdrop of the Colorado Mountains. "Red room of what?"

"Haven't you read *Fifty Shades of Grey*? I mean, where do you take all the women who beg you to hurt them? I wouldn't want to walk in on something by accident."

Thirty seconds alone and she was already prying into *that* part of his life. Liam was discreet, but he hadn't kept his sensual preferences from his friends—and he knew that Jaz knew as well. So much for hoping that common courtesy would prevail.

"I don't play in the house, so don't worry about it," he said flatly.

The fact that he wasn't playing at all nowadays was none of the woman's business. He pointed to the front door. "Here are the rules: The dead bolt stays engaged at all times. Brief me the night before on your agenda. You control the daily activity, I set the security. No games."

Jaz walked over to the kitchen and hoisted herself up to sit on the edge of his island countertop, her crop top swaying just enough to show a tanned midriff. Her feet were bare, and her manicured toenails shone with a bit of sparkle that wasn't unlike the bits of stone in the quartz countertop on which she sat. Crossing her thighs, Jaz flicked the tip of her tongue between her lips and gave Liam a coquettish flicker of long lashes. "I'd never play games with you."

Fuck. Despite knowing full well that Kyan's demon of a baby sister was just pushing buttons on purpose, Liam still felt all the blood in his body rush down to his groin. The pulsing sensation was so intense, his jeans suddenly so tight, that for a moment, the pressure made him outright light-headed. He was a SEAL and a professional, but he was still human, and something about Jaz Keasley made his body rebel against his better sense. It always had. The woman had been his kryptonite since teenagehood—which was why Liam had always kept his distance from her.

Now, distance was impossible, and Liam's hands itched to wring her neck for this move. Her lovely, long neck.

Jaz curled a strand of hair around her finger. "But so long as we are talking about rules and expectations, I did have some questions… What are you going to do if I have a doctor's appointment? Say, a gynecologist. Will you go in for the exam?"

Seriously? Fine. He could wait this out. Eventually, Jaz would run out of steam. "I'll stay in the waiting room." Liam crossed his arms. "Next question?"

She smirked. "Those seats are usually reserved for boyfriends and husbands."

"If someone asked, I'd tell them I'm your brother."

"That just sounds incestuous. What if I go on a date?"

"I'll find a table at the restaurant where I can keep you in my line of sight. I'd also want you to choose a corner table."

"What if my date and I want to have sex?" She leaned forward to say the word in a dirty way. "Can we agree that if you watch, you keep any commentary to yourself?"

Goddammit. And for a moment there, Liam thought he could still steer this conversation back to normalcy. He turned on his heels and attacked the coffeemaker with more vigor than it deserved. He wasn't squeamish about sex, but that topic didn't belong in the same thought as Kyan's sister. "I'd consider it a personal favor if you strove for celibacy for two damn weeks."

"That will be very difficult," she said. "Will you be making a similar sacrifice?"

The woman got a kick out of goading him, but what bothered him most was how easily she succeeded at it. How he could never seem to get a solid read on her. He prided himself on his ability to take in any situation at a glance, assess the people and assets involved, boil down the variables, make a quick decision. He'd excelled at this throughout his time as a SEAL and while building his security business. But something about Jazmine Keasley eluded him.

Maybe he'd been going about this whole thing the wrong way. He'd tried the straight-up aloof professional route so many times, he was blue in the face. Maybe what he needed to get her to back off was a good offense.

Leaving the coffeemaker alone, Liam turned back to where Jaz still sat on the edge of the kitchen island and stalked slowly toward her. Braced his large hands on either side of her hips, not touching, but enough to invade her space. Then he leaned in, his shoulders spread, his internal dominating power pulsating through him. He was so much taller than Jaz's petite five-foot frame that even in her perched position, he managed to look down at her. To let her breathe in his masculine scent of musk and fresh shampoo.

Jaz swallowed, her pupils widening slightly. She didn't quite squirm, but Liam knew how to pay attention to the smaller signs. The tensed muscles. The shift of weight. The slight color that touched her cheeks. She was aware of him. Uncomfortably so.

Holding that pressure, Liam waited. Watched the indecision of whether to go nose to nose with him or ask him to back up warring in Jaz's gaze.

"Am I supposed to be impressed, scared, or aroused?" Jaz asked.

Fighting words, but Liam could read her body language well enough to know she felt all three just then. She was just too competitive to admit it. To ask him to back off. So he didn't.

"Two can play this game, Jazmine. Stop baiting me." He let his voice drop to a thick, sensual gravel. "If you're curious about power play, google it. You and I, we're not friends. We're not fuck buddies. We aren't anything other than business associates. Your brother has saved my life more than once—I have a responsibility to him. So I *will* keep you safe. The sooner you stop acting like a spoiled teenager who didn't get Daddy's car keys, the smoother this will all be for everyone."

Liam let the words simmer in the charged air between them for several heartbeats, then pushed himself away to finish making coffee. His heart was pounding, and though he went through the motions of grinding beans and turning dials, all his self-control was focused on breathing and staying still as he heard Jaz slip down to the floor behind him. The kitchen was empty by the time he let himself turn back to the island, and the uncomfortable sensation that he'd hit Jaz deeper than intended grazed unpleasantly along his chest.

JAZ

*S*tepping into Liam's guest room shower, Jaz leaned her head against the cool tile while scalding water rained onto her back. Liam's words played in her head like a loop.

A spoiled teenager who didn't get Daddy's car keys.

She felt like that young girl all over again. Stupidly thinking she could go head to head with Liam Rowen, that she'd be allowed to play on the same teasing playing field where he'd welcomed her brother and his friends. That Liam might look at her and see an equal.

She hated her arousal to Liam's gorgeous face and low voice. To his powerful body. His powerful everything. She hated how, when he'd bracketed her on that kitchen island, his very presence taking up all the air in the universe, she'd felt her heart quicken and moisture gather between her folds. He'd taken her high without ever touching her.

And then he tossed her away to shatter. Because she didn't matter. She was a favor Liam owed her big brother. Irrelevant for herself. Worse than irrelevant. *A spoiled teenager who didn't get Daddy's car keys.*

She was twenty-five to his thirty-one now. Leaning her head

back, she let the water rush through her hair and scolded herself. Eleanor Roosevelt said that no one can make you feel inferior without your consent. Through that lens, Liam wasn't the problem at all. She was, by giving him that power over her.

That would stop this very moment.

The following morning, Jaz got up at her usual dawn hour, printed out a copy of her training plan, dressed herself for a run, and strode into the kitchen just as Liam coaxed a cup of coffee from his high-tech machine. He turned and looked at her wearily.

"Would you like some coffee?" He held out his cup.

"No, thank you." She handed him the schedule and started rooting around the kitchen. "Where is your blender?"

"How do you know I have a blender?"

"Same way I know you pee standing up." She hadn't meant to joke around with him, but some quips came naturally and she wasn't going to self-censor herself either.

Liam snorted and pointed to a cupboard. Jaz pulled out the appliance, protein and nutrition powders she'd brought from home, and some ice. Getting the fuel just right before a workout was part of her training routine. "Is there anything on the agenda you feel uncomfortable with?" she asked as she poured her breakfast shake into a glass. "It won't leave you much room to do other work. The on-site climbing locations have no Wi-Fi signal, but I can shift some of the workouts indoors if you need a computer."

Liam studied her the way one might consider a new species, then cleared his throat. "It's all fine. The main company movements are with Trident's legal team now, so between my phone and home computer, I can be remote for a couple of weeks. Getting out from behind the desk once in a while is good for me." He glanced at the grid again. "Endurance work, two-a-day practices, skills training, strength training—this is enough to make a pro-football player cringe."

Now he sounded like her father. In Hugh's eyes, football was a profession. Climbing was a good hobby.

"Then good thing I'm not inviting any football players to join me. I wouldn't want to make them feel bad."

"I played football," said Liam. "We had to play a sport at the academy, so I played football."

"You won't need to join either, beyond the runs. Sebastian helps me train and will belay me at the Clash."

"He is your pro coach?"

"Something like that." Unlike pro football where the athletes got crazy salaries for training, Jaz's money would come from endorsements and prize money. Even Vector Ascent, who was covering her gear and providing a small living stipend, wasn't going to spring for a coach. That had to come out of Jaz's empty pockets. Fortunately, Sebastian was a champ and a better climbing partner and supporter than most pros. Time to change the subject. Better yet, to stop talking altogether.

With a few big gulps, Jaz finished her green shake, made a face of disgust, and went to the sink to clean the blender and her glass. "Can you be ready to leave in five?"

As JAZ WOUND the running route along the sidewalks crisscrossing downtown Denton Valley, she wondered whether Percey and Harkness had given Liam a heads-up about the morning routine. Or maybe, despite his larger size, Liam was used to long runs. Either way, he appeared unsurprised by either the pace or distance and kept up with little show of effort. Which was, Jaz had to admit, somewhat disappointing.

But it didn't matter. She was not thinking about him. She wasn't.

Jaz's phone rang about two miles into the run, and she tapped her earbud to answer, knowing exactly who it would be. "Bastian! Good morning."

"Good morning, beautiful. Where did you sleep last night? Was he gorgeous?"

Jaz cringed. Sebastian sometimes joined her for the runs, and with everything going on, she'd forgotten to get him caught up on the *Liam Situation*. She did so now as she ran, acutely aware that the Liam in question was keeping pace about a step behind.

Sebastian listened with unusual lack of comment until she

finally came to the end. At which point, he cleared his throat. "I can officially say I'm not qualified to have an opinion on this, but what about Friday night?"

"Friday night?" said Jaz.

"The set-up date you agreed to go on," Sebastian exclaimed. "I have it all set up with Devante and if you think of backing out now, I'm going to crazy glue your climbing shoes."

Jaz barely remembered agreeing to something like that before the whole fiasco with Liam started, but she knew better than to blow it off now. Sebastian took dates seriously, and she didn't want to jerk him around. Though perhaps there was still a way out of this. "Of course I'm not backing out. But my shadow and all that. Wouldn't it be awkward with three people?"

There. Not her fault at all that this wouldn't work.

Sebastian groaned, and she could imagine him raising his hands dramatically on the other end of the line. "Can't he wait outside the door or something?"

"I wish. Plus, even if he could, it would still be awkward. I would rather not start a potential relationship with an explanation of a security detail."

"I see your point."

Jaz breathed a sigh of relief, though she kept the sound quiet enough to not be picked up on the phone.

"Let me talk to him," said Sebastian.

"Yeah, tell Devante I'm sorry and maybe another time."

"No, not him. *Him.* The asshat."

"To Liam?" Jaz nearly stumbled over her own feet. "Why?"

"I have an idea. And you know I'm going to be cranky if you don't let me give this a good shot. Not after you agreed." Sebastian's tone took on a stubborn note Jaz knew well. For a moment, she was going to protest, but then realized there was no point. Sebastian usually got his way somehow, and really, what did she care if he and Liam talked?

Without breaking stride, Jaz took her phone out of its armband and disconnected the AirPods. "My friend Sebastian wants to talk to you," she told Liam.

Liam took the phone and pressed it against his ear without breaking stride. "Yes," he said after a while. Then, "Seems rude." More silence as Sebastian talked. Finally, Liam barked a "Fine" into the line and disconnected.

"Your friend is going to find a fake date for me on Friday night," Liam told Jaz as he handed her the phone back. "He very insistently wants you to keep your rendezvous with some Devante character and thinks that making it a double will keep things less obtrusive."

"And the prize for creativity goes to..." Jaz muttered before shaking her head. That was Sebastian for you. She glared at Liam. "Wait. Why the hell did *you* agree to that?"

Liam shrugged. "I'm here to run your security, not your social interference. If you don't want to go, tell your friend to call off the event."

Fine. Be like that. "Do you even know who you're going with?"

"Don't know, don't care." Liam shrugged a shoulder, the slight sheen of perspiration along the muscle grooves shimmering in the sun. "I won't be there for romance, so it doesn't matter."

8

LIAM

*B*y Friday, as Liam secured his Glock into an ankle holster in preparation for Jaz's date, he admitted to himself that few people could keep up her training regimen. Her schedule, which she printed for him each morning, wasn't a spoiled brat's journal—it was a professional athlete's. Jaz pushed herself as hard as any SEAL, but she was smart about it too. Strategic. Professional.

She was also perfectly reasonable toward him. Considerate, even.

So why did it irk him?

Because it was bullshit, that was why. Jaz hadn't changed her mind or her ways, she simply shut Liam out. The two of them never been apathetic toward each other. Angry, irritated, downright homicidal—yes. Apathetic—no. Not until Liam had crossed the line and crowded her on that kitchen island. He'd tricked her body into an arousal he knew he could elicit and then he turned his back. He knew better than that.

But when it came to Jaz, he broke all his own rules.

And in response to his misstep, Jaz had done the one thing that Liam hadn't realized would bother him—she'd shut him out of her emotions completely. Raised a shield of professionalism that he couldn't get through. And Liam was surprised how much he hated that.

As Liam was shrugging into his sport coat, he felt his phone vibrate. He checked the caller ID. His mother. For a second, he worried that he'd gotten his days confused. Was it Saturday? No, of course it was Friday. Double-date Friday. So why was his mother calling?

"Ma? Everything all right?" He glanced at his watch. Five minutes until they needed to go. "Did Lisa get the car fixed?"

"That's actually why I'm calling."

"This isn't the best time." He could hear Jaz in the living room and walked down to meet her. "Whatever additional work needs doing, just have the mechanics go ahead and put it on the same card, all right?"

"No." Of course Patti would choose now to be difficult. Probably because he'd told her it was a bad time. "Liam, you need to stop paying Lisa's bills. In fact, stop the stipend you send."

"What? No. Never mind." He wasn't going to go down a rabbit hole of conversation with her. "Look, I can afford it. It makes me feel better to know you two are taken care of, all right? So just consider taking the money as a favor you're doing for me." Walking into the living room, Liam found Jaz gazing out the bay window into the mountains. The setting sun brushed the outlines of her athletic silhouette, giving her an ethereal glow. "I really need to go."

"This isn't about you," his mother continued as if he hadn't spoken. "Lisa is thirty-five years old. She's not going to school. She isn't looking for a job. You paying for everything is enabling her to just…drift. She has no goals. She isn't dating—"

"Ma, I don't care how badly you want grandchildren. Lisa has a damn good reason not to date."

"That's not—"

"The irony of you of all people protesting a payoff is overwhelming. Lisa will start seeing someone when—*if* and when— she's ready. She and I may not like each other much, but don't think I'm going to turn my back on her. That's your MO. Not mine." He turned the phone off with nearly enough force to crack the screen and stuffed it into his pocket.

Jaz turned from the window, her expression confirming she'd heard the tail end of the conversation. Absurdly, Liam wanted her to ask what it was about and who Lisa was—just so he could tell her to mind her own business.

For a moment, that noisy, bubbly curiosity flickered in Jaz's intelligent eyes. Their gazes met. Jaz's flickered toward the phone.

"Is—" She hooked her clutch over her wrist. "You look nice."

He glanced down at himself. Growing up dirt poor, he'd never developed a sense of what to wear to nice places—so he'd hired a discreet stylist. Tanille had put together a dozen outfits for different occasions and issued strict orders not to deviate from the packages. Orders that Liam happily followed since his profession required him to fit into his environment, even when that environment was a five-star restaurant.

Unlike his blend-me-in outfit, Jaz's soft pink dress had a deep V neck, clung to her torso in the most sinful of ways, and had a flouncy skirt that hit her about three inches above the knee. The lace overlaying it was something unusually feminine for her, but the contrast of the light color against her tanned skin was so show-stopping spectacular that he forced himself to refocus on another less alluring part of her figure. He jerked his chin at her feet, which were clad in impractical four-inch-heel contraptions strapped on with thin bands of leather. "I hate your shoes."

Jaz wiggled a manicured toe. "Then don't wear them."

"They aren't practical."

"Noted. What would you have preferred I'd worn?"

"Kevlar," Liam muttered and started for the door.

They arrived at The Cellar, a five-star restaurant and winery at the heart of Denton Valley, just before seven in the evening. Liam got out of the car first, opened Jaz's door, and tossed the keys to the valet. He didn't like the place already. It was little and cute, on a small side street filled with other little and cute places—and enough small roads and shadows to hide a guerilla army.

As the hostess guided them through the vineyard-themed

establishment, Liam surveyed the inside, marking the locations of doors and windows, absorbing the customary noises, and considered the patrons. As they approached the back corner table he'd asked Sebastian to reserve, Liam shifted his focus to their upcoming dinner companions—and nearly tripped over Jaz, who'd suddenly stopped short of the table.

A heartbeat later, he understood why. Jaz's date, a hippy-looking man in a bespoke suit with rows of braids in his hair, was already on his feet to pull out Jaz's chair. But the person seated across from Liam's spot wasn't a leggy blonde, redhead, or brunette. Well, it *was* a redhead, but with a rather important caveat.

Replaying the conversation with Sebastian in his mind, Liam had to give the guy props—Jaz's best friend had never actually specified that Liam's date would be female.

"You must be Liam." Sebastian stood and pulled Liam's chair out for him, just as Jaz's date had done for her. "And you're as absolutely stunning as Jaz described you."

Liam remained standing. And contemplating the many, many ways he could dismember Sebastian, who was grinning like a cat with cream.

Jaz excused herself through a small coughing fit, then found her voice. "Liam, this is my dear friend Sebastian Bridgeport," she said cordially. "Bastian, this is my brother's friend and colleague, Liam Rowen."

"Nice to meet you." Sebastian offered his hand.

Yanking himself out of his stupor, Liam shook it, squeezing all the bones. "Likewise."

Sebastian grinned and returned the crushing shake. Damn climbers and their grips.

They sat, Sebastian formally introducing Jaz and Devante Jackson, who was both a professional musician and amateur rock climber. Just as Sebastian finished the final introduction, a server appeared to take dinner orders and offer a selection of the whites, reds, blushes, and Shirazes available.

Liam ordered a Diet Coke.

Sebastian waggled his brows at the drink. Fuck. What exactly had Jaz told her friend about him? If she mentioned anything about his personal life, she wouldn't need protection because he'd strangle her himself.

"I'm an enormous fan of yours, Jazmine," Devante said as the aroma of wine filled the table and the scent of someone's lamb order drifted in to tickle their appetites. "Vector Ascent was brilliant to have signed you. I've watched every one of your climbs over the past year."

Liam felt Jaz tense beside him. She hated her full name. *Loathed* it.

"You have?" Liam prompted, wondering whether he could get Devante to say it again, just so he could watch Jaz be irritated. "Where did you stream the events?"

"Stream? Oh no." Devante grinned, showing perfect teeth. "I was there in person. Jazmine is kind of a hero of mine. Or I guess I should say heroine." He turned to her. "Your speed and agility on the mountain are well known all over the beginner's circuit. It's kind of inspirational."

Jaz blushed. "That's kind of you to say."

"Nothing kind about it when it's the truth."

"So you've essentially been stalking her?" Liam asked.

His three companions looked at him awkwardly.

Liam stared Devante down.

Jaz kicked him under the table, catching his shin with those heels of hers. He hissed in pain, covering it up as best he could by taking a sip of soda. Jaz's tiny pointy things did more damage than he'd given them credit for.

"So Jaz, have you gotten the official details for the Clash of the Titans Challenge Exhibition?" Sebastian volunteered in a rush, emphasizing the correct pronunciation of her name. "Last I heard, it's nothing like a normal competition. Five challengers on live routes, and the first to the top gets a hundred grand."

"That's about right," said Jaz. "But since we'll all be climbing real rock faces at the same time, five equitable routes have to be marked first."

"Why don't you just go one at a time?" Liam asked.

Devante gave him a condescending look. "The routes are three to five hours—the weather and light changes would make it inequitable."

"Route selection is also a part of the challenge," Jaz told Liam. "The marking period starts the first of the month. All the competitors get a week on location to mark five routes they believe are of equal difficulty. The judges will pick the set that is most interesting and equitable to use for the challenge."

"So whoever finds the best five equal routes gets the advantage of having previewed the route?" said Liam.

"Exactly." Devante pushed his way back into the conversation, shifting slightly in his chair to claim a great part of Jaz's line of sight —though the effort was somewhat spoiled by the arrival of their meal.

The conversation shifted to Devante's music and his admiration of all things Jaz. In short, he admired her skills, her looks, her support of Girls Aflame, and the fact that—according to an interview with *Climb*—she loved miniature poodles.

Liam probed Sebastian on just how well he knew Jaz's date. The short answer was not very well, and Liam gave Sebastian a reproachful glare.

Instead of looking repentant, Sebastian speared up a piece of his lobster almondine and offered some to Liam on a fork. The buttery morsel hung in the air between them, the grin in Sebastian's eyes matched only by the one in Jaz's.

Oh, for God's sake. Neither of the two of them had any idea what they'd be in for if they played Liam's version of sensual games. Not like he was playing them nowadays either. Liam took Sebastian's whole fork and fed himself, then decided to take control of this runaway train of a double date.

"So, Devante," he said, pointing Sebastian's fork—which he had no intention of returning to its owner—in Devante's direction. "Did you see the photos of Jaz from the Special Needs Charity Gala trending on Twitter? She's becoming quite a social media sensation."

Jaz narrowed her eyes at him.

Liam kept his attention on Devante, who dutifully opened his phone. Per the text Liam received from the office, the photos from the gala had been posting and getting attention on various channels. The attention had more to do with the charity event than Jaz, of course, but Liam didn't mind a bit of a twist for a good cause.

"Hey, that's you and Jazmine," Devante said, flashing an image from the gala to the rest of the table's occupants. "Jazmine looks lovely of course. Who are the other men?"

"That's Kyan, Jaz's older brother." Taking Devante's phone, Liam flicked to another gala image—this one showing all four of the massive Tridents standing near Jaz, with Kyan wearing a particularly murderous expression. "Then me. And the other two are our best friends. The four of us served in the navy together."

Devante gave a tense laugh. "You make an intimidating bunch."

"Only to those who wish us harm." He shrugged. "Or to hurt our family. Jaz is sort of everyone's sister." He gave Devante a very pointed gaze, holding it until he was sure the man got the message.

Devanta shifted in his seat. "Right. Good to have brothers. I always believe in supporting family, you know."

"Will you excuse us for a second?" Jaz grabbed Liam's arm and hauled him off to the side. Her tanned skin was a shade darker than usual, and displeasure shot like lightning from her large eyes. Oddly enough, he preferred the angry-at-him Jaz to the distant one. "What the hell are you doing?"

"Informing your stalker that you aren't as defenseless as you look."

Jaz's fingers curled at her sides. "One, I'm not defenseless. Two, Devante is my date—and I happen to like him very much."

"I don't think you do, *Jazmine.*"

"Seriously?" She pointed her finger at Liam's chest, poking him right in the sternum. "Let's try this again, using simple words. Devante is my date. You're hired muscle. So shut up, sit down, and stay out of my personal life."

"Anything else?"

"Yes. Give poor Bastian his fork back."

"I'll think about it."

After dessert—which Sebastian didn't try to feed to Liam—the four of them finally ambled toward the exit. Devante had his hand resting on Jaz's lower back. Liam silently dared the man to slip it to her ass and give him an excuse to accidentally shove him into a wall. He didn't. In fact, after pointedly not looking at Liam, he gave Jaz a chaste kiss on the cheek and promised to call before walking off with Sebastian.

Jaz crossed her arms and stared at her date's retreating back, but it was hard to make out her thoughts. Liam handed the valet his car ticket.

"I'll be right back," Jaz said.

"I'll come with you."

"No!" She held up a hand, the other rubbing her creased forehead. "I just want to catch up with Devante and thank him for the evening. And I want to do it without you glaring over my shoulder and scaring the piss out of him."

"I didn't—"

"You did and you're proud of it. And now, to make up for that, you're just going to stay here and wait for the car. He's literally two blocks away, and you can see everything." Without waiting for Liam's consent, Jaz turned and jogged off.

Liam gave her a five-second head start and jogged after her anyway.

Right in time to see a man step out from one of those small side alleys Liam hated and grab the clutch hanging off Jaz's wrist.

9

———————

JAZ

*J*az's heels made a crunching noise on the gritty cement as she took a breath of fresh Colorado night air and hurried after Devante. Jaz hated her stilettos. She'd never paid much mind to road cracks before, but having needle heels for footing while trying to make haste changed her perspective. With her attention divided between hurrying and keeping from sprawling on the sidewalk, she'd no notion that someone was near her until a rough hand jerked hard on her clutch.

The wrist strap dug into Jaz's skin, the force yanking her sideways. She tried to pull back against it, but the damn shoes gave way. Her balance faltered together with her breath. Then she was falling onto the pavement, the clutch strap still digging into her wrist. Dull impact, then stinging pain and a rush of terror pounded Jaz in rapid succession. She gasped for breath and gagged on a mouthful of putrid air.

"Let go, bitch." The scruffy face of a dirty thug in stained camos came into focus. He stank of urine and booze, and his grubby hand was still tugging on Jaz's clutch. Behind him, a similarly bedraggled man was looking around in jerky motions.

Jaz gripped her wrist strap tighter and screamed. A barrage of fury and fear pounded through her, her vision narrowing to her tiny slice of the alley. To the stench of the putrid man yanking on her clutch, the pain of pavement scraping skin, the outlines of garbage cans disappearing into shadows down the road.

The thug raised his booted foot, the heavy heel aimed to stomp down on Jaz's wrist. She tried to scramble back from the coming pain, but before the thug's boot could connect, another foot cut into her line of vision. Moving faster than Jaz thought possible Liam kicked the thug's knee, sending the man to the ground. Another crisp strike uppercut into the bastard's chin had him releasing Jaz's purse.

Moving smoothly as a predator, Liam spun toward the second man—who'd picked up a brick somewhere. Seeing Liam's attention focused on him, however, the brick man dropped the makeshift weapon and took off down the alley. Thug one scrambled to his feet and limped after him into the shadows.

Liam shifted his weight, as if considering going after the men. The thought of being left alone sent a new wave of terror through Jaz. She kicked her feet, trying to get off the damn high heels that had tripped her, but they were strapped on with leather. She clawed at the straps. Around her, someone was shouting something. Maybe several people. She didn't know. Her knees stung. Her hands stung. Most of all, her whole ordered world was spinning about.

"Jaz! Are you all right?" Sebastian was there, doubled over out of breath.

She didn't know what to answer. If that boot had come down on her wrist, if Liam had been there one second later, her whole world would have ended.

"You're all right." Liam's stone-calm face filled her vision. Unlike Bastian, Liam wasn't asking—he was telling. And he was so certain about it that Jaz couldn't argue. Strong hands closed around Jaz's shoulders, lifting her to her feet. Still holding on to her, Liam surveyed the alley and street. They had a small crowd gathering about them now, Devante staying somewhere in the back.

Jaz's heart pounded, and every muscle in her body thrummed.

"Sebastian. Get my car from the valet." Liam ordered. He wasn't even breathing hard. One arm still around Jaz, he pulled out his phone and pressed a few buttons to call in the assault. He listed the details to the police with the kind of matter-of-fact detachment people reserved for household chores and grocery lists and, despite having been on scene for less time than she, managed to capture the details of height, weight, and facial features she didn't remember at all.

Even spoken calmly, the word "attack" made her feel cold, as if someone had dunked her entire body into a frozen-over lake.

Cradling the phone against his shoulder, Liam pulled off his jacket and wrapped it around her.

"I'm fine." Her protest was halfhearted. She realized her dress had been torn so that her less-than-ample cleavage became far more pronounced. She moved her arm to cover it, then noticed that her palms were bleeding. The gashes weren't deep. Scrapes, really. But they stung.

Sebastian pulled up, and Liam shuffled Jaz into the passenger's seat before taking over the wheel and driving them home. They didn't say anything all the way to his place, and Jaz was grateful for the silence as she wrangled her errant thoughts into place. Once inside, however, Jaz wedged herself into the corner of his couch instead of retreating to her room. "Was that my hate mailer, you think?" she asked. "Or someone else trying to keep me from competing?"

"I don't think so." Liam retrieved a first aid kit and a wet washcloth. "I'll look into it and see what we can find for an ID, but from the scent and looks of it, they were after your wallet, not your career."

"Just a random mugging," Jaz said softly. "If I'd just let them have the damn purse, they would have left."

He settled next to her, his hazel eyes scrutinizing. "You could shift your training schedule to work in self-defense practice in place of a few weekly runs."

Jaz shook her head. Liam meant well, but he didn't understand how much of her life was riding on that Clash of the Titans Challenge. "I can't risk it. Same way I can't risk going rollerblading or playing soccer. There's too much of a chance of getting hurt."

"I'm not going to go after you the way I train with Kyan." Taking her wrist, Liam dabbed at the scrape. She pulled back from the sting, but his grip was unrelenting. It was comforting and annoying at the same time. "Contrary to popular opinion, I can use my brain when forced."

"Things still happen. A tweaked wrist. A turned ankle. I can't. Not now."

"I swear, sometimes I think you take some perverse pleasure in being difficult." Finishing with her palm, Liam took hold of Jaz's chin and turned her face for a better look. His thumb rested on her cheek. The spot was tender, as if bruised. It probably *was* bruised. "And for the record, you're the most insufferable, bullheaded, and frustrating woman I've ever met."

"I..." She trailed off, not knowing what she'd been about to say. Liam's presence, his touch, made her feel safe. Which was stupid because there was nothing safe about him. But her body wasn't listening for a better reason just then.

Liam's other hand tucked a piece of stray hair from her face, then dabbed carefully at a small cut over her brow she didn't remember getting. She smelled something woodsy, a scent that was barely there but definitely coming from him. This close, she could see the fine stitching along the collar of his button-down shirt, the five o'clock shadow along his square jaw. Around them, the apartment's normal sounds drowned out the occasional car passing on the street below. The low hum of the air ducts. The vibrations of the phone Liam wasn't answering.

His eyes were on hers now, their gaze potent and dangerously powerful. But safe too. She'd never been in such close proximity to him until now, not even when he'd cornered her on his kitchen island. Her heart quickened, her lips parting with shortening breaths.

Liam's fingers were frozen on her now. His entire body coiled into absolute stillness.

Jaz couldn't tell who had moved first or if they each moved in unison, but the bit of distance remaining between them became less and less as their mouths zeroed in on one another. Closer. Hotter. As unstoppable as it was wrong.

10

JAZ

*T*heir mouths connected softly, but once Jaz's lips parted in invitation, Liam's tongue invaded her with powerful strokes. One of his hands slipped behind her head, the other bracing her ribs with a strong hold. He held her with a secure, powerful confidence that washed all doubt from Jaz's mind, letting her lose herself in the flood of sensations of the now. In the way heat pooled low in her belly and spread in waves of pulsating need all the way through her body.

Liam's kiss was like nothing she'd ever experienced. His mouth didn't ask permission, it laid its claim and took without hesitation in a way that made her feel wanted. Savored. Special. Jaz's heart hammered against her ribs, her hands grabbing Liam's shoulders and finding coiled hard muscle beneath. More heat built where his palms lay against her skin, the sensation joining with that in her belly and mouth. In this moment, she was alive and awake and present with every hungry fiber of her being.

Liam's hold softened as he slowly pulled away, his own pulse beating strongly enough that she could see it in the side of his neck. For a long moment, he just looked at her, his hand still on her face. "That was…" He trailed off.

Mind-blowing. Erotic. Amazing.

The beat of silence between them stretched.

"Wrong." Liam pulled his hand back and stepped away. "I was out of line. I apologize."

It was ironic, but the apology somehow stung more than pavement smacking skin.

Jaz shrugged, giving her hair an irrelevant little flip that was right out of acting class. "It was nothing." The distance between them suddenly felt miles wide. Like there was too much open air and no solid rock to anchor into. "Just that kind of night, you know?"

Liam slid his fingers into his back pockets, his gaze as intense as always. "Are you all right?"

Now wasn't that a loaded question. She'd been assaulted for the first time in her life. And then been kissed just as potently. "I'm tired, is what I am." Assuming her signature bouncy step, Jaz strode up to Liam, stood on her toes, and kissed his cheek. "My purse and I both thank you for the save today. I'm going to bed."

LIAM WAS ALREADY in his running shoes when Jaz slipped out of her room in the morning, her wet hair from the shower tied in a ponytail high on her head. They didn't say much as they headed out to the elevator together and onto the sidewalk leading to the jogging path that started about half a mile from Liam's building.

That was when the reprieve ended, with Liam pulling up to run beside her. "We should talk about last night."

Jaz increased her pace. "You really want to hear me admit that you were right about a protection detail? I'm not sure a couple of drunk bums qualify as a world-shattering danger, but if you need to hear a word of undying gratitude, I'll send you a Hallmark card."

"Just to save your purse?"

"What else would I be thanking you for?"

"Sweeping you off your feet with my technique. I'm an excellent kisser."

"And highly modest."

"That too." Liam's voice lowered to somber tones. "Jaz. I meant what I said. I was out of line last night, and I know it."

She ran faster still. "Last I checked, it took two to tango. Stop acting as if you forced something."

"Not directly, maybe, but I knew you were vulnerable. It wasn't right. Kyan's sister deserves better than my behavior last night."

Great. She was back to being Kyan's little sister instead of a person in her own right. And here she'd thought the aftermath of the kiss couldn't get much worse. "Just so I'm clear, what other privileges does Kyan's little sister get as opposed to a regular mortal woman who walks the earthly planes?"

"I have to be nice to you at family functions."

"You aren't nice to me at any function."

"I never said I was perfect."

Jaz couldn't take it anymore. Taking a quick few sprint steps, she stopped in front of Liam, who nearly stumbled to keep from crashing into her. "Look. Liam. You and I, we don't like each other for a good reason. Yes, you're physically attractive—my opinion on that hasn't changed since you humiliated my little twelve-year-old self. But unlike that twelve-year-old, I'm perfectly capable of telling the difference between the heat of the moment and sincerity." Lie. She was terrible at it. But she could fake it with the best of them. It was one of her Hollywood-brat superpowers. "Lots of things happened last night. We kissed. There are probably five seventh graders in that middle school a mile away who are doing the same thing right now. Don't think I imagine it as anything more than it was—or that just because I'm a woman, I don't enjoy a mindless pleasure."

Jaz stepped out of Liam's way before he could reply and picked up the run again, her sneakers landing softly on the dirt-packed trail. She couldn't keep doing this. Pretending that nothing bothered her. It was better to put a nail into that coffin once and for all. That, and to wipe that whole bullshit thought line about how he was in charge from Liam's mind. "I think it's me who should be apologizing to you, if I gave you the impression that something could have meaning beyond the moment. For the record, I find how you treat women repulsive."

Instead of flinching like he was supposed to, Liam cocked his head in humored curiosity. "You keep bringing this up. All right. Let's have it out. What exactly is it that you think I do to women?"

Shit. That was not what she'd meant to step her foot into. Her face heated. Despite the tan, she blushed with embarrassing ease. And she was not talking about this. Except she had opened the damned door, and running away now would make her look like a coward after all that nonchalant talk about sex. "Like I said before, *Fifty Shades of Grey*. Though you probably can't count that well, so it's forty-nine or fifty-one just to be extra contrary."

"I find women too vulnerable and uncomfortable to say no to abuse, and then hurt them for my own sexual gratification?"

That sounded downright disgusting, and Jaz made a face. "Ew."

Liam's curious gaze turned penetrating, as if some part of him wasn't quite certain of Jaz's answer. Was afraid that she did think that of him.

"I think you're a certifiable asshole," Jaz informed him. "But no, I don't think abusing women is in your nature. What people do in bed is their own business. I'm just saying that your idea of a good time and mine are different." She turned her face up to the sky, where a light sprinkling of rain was starting to descend. "Yesterday was a fun little interlude, but now I see that it affected you a great deal more than it affected me, and I promise it will never happen again. Plus, two weeks are up next weekend. Unless those bums are behind the creepy newspaper-script letters, I'm free of you."

"Sounds like you haven't checked your email lately."

That didn't sound good. Pulling her phone from the armband she had it in, Jaz scrolled to the incoming messages, her gaze snapping to the starred one from her handler at Vector Ascent. Amid the usual disclaimer and a signature line that took up two paragraphs, the fatal words stared out at her from the screen.

Jaz, given the uptick in threatening comms, we'd like you to stay with Trident Security through the competition. We're picking up the tab on it as of Friday. Stay safe and climb on.

She scrolled through the message again. It stayed put. Her jaw clenched. They'd had a deal with Liam, and he went behind her back by secretly contacting her sponsor. By taking all choices away from her. This wasn't even a reaction to last night's attack—from the dates of the emails in the chain, he'd started this train into motion a week ago.

"How could you?" she demanded.

"How could I what? Make a professional recommendation about the security of a woman who has less than zero situational awareness and thinks learning self-defense carries too great a risk of pulling a muscle?" Liam snorted. "To be blunt, I did it without hesitation or a second thought."

LIAM

*L*iam, Jaz, and Sebastian arrived at Los Angeles International Airport the day before the route-marking part of the Clash of the Titans Challenge was set to start. After collecting the oversized gear bags from baggage claim, they made their way to the car rental counter.

"Give me that." Liam extended his arm to take Jaz's bag, which wouldn't fit onto their overfull trolley. "It's bigger than you are."

"I can handle my own gear."

"You can also pee behind a bush. Are we giving up indoor plumbing on that count?"

"Technically, yes. Unless you want to haul a potty into the mountains."

"Children." Sebastian's voice was singsong as he tilted his head toward the rental counter, where an associate was waiting. "We are in public."

"Tell him to stop trying to control me, and we won't have an issue." Jaz walked up to the counter, giving her name for the reservation. Liam was right behind her, rejecting the more fragile Corvette they were offered in favor of a slate-gray Ford Fusion with tinted windows.

"I'm not controlling you, I'm controlling the environment. That's my job." Liam grabbed the keys from the attendant before Jaz could. His lower body tightened involuntarily, letting him know just how much it wouldn't mind *controlling* this woman for a while—which was out of the question even if Jaz had been interested. She was Kyan's sister, and that made her off-limits.

He still hadn't told Kyan about that kiss. Liam told himself he was waiting until they were at a gym with a proper sparring ring so Kyan could pound on him for it—but that wasn't the whole truth. The real problem was that instead of satiating the pull Liam felt toward Jaz, the kiss had only magnified it. He could still taste the sweet surrender of her mouth, the arousal he felt taking over her body as she dug her fingers into him. There was a part of Jaz's sexuality that enjoyed erotic control, though she would no doubt try to skin Liam alive if he pointed that out.

And that was the crux of the problem. Now that Liam knew she enjoyed it, his own urges were assaulting his cock every time he allowed an errant thought into his head. Maybe he should have gone to one of those parties Sandy tried to coax him into attending. Released some tension. Cleared his head. But he hadn't gone. Didn't want to. Couldn't make himself interested in casual play.

So he threw himself into his work—and when the Clash of the Titans was over, he'd step away to the distance he'd always maintained between them. For now, though, nothing—*nothing*—was going to happen on his watch. He didn't care how much it chafed Jaz to have a babysitter. The day Liam's sister had been assaulted by a rich high school senior was branded on Liam's soul. He'd been too small and weak to stand up to the football player then, but he wasn't that little boy anymore. Now he made the rules. And enforced them.

"Ready for the press conference?" Sebastian asked Jaz as they piled into the Fusion, Liam taking the wheel. "I hope there are blow-dryers at the hotel. Gotta look my best in case the camera swings to show your lovely support team."

"I'll be fine. Not my first round in front of a camera. Just try to keep the paranoid boy from interrogating the other competitors and making a fool of everyone."

Liam ignored the jab. Vector Ascent had sent him profiles on the four men Jaz would be competing against. A couple had a few minor misdemeanors on their records, but since each Titan was backed by a national brand, they were trying to stay on the straight and narrow. The online rhetoric from people upset about Jaz taking Roman Robillard's spot and about Girls Aflame in general had been holding steady, but without any specific threats.

"Did the PD ever track down Jaz's purse snatchers?" Sebastian asked from the back.

"Negative." Liam hadn't really expected them to. A pair of drunken bums who failed to snatch a purse in a cameraless alley were never going to be a priority. Ignoring the GPS's insistence on a direct route and the grumbling of his annoyed passengers, Liam took extra time to drive around and get a solid lay of the area. Yes, it turned a short drive into a long one and made a part of Liam's left ass cheek fall asleep, but the inconvenience was worth it.

Ontario, California, was a large small town with great access to the San Gabriel mountain range, where the competition was being held. Despite being located in SoCal, the partially wooded peaks would be covered with pristine snow over the winter months. The slabs of stone sliced up from the earth like the vertebrae of some enormous many-backed beast. In counterpoint to such monstrous imagery, birds chattered overhead, including the repetitive, high-pitched pips of bald eagles. When Liam peered upward, he saw two of them wheeling above, the telltale white of their heads and tail feathers visible. There were a few restaurants in the area and a number of establishments that catered to the tourist industry. The Cucamonga Peak Inn the Titans were booked at already had five utility task vehicles or UTVs parked outside, each shiny washed car painted with the words RZR XP 1000 Dynamix on the side.

"Our trusty mountain steeds," Jaz announced.

"They don't look trusty," said Sebastian. With a steering wheel and two seats, the UTV's open structure consisted of a roll cage instead of a traditional roof. The vehicles also sported a short snub-nosed body, high undercarriage clearance with higher, large off-roading tires. "And they only have two seats. If someone has to sit on Liam's lap, I call dibs."

"Yes, exactly how are we going to explain why I'm squeezing an extra person into a vehicle?" asked Jaz. "Competitors are allowed one support person and belay while we mark the routes. I don't need to be disqualified before the competition even begins."

Liam gave her a sideways glance. He'd already discussed as much with Vector Ascent, who'd cleared it with the event organizers. Did she think this was his first detail? "The UTVs only get competitors to the trailhead," he said with exaggerated patience. "I'll take my own vehicle. The seven days after that are all hiking and climbing on your own power. I'll shadow you and Sebastian with my own gear, but won't interfere or engage with you about anything."

"How will we ever pitch a tent without your sage advice?" asked Jaz.

"Badly, I imagine." Getting out of the car, Liam walked around and opened Jaz's door for her, which he knew would piss her off. Small pleasures.

The rustic hotel was tastefully decorated like a hunting lodge, with rough wooden walls like a cabin, antlers decorating the lampshades, and brown-and-white curtains that resembled legitimate cowhides. The place gave off the scent of leather, so maybe the resemblance was real. They were checked into the event and given two adjoining rooms, each with two double beds. Liam made himself comfortable in Jaz's quarters quicker than she could offer a protest.

They'd barely gotten a chance to shower and change after the trip before the schedule had them in the hotel's single meeting room, where a podium for the competitors and chairs for the press were already set up. Behind the podium, banners of the sponsoring brands proudly bracketed large windows with the view of the San Bernardino National Forest. Taking up a post next to the door, Liam watched Jaz stride confidently into the lions' den.

She wore Vector Ascent's top gear for the event, the athletic clothing hugging her lithe figure as she smiled for the photographers and smoothly discussed her gratitude for the well-placed jacket pockets and oversized hood that fit over a climbing helmet.

"You know, I almost feel bad for the rest of them." Sebastian leaned on the wall near Liam, watching the reporters huddle around Jaz while the rest of the climbers shifted their weight uncomfortably. With her smiles, sound bites, and honed yet natural-seeming camera poses, Jaz positively owned each square inch of the limelight. It was difficult to imagine her and shadow-loving Kyan growing up together.

Yet how much of this attention she loved was also fueling the danger against her?

"So when did it happen?" Sebastian crossed one ankle over another.

"When did what happen?"

"When did you fall for my Jaz?"

Liam's head snapped to the side. "I'm the hired help, Sebastian. That's where my relationship with her starts and ends."

"In my experience, hired help tends to have limits. And being set up on a date with me would have crossed them three times over."

Liam returned his attention to where it belonged—watching the room and his charge. "I'm a professional."

"A professional owner of an international security firm. Your job is to send teams all over the globe, not play bodyguard. You're here because you can't make yourself not be."

This was getting ridiculous. He wasn't going to explain his need to get out and stretch his legs in the field to some kid from Jaz's climbing club. "You've got it all wrong, Bastian. It's you I'm head over heels in love with. Jaz is just an excuse."

Sebastian laughed, but his rich voice soon quieted into somber tones. "Don't underestimate how hard she fights to stay strong. She makes it look easy, but she is fighting every moment of every day."

Liam opened his mouth to ask what the hell Sebastian was talking about, but the whine of a microphone cut him short. The conference was starting, and the five competitors took their seats behind a cloth-covered table. The organizers made a few short remarks, then released the sharks.

"Ms. Keasley." The first reporter went right for Jaz. "You're the only woman at the table. How does it feel competing against all men?"

"We are all competing against the mountain," Jaz answered. "I'm honored to be in the company of fellow athletes who love the sport." She grinned. "That, and we're all adrenaline junkies, so there is that."

The room chuckled appreciatively, but the next reporter was already up on his feet and digging for trouble. "Ms. Keasley, you're an eleventh-hour substitution for the long-standing champion Roman Robillard. Can you speak as to why the change was made and whether you and Roman discussed the situation?"

"I don't get told inside baseball," Jaz said with a self-deprecating grin that Liam would never have managed in her place. "What I can tell you is that Roman is one of the most skilled climbers I know, and it's my hope to do his legacy—and Vector Ascent—justice."

Not bad at all.

"What about the rumors that Girls Aflame, which you very publicly support, has garnered unwelcome attention from a certain extremist group?" A third reporter jumped in, tightening the loop around Jaz despite the other competitors starting to shift their weight restlessly. "Does that worry you? Will it affect your ability to focus while up there on the mountain?"

Humor left Jaz's face as she twisted toward the reporter and held the silent pause just long enough for the air to zing with tension. "Does it worry me that terrorists overseas want to see women and girls denied an education? That should worry every single one of us. Hateful groups spread hate. That's what they do. Nothing they might say will stop me from supporting such a deserving cause."

Once the reporters saw they were unable to get under Jaz's skin, the conference turned technical and Liam allowed himself to relax as the sharks stopped circling. Which brought Sebastian's comment back to the forefront of his thoughts. He wanted to probe more into this fighting thing Jaz's best friend thought she was doing, but it was wise to presume that anything he said to Sebastian was going right back to Jaz. Taking out his phone, he tapped a message to Aiden back in the office.

Can you take a quiet look at Jaz?

Aiden: *What am I looking for?*

Liam hesitated. *Skeletons in the closet. Anything that could be used against her. Get personal.*

A pregnant pause. Then, finally, a reply.

Aiden: *Roger.*

Liam put away his phone, his chest tight. He could explain this away with all the logic in the world, but the reality was that he'd just stepped over the line. There was nothing in what he'd seen to warrant that kind of intrusion into Jaz's privacy, and if Jaz ever found out, she'd be furious. And rightfully so. But fuck it, Liam couldn't bear to take any chances. Not with Kyan's sister. Not with Jaz.

Guilt was still gripping Liam's conscience as the conference ended and Jaz returned from the fray. Sebastian swept her into an unapologetic hug, his tall, lanky body engulfing hers.

"Good job, killer." He kissed the top of her head. "Ready to see what this exciting city has for restaurants?"

"I'm ready to test out the mattress," Jaz told him. "I'll grab a sandwich at the marketplace and hope I can stay awake long enough to chew."

Liam was glad to hear that, but Sebastian looked disappointed.

Jaz seemed to pick up the same vibe because she pulled the car keys—that she'd taken away from Liam earlier—from her pocket. "You should totally go out, though. Do some recon for when we come back from the field and are starved for something cooked on a real stove."

"You sure?" Sebastian's hand was already wrapped around the keys, his eyes alight. "I'll bring you something back. In case you wake up hungry. I can even pick up something for your pet bear."

Liam didn't indulge that with a reply.

"Sounds perfect." Jaz laughed in that easy way she had around her friend. The kind she and Liam would never share. "Have fun."

True to her word, Jaz stopped at the little market shop near the check-in counter for something that claimed to be a chicken salad wrap, set her alarm for four in the morning, and dropped into bed.

Keeping the lights low, Liam pulled out his laptop and settled behind the writing desk to catch up on work. Which was how, at 11:00 p.m., he saw the call from the Arrowhead Regional Medical Center in San Bernardino flashing across the screen of Jaz's charging phone. Since he'd checked the lay of the land before leaving on this trip, he knew that hospital to be a fairly short drive from their current location.

"Hello?" Liam answered without hesitation.

"Good evening," a no-nonsense voice on the other end said calmly over the line. "This is Naomi, the charge nurse at the Arrowhead Regional ER. I'm looking for a Jaz Keasley."

"I'm Jaz," Liam told Naomi. "What's going on?"

"Mr. Keasley, your friend Sebastian asked me to call you. I'm afraid there's been an accident."

JAZ

*J*az rushed through the doors of the Arrowhead Regional ER, Liam's words when he woke her replaying on a loop in her mind.

There was an accident. A hit-and-run that T-boned Sebastian's car. Sebastian was in surgery. There was an accident...

"Can I help you?" A woman behind a semicircular desk with an Information sign hanging above it asked with too great a calm.

Jaz drew a breath. She didn't like hospitals. Didn't like the clean walls and wheeled beds and the antiseptic smell. The signs pointing to different circles of hell, like *oncology* and *intensive care, burn unit.* Hospitals were places where people changed. And now Bastian, her kind, sensitive best friend Bastian, was in one.

"What are you looking for?" The woman prompted again.

Liam put a hand on Jaz's shoulder, speaking with the confidence and authority of someone who considered himself at home in such places. Of course he was. He was a medic just like Kyan. The woman at the information desk gave Liam an appreciative sort of smile, which he ignored, and started tapping away on the computer. Thirty seconds later, Liam had directions and was steering Jaz along in a daze.

They sat in silence in the waiting room, Liam throwing a jacket he'd somehow thought to bring along over Jaz's shoulders. An hour passed. Jaz stared at the bland wall. Liam tapped away on his phone. Finally, a doctor-looking person in scrubs and a cap covering her hair appeared in the door.

"The car that hit your friend's vehicle struck on the driver's side," the woman explained in a soft voice. "It fractured his leg in several places. For a little while there, we were worried about the femoral artery, but fortunately, it was spared. Sebastian will have a long road to rehab, but he'll be all right." She paused. "He's out of surgery and coming out of anesthesia now. Would you like to see him?"

"Yes," said Jaz.

"Would you give us a moment first?" Liam asked.

"Of course." The doctor stepped out.

Jaz wheeled on Liam, her heart throwing itself against her ribs. "What are we waiting on now?"

"For you to start breathing." Liam invited himself into Jaz's space, taking her chin in that way that he had. The one that made her feel safe and infuriated all at the same time. "The last thing Sebastian needs right now is for you to go in there and fall apart."

Jaz tried to pull away.

Liam didn't let her.

"You don't know what he needs," she said through clenched teeth. "You don't know anything." She shoved Liam right in the chest.

Liam's hands slipped to Jaz's face, his thumbs tracing her cheekbones. "Listen to me. Sebastian is going to have a hard road to recovery. Do you want him to feel like a victim or a survivor?"

Liam's words finally penetrated Jaz's haze, and she nodded. She could do this. She'd act if she had to, but she could do this. With Liam's hand steady on her lower back, she allowed herself to be guided into Sebastian's room.

Sebastian was half reclined in a bed, his face scratched and his leg in an elevated sling attached to the bedframe. He gave Jaz a weak smile as she stepped in.

"The doc tells me you're hard to kill," she told him as a way of greeting.

"Kill? 'Tis but a flesh wound." For someone just coming off anesthesia, Sebastian did a fair imitation of the British knight from Monty Python. Regardless, he looked pale beneath his freckles. "And I did get a nice airlift ride here. I just wish I'd been conscious to enjoy more of it. That and, hey, if a glorious man's gonna shear off my pants, I'd prefer he at least take advantage of my naked body." Sebastian waggled his brows. "How did you get here anyway? I hate to tell you this, but the rental Vector Ascent leased for us is absolute toast. I hope that doesn't damage your sponsorship."

Jaz realized she hadn't even noticed that Liam had procured another car somewhere. He was right—she was a wreck. "Never mind about the car. You scared the shit out of me, you know." Though she was trying to hide it, all the pent-up adrenaline was making her hands shake. She stuffed them behind her back. "Do you remember what happened?"

His grin slipped. "I was circling what passes for main streets around here, got lost. The next thing I know, this huge ass SUV is flying out at me. Then, boom, crack, airbags. The last I saw of the bastard, he was backing away and speeding off."

"Why would someone do that?"

"Could have a record or a warrant out for their arrest," Liam said, staring at his phone.

"I'd hate to think of it like that," said Sebastian. "Maybe it was just a kid who got freaked out and didn't know what to do. Maybe they'll end up confessing everything to their parents and showing up at the police department later."

"Yeah. Definitely." Liam's voice was dry. "Did you stop anywhere before the accident? Have an argument with anyone?"

"No. I hadn't even gotten out of the car to get dinner yet. Was still driving around looking for a place." Sebastian switched his attention back to Jaz. "The bad news is that I'll be out of commission for tomorrow. I won't be able to spot you for the Titans thing."

Jaz immediately pressed a kiss to his temple. "It doesn't matter. Did you see those climbers yesterday? I wasn't going to be winning anything anyway. Plus, who cares about this round? It's just route selection."

"Route selection is half the battle," said Sebastian.

"Wrong again, G.I. Joe." Jaz forced that acting smile back onto her face. "*Knowledge* is half the battle. And since you're proving so difficult to get rid of, you and I are going to be poring over maps together."

Sebastian shook his head, though it made him wince. "You need to get out there. Is there anyone we can fly out here?"

There wasn't. Jaz had already gone through that calculation in her head. Even if one of her climbing friends could drop everything right this moment, by the time they could catch a flight to California and drive all the way to the San Bernardino Forest, the event would have been way past started.

"What about him?" Sebastian pointed at Liam, who was on his phone again. "Wasn't he in the air force or something?"

"The navy," Jaz corrected automatically. "SEALs."

Bastian grinned. He'd known and had baited her. "Right. SEALs. I hear they can handle a rope if you give them enough training and treats."

Liam raised his head. He looked harsh and unapproachable, his chiseled face a study in male perfection. Worse still, the moment Liam put his phone away and gave his full attention to the conversation at the bedside, his presence somehow filled the room. The effect was so immediate and potent that Jaz wondered whether Liam had been playing with that phone on purpose, just to keep from imposing too much on the room's air. He crossed his arms over his chest. "I can handle a belay."

"Excellent." Sebastian made a good effort at sounding enthusiastic, but Jaz could see that all the talking was getting to him. "Liam has me by twenty pounds, but we're about the same height. Most of the gear should fit with a few minor tweaks."

"But…" Jaz bit her lip. The thought of seven days alone with Liam filled her stomach with a fluttering sensation she didn't care for at all. This was all too much. *He* was too much. But Sebastian was right about this being the only way forward. A chain of events had hung everything—her finances, her career, her future—on the Clash of the Titans. If she backed away now, she would owe Vector Ascent money that she didn't have. That meant bankruptcy, crawling back to her parents, proving that everything her father thought about her was true.

Not to mention it would be sheer cowardice.

"All right, then." She gave the two men her signature energetic Hollywood grin. "If the SEAL can keep up, I guess he can come along."

Sebastian's returning smile took more than it should have. "Go and fight like a girl, Jazminator." He felt for something at the side of his bed.

Wordlessly, Liam stepped up and placed a small push-button device in his hand.

Sebastian gave Jaz a sheepish look. "Morphine. Do you mind if I talk to Liam for one second? I want to make sure he knows I'll kick his ass if he screws this up for you."

"Get better, Bastian." Pushing herself up on tiptoes to get the right angle, she gingerly gave her friend one final hug. "I love you."

Liam followed and joined her in the hallway only a few seconds later, on the move as always.

"Hey, thank you for—"

Liam cut her off. "Start at eleven a.m. tomorrow?"

"It is. Why?"

"Can you manage four hours of sleep?"

"Yes. Again with the *why*?" It was two in the morning, which would put them back at the hotel by three, and then a luxurious seven hours in the sack if she wanted.

"Because while we were chatting up Sebastian, someone tried to return a black SUV with a damaged front end to Mountain Rent-a-Car. Said he'd hit a deer."

Jaz grabbed Liam's arm, her heart skipping a beat. "The hit-and-run driver?"

"It looks like it. The PD has him, and if we get there at seven a.m. tomorrow, we may be able to speak with him."

Jaz frowned. "Why do you think he'd agree to speak to us all?"

"Because of you." Liam caught Jaz's eyes. "The man the PD picked up, it's your date, Devante."

13

JAZ

*a*t seven in the morning, just four hours before the first challenge of the Clash of the Titans was scheduled to kick off, Jaz followed Liam and Detective Dan Kilauea through the bowels of the San Bernardino County Police Department.

"Through here," Kilauea half growled in the tone of overworked employees everywhere, skirting metal desks, uniformed personnel escorting handcuffed arrestees, and a pair of adolescent boys along the sidelines looking in turn sheepish and defiant. The place smelled vaguely of sweat, bad coffee, furniture polish, and, for some reason, grapefruits.

"Don't know why he agreed to talk to you, but I always say that we only catch the stupid ones." With his gruff voice, mustache, and ruler-trimmed straight black hair, Kilauea looked like he walked right out of central casting for an old detective film. "Devante Jackson is going to see the judge at eight. Will be out by noon, provided he makes bail."

Jaz wrapped her arms around herself. "How can they let him out on bail? Isn't a hit-and-run the very definition of a flight risk?"

The detective gave another noncommittal grunt that probably meant *not my department* or maybe *welcome to reality.* "Do you have any reason to believe Mr. Jackson targeted your friend on purpose? Any bad blood between them? Arguments?"

"No. They were friends."

"Acquaintances," Liam corrected, though the distinction seemed petty just now.

"When was the last time you saw Mr. Jackson?"

"Just over a week ago. Sebastian had set us up on a blind date. Mr. Jackson texted me once afterward, but I never replied."

The detective gave Jaz a hard look that sent a chill down her back. Did he somehow suspect her in this mess? Sticking her hands in her pockets, Jaz fell back to stay in step with Liam.

The grapefruit scent increased as they edged down a narrow hallway and past a potted citrus tree peeking out of an open door in one of the offices. Another turn and Kilauea opened a door into a small room furnished with a table, two chairs, and what had to be a two-way mirror. Devante was already there, one wrist handcuffed to the table. He was wearing a pair of jeans and a T-shirt that looked slept in—and probably had been.

"Jaz." His face lit up in a smile, which faded the moment Liam came into view. "Sorry, I'm not into threesomes."

Jaz was about to tell him just how little she cared about his preference, when a soft squeeze from Liam reminded her that Devante didn't have to talk to them. And once his attorney got involved, he wouldn't be doing any chatting at all. If there was any clarity to be gained, this was their one chance.

Jaz nodded.

"I'll be outside," Liam said.

Stepping forward, Jaz took a seat in the folding chair opposite Devante and tried to think of something useful to say. "So, are you all right?" she managed, trying not to look at Diante's handcuffs, which were clipped to a bolt in the middle of the table to limit his motions. The room was chilly, and she rubbed her hands over her arms. "Did you get hurt?"

He gave her an appreciative smile. "A little banged up. I was lucky."

Sebastian hadn't been.

"Jaz, listen." Devante leaned in toward her, the movement hampered by his cuffed wrist. "You know this is a huge misunderstanding, right? Everything yesterday was an honest-to-God accident. I swear. You have to believe me."

"What are you doing in San Bernadino anyway?"

"Coming to see the start of the Clash of the Titans, of course." Devante spoke in the same reverent tones as he had that night. "I told you I always come to watch you climb. I pick up something new every time I do." He reached for her hands in his handcuffs as if imploring her to grasp his fingers.

She didn't. "Why, Devante? Why would you just drive off like that after hitting Sebastian? He's your friend."

"That's not what happened."

"What happened, then?"

"I didn't even know Sebastian was in the car, much less hurt. What I remember—I think—is suddenly recognizing the Ford Fusion as possibly the one the guy at the airport rental counter told me you rented. I just wanted to speak to you. I tried to pull up close, to check if it was really you, but then lost control."

He'd interrogated the rental counter guy for which car she'd rented? Holy crap.

"You have to know I'd never hurt you or Sebastian," Devante continued. "I just sort of blacked out. I must've banged my head or something because I don't recall the next few minutes. Next thing I know, I'm driving toward town with no memory of how I got there."

"I'm sorry, Dev, I want to believe you, but it sounds like the most convenient amnesia ever." Jaz rubbed her face. "So why didn't you turn around when you came to? I mean, if you thought I might be in the car you just hit, why didn't you go back to check if I was okay?"

"I wasn't thinking like that. When I, you know, came to, I wasn't really hurt—so I figured the other driver must be in the same shape. Maybe I somehow knew you weren't in that car I hit. I was disoriented and my thoughts were all scattered. I felt really tired, though, so I pulled off on one of those trails and drifted off. When I

85

woke a few hours later, I didn't know where I was or why. I guess I hit my head harder than I thought, right? Anyway, I got out and saw the damage and figured I must've hit a deer. So that's what I told the rental car place."

"You woke up in a damaged car in the middle of the night, had no idea how you got there, and instead of going to the ER to get checked out, you went to return your rental?" It was difficult to even repeat Devante's bullshit back to him with a straight face.

"Like I said, I was confused. I probably had a concussion. I'll get it checked out." Devante shifted in his seat and laid his palms on the table as if in supplication, the chains from the cuffs clanging stridently against the wood. "Look, I panicked, okay? Not everyone has nerves of steel. I was freaked out and had a head injury. When I woke, the deer explanation made more sense to my jumbled brain. Even knowing, it all feels like a dream. A bad one."

"Yeah." Bad dream seemed a very apt description of Jaz's own feelings.

"Sebastian needs to tell the police that he doesn't want to press charges. He probably didn't think of that with all that's going on, but this is important. You need to explain things to him, and tell him to tell the PD about the no-charge thing. We're friends. What happened was terrible, but it was just an accident. I know he wouldn't want to make it even worse all around. You'll get him to call, won't you?"

"Yeah." Jaz lied and didn't care. "I'll talk to him."

Devante leaned forward. "Today, all right?" The reverence in his voice was creeping toward demand. "This is my life we're talking about."

"Of course." She pushed away from the table. Maybe someone as cool minded as Liam would think of something clever to ask just now, something that would seal the case against Devante once and for all, but all she wanted was to get out of the room. "Let me go make some calls before the challenge starts, all right?"

Jaz walked out of the interview room, shivers still rushing over her skin. Liam held out his arm, and Jaz pressed herself gratefully against his chest, her head fitting perfectly into the nook of his large shoulder. "I don't understand," she said. "I know people do stupid things when they panic, but there's no way he could think Sebastian wasn't injured. I mean, he crashed the front of a huge-ass Suburban into the driver's door of a little Fusion."

Liam brushed the back of her head, and Jaz had to acknowledge that the man he'd grown into bore little resemblance to the teenaged asshole who'd humiliated her all those years ago. She was fortunate to have him here. Fortunate to have him as her partner for the coming week.

"Before I left his room, Sebastian told me something. I need to know if it's true." Liam's voice was just loud enough for Jaz and the detective to hear. "When you and he go places together, who drives?"

"I do," Jaz said reflexively. "It's a running joke between us because I always pull the seat so far up that if he gets in after me, he bangs his knees. So he always lets me snatch the keys. I like having the wheel, so… Oh God. The rental was in my name, and with tinted windows—you think Devante assumed I was driving? That he wanted to hurt me on purpose?"

"I think there are several possibilities to consider," Liam said firmly. "To Detective Kilauea's point, one can't rule out sheer stupidity. But yes, one of the scenarios is that this wasn't an accident at all."

14

LIAM

*T*he Clash of the Titans' first challenge kicked off from one of the most gorgeous—and photogenic—spots on the West Coast: San Gabriel Mountains. As an added bonus, Mount San Antonio, or as the locals called it, Mt. Baldy, with its ski resorts and crests rising over the valley cities made its stand to the east. Jaz and the other four competitors knelt beside their gear, carefully rechecking it. Not because they needed to, but to give the photographers plenty of time to get just the right picture of the brand they were representing. Liam had to give Jaz props for at least making it look natural instead of coiling and uncoiling the same piece of rope for the fifth time like Nike's champion was doing.

Despite the remote location, there was a bevy of spectators, along with chance hikers going in and out of the zigzag of pine-lined trails. Fortunately, the event organizers had set up a secure perimeter with competent men at all entrance points. Which all left Liam with time on his hands to get a bit of work done.

Angling his body discreetly away from Jaz and the others, Liam took out his phone and scrolled through the recent emails. Electronics were forbidden for the challengers, who had to rely on maps and skill to navigate, but Liam wasn't a participant. So ethically, he was okay with it.

The email from his mother was at the top of the chain with another admonishment to stop enabling his sister's behavior. Then a bill for his credit card, which Lisa had run up. He let out a breath, then with one click approved the payment of the balance in full. Next, Aiden needed an update about the whole Devante debacle, so he tapped out a few keystrokes to give the lay of the land. Then there was a legal cease-and-desist notice from Obsidian Ops trying to keep Trident Security from expanding into a field his company had every right to expand into. A couple more swipes on his screen and that nasty tangle of weeds went to his lawyer to deal with.

Done, done, and done.

"If you don't knock that off, I'm going to personally kick your ass." Still smiling for the cameras, Jaz whispered the threat under her breath as she walked by him.

He gave her an innocent look and slipped his phone discreetly up his sleeve.

Her answering warning scowl would have done a Catholic nun proud.

The photo circus finally came to an end with the Clash of the Titans host coming up to the podium for an official welcome and walk down memory lane. A very long walk. Liam pulled his phone back out, caught Jaz's blazing glare, and made short work of slipping the phone right back where he got it. His hands rose in open-palmed innocence. *Nothing to see here.*

"That little girl is so out of her league." The low mutter sounded from Liam's right, where the other four support people were standing in wait to get the show on the road. The guy who'd spoken had his arms crossed over his chest and wore the kind of condescending scowl that Liam itched to punch off his face. Not just because he disliked anyone disrespecting Kyan's little sister, but because he disliked anyone disrespecting his partner. It appeared that in stepping up to fill Sebastian's place, something had shifted inside him. He wasn't sure what, exactly, but there was one thing he knew for certain: only *he* was allowed to give Jaz a hard time.

It was a change that would take some time to acclimate to.

Finally, after an hour of bullshit and admonishments on safety, the climbers got the official send-off. Each pair took the direction they thought would lend them most luck. For the next seven days, it would be Liam, Jaz, whatever they carried on their backs, and the mountains.

They'd spend the rest of the day getting to the base point of where Jaz had intended to mark at least two of the routes. The straps of Sebastian's pack dug into Liam's shoulders. He wished he had his own gear, but he hadn't brought a large enough pack to carry all the climbing paraphernalia along with the power cell banks and range extenders for his cell. That part of the packing he'd kept on a need-to-know basis, and Jaz *didn't* need to know. He wasn't a challenger, so he figured he could have his toys.

Once they reached their first camp location, Jaz wasted no time getting herself up on the rock face. The place she'd chosen rose toward a large circular overhang that hugged the mountain. The protrusion was aptly named Ballerina's Skirt, and she was adorably vocal about her excitement to lay routes cutting through it.

With her neon-pink—of course they were pink—Vector Ascent garments and bright orange ropes juxtaposed against the slate gray of the cliff, she looked like a phoenix swooping up the mountain face with more speed and grace than any mortal should be capable of. As Liam held her safety line, he recalled Jaz's father calling her climbing *a goddamned hobby* that she *should have grown out of a decade ago* and decided that Hugh Keasley was a blind idiot.

But at least Hugh and Lola hadn't sent Jaz off to military school when she was twelve, the way his own mother did to him. If she'd done it because he was a troublemaker or because she believed in service, or even if she'd just thought it was the best thing for him, he'd have understood. But that wasn't why Patti had done it. She sent Liam off because the rich parents of the high schooler who'd raped Lisa had paid her to do it. Because even at eleven, Liam didn't think rape should be ignored and refused to keep his mouth shut.

Liam had cried himself to sleep for the first year away. He'd called every day begging to come home, even when Patti's newest boyfriend threatened to beat his ass if he bothered his mother again. But Patti had eventually found a more effective solution—she stopped taking his calls. Stopped answering his emails. Signed him up for summer camp, paid for, courtesy of the very same rapist's parents.

It was the first time Liam had learned that affection and belonging had a price tag attached. That there was always a return-on-investment calculus. That once keeping him around became too costly, he would be shuffled away. At least the military was upfront about it. Told him all the rules.

Liam shifted his weight and took the slack out of the line he held. That was ancient history. Had he been able to protect Lisa to begin with, none of it would be a problem. Now he ran a whole security company and rescue outfit. He really couldn't complain. He'd gotten a top-notch education, both in a prestigious military school and the one in life. He learned. He grew. He had the Tridents, and that was all the real family he needed.

"Doing okay up there?" he hollered to Jaz, who was shaking out her arms after defying an overhang. They were high enough that the elevation was thinning the oxygen, and it took less exertion to reach fatigue. Not that such things were slowing Jaz down at all from the pattern they fell into.

Jaz lead climbed, hammering the pitons into position as she went. He anchored himself in and fed out the rope until she reached a wide enough landing to reset their belay system. Then he'd climb up to join her, and they'd rest a few moments, the breeze drying the perspiration from their faces while they drank water. Pulled up the gear. Reset and started again. With the fog in the valley still visible below them, it felt like they were scaling their way to the heavens.

But if they didn't get back down soon, they'd lose the light.

"I'm good." She flashed white teeth as she peered down at him. "Am I keeping you from playing Candy Crush?"

"You're keeping me from a nap. Have you checked the time lately?"

She turned over her wrist and swore. "You better be faster going down than going up."

Liam snorted. Airborne school, search and rescue, ziplining from helicopters. "I'm rappelling. You're the one picking up gear." He knew better than to offer to do it for her.

They returned down to the campsite in the same amiable silence. It'd been a while since Liam climbed like this, and years since he'd made a straight descent without having an objective or a victim strapped to a Reeves basket to worry about. This was sport and velocity, and he lost himself in perpetual motion. It reminded him of a runner's high, and the intense but content look on Jaz's face said she was feeling it too.

The serenity was shattered by the time they finished the descent, the glorious-looking clouds having decided to take away some of the light they'd counted on. Jaz was stressing she hadn't gone farther on the first day. Liam was frowning at the tent they were going to be sharing. A nice lightweight and durable contraption that saved ounces by being, well, small.

He and Jaz would be in closer quarters tonight than he'd realized. Close enough that Kyan would probably have his head for it.

Not a problem, Liam told himself firmly. Except for actual sleeping, all other camp chores could be done outside. And hell, there was nothing wrong with sleeping beneath the stars either. With that in mind, Liam went to pull his bedroll out into the clearing.

And felt the first drops of light rain land on his cheeks.

JAZ

The *pow pow pow* of rain beating down on the tent sounded like gunfire. It shook the fly and ran in rivers along Vector Ascent's high-tech fabric.

"No, no, *no*." Jaz rushed over the sleeping bags and Liam and stuck her head outside the tent.

The light hint of rain from earlier in the evening was gone. Now, water slapped her skin with huge drops, soaking her hair and running down the front of her shirt at once.

"What the hell are you doing?" Liam hauled her back and rezipped the tent. "I prefer not to spend the next twenty-four hours trying to keep my gear from drowning. Been there, done that."

Jaz shoved back her water-slicked hair. "I needed to see how bad it was."

"Really?" Liam waved his hand toward the tent roof, which trembled beneath the downpour. "You couldn't use your imagination?"

The sky lit up with lightning to punctuate Liam's words, thunder following suit a few seconds later. Jaz groaned and lay back on the sleeping bag. There was no going out in this weather.

"Strategically speaking, the rain works to your advantage." Liam readjusted his sleeping bag and lay back down. "No one will be able to go out in this, and given last night's adventures, you need the rest more than the others do."

Jaz closed her eyes. Liam had a point. But it also meant that she'd have to move a great deal faster than she was planning during the remaining days—and she preferred technique to sheer speed. "None of the others will be stuck with you for the day, though."

"It's karma," Liam muttered. "The universe is inflicting penance."

"For what?"

"I'll make a list."

Jaz snorted, but nestled back into her own down bedding, the heat from Liam's body just inches away from hers filling the otherwise chilly tent. If someone had told her two weeks ago that she'd be happily dozing next to this man, she'd have called them mad. Yet here they were. A warm tent, a rainy day, the rhythmic pattering of the drops. With a fatigue-laden sigh, Jaz let herself fall back asleep.

The weather showed no sign of easing come morning. After sleeping in late, making coffee and breakfast oatmeal on a carefully contained stove, and spending several hours poring over maps and routes, eventually reality settled through the tent. They were stuck together for a while yet, and all solitary entertainment options had run out.

"Truth or dare," Jaz said into the silence.

Liam rolled onto his side and propped his body onto his forearm. "You've got to be kidding."

"I'm bored."

Liam dropped back and stared at the ceiling, as he'd been doing all morning. "Watch the spider between the tent and the fly, see how far out you can calculate pi, write a poem."

"I never took you for a coward."

As if touched with a hot poker, Liam was up again in a moment. His eyes flashed with challenge and a slice of something Jaz hadn't seen him show before. Mischief. Unabashed mischief. "Don't say I didn't try to give you a way out. Truth or dare, *Jazmine*."

"Oh no, you don't." She pointed her finger at his chest. Unlike Liam, with his six-foot-two frame, she found the tent spacious, and now lengthened her back to full height as she sat cross-legged. "I asked first. Truth or dare."

He didn't hesitate. "Dare."

"Go outside and sing the national anthem at the top of your lungs."

Liam started toward the tent flap, then stopped, swearing softly under his breath. No one wanted wet clothes in the backcountry, and with the heavy downpour, going out meant full rain gear or… Sitting back down, Liam pulled off his socks and shirt, revealing defined pectorals and washboard abs. His pants came next until he knelt on the tent floor in nothing but black trunks stretched tightly over a well-muscled ass.

Jaz's thighs twitched a little. She was used to men in good shape, but Liam's body was something else altogether. She took a careful breath to keep her thoughts from showing. At least the trunks weren't that white material that turned see-through when wet.

"Turn around," Liam ordered. "I'm not getting my shorts wet."

Now that was an idea. Jaz grinned, her voice dripping with sympathy. "Yes, walking around with wet undershorts all day tomorrow will be a little annoying, won't it?"

Liam glared. "You think I'm going to be made miserable just so you can be entertained?"

"That sounds about right, yes."

He snorted. "That only goes to show that you were never in the military. Modesty takes a far, *far* second place to comfort." With no further hesitation, Liam stripped off his underwear, giving Jaz a good view of his smooth butt cheeks as he let himself out into the rain. A moment later, the most off-key version of the "Star-Spangled Banner" filled the sky.

Jaz covered her face with her hands, laughter bubbling out between her fingers. She'd never expected the stinker to actually go through with it—not really. But he had. Unabashedly. Liam Rowen—Liam—was out there buck naked and making up in volume what he lacked in musical talent.

Thunder answered Liam's rendition of Francis Scott Key's masterpiece, nature making its opinion of his voice known.

As Jaz's laughter ran its course, heat started to fill her still-shaking cheeks. She could see the outline of his naked body through the tent's blue fabric, the silhouette showing a large endowment that was impossible to ignore.

Jaz's thighs clenched, heat trapped between her folds starting to trickle into the channel of her legs and back. She hadn't meant to go here with her silly dare. Wasn't prepared for her physical response, for the unrelenting volley of need and lust that now assaulted her. Damn. She wouldn't mind a little walk through the cold rain herself just now. Just to settle down. To be able to think.

Liam finished torturing the national anthem and made his way back to the tent.

In the spirit of good sportsmanship, Jaz held out a towel for him and very precisely kept her gaze on his hair as he roughly rubbed himself dry. Wrapping the towel around his hips, Liam settled triumphantly on his sleeping bag. "My turn." He rolled his shoulder as if to work out the kinks. "Truth or dare."

Jaz's stomach clenched. "Truth."

"Coward."

"Fine. Dare. Happy now?"

Liam raised his chin and studied her from above. "Show…me… Your most embarrassing tattoo."

"How do you know I even have a tattoo?"

His brow twitched, his face intense and penetrating. "A hunch."

Right. Closing her eyes, Jaz twisted around, slightly raised the back of her shirt, and tugged down on the elastic band of her shorts. She was only revealing a couple of inches of skin, but it made her feel naked. Vulnerable. Liam made her feel vulnerable. Her pulse fluttered.

Liam's heavy palm pressed between Jaz's shoulder blades in a silent instruction to keep still while he ran his callused thumb over a small inked patch of skin. "A polar bear?"

"Yes." She pulled away, tugging her shirt back into place. "A polar bear. All right? It's a polar bear."

"Because…?" Liam prompted.

Jaz face blazed. She'd gotten the tattoo years ago, and it had made good sense at the time. She never thought she'd be explaining it this way, though. Still facing away from him, she drew a deep breath. "Because of what polar bears eat."

"They eat everything," Liam paused, and Jaz knew he'd figured it out. "SEALs. Polar bears eat seals."

"Yes, well, you were all annoying assholes at one time." Jaz twisted back around and raised her face defiantly while Liam tried and failed to conceal his laughter. "I'd just read something that said the best way of getting goals accomplished was to write them down. Then there was alcohol. And—well—the self-pledge made great and noble sense at the time. So polar bear. Truth or dare, SEAL."

"Dare."

"Coward."

Liam snorted. "Truth. What do you want to know?—And please don't go into *Fifty Shades of Grey* again."

She wasn't planning on it. Being this close to a nearly naked Liam was difficult enough without talking about hot, kinky sex.

"Tell me about your scars." Jaz reached out toward Liam's torso, where all sorts of marks had left a history on his flesh. She traced a jagged white line with the same care he'd used on her tattoo. "Are these all from Afghanistan?"

Instead of the expected resistance, Liam shrugged a muscular shoulder and spoke easily. The one Jaz had pointed to was from a cut of an edge of a rusted-out ship's hull he'd gotten caught on while scuba diving in training. There was a surgical mark on his knee from an ACL repair. Several more marks were badges from when he'd been captured by a tribal war band on a combat deployment.

"Don't get me wrong, it was an unpleasant two days," Liam said matter-of-factly, "but there was too much of a language barrier for them to bother with interrogation, and I knew we had a team nearby. Aiden McDane was nowhere near so fortunate."

"And this one?" Getting up on her knees, Jaz touched a small scar cutting into Liam's left eyebrow. Unlike the others, it was nearly invisible beneath the dark hairs, and she'd only spotted the mark now.

Liam caught her wrist and shook his head. *No. Not that one.* There was a seriousness there, lurking behind the silence. The kind that told Jaz she'd stumbled onto something that wasn't meant as fodder for a game. She didn't think anything could hurt Liam Rowen, wasn't even sure he was capable of feeling pain, but now, in this moment, she knew she was wrong.

Quietly, slowly, Jaz leaned forward and brushed a soft kiss over the small scar that summoned a light smile. "Fine, but I get an extra question. Favorite movie scene."

Liam snorted softly. "'Circle of Life' song from *The Lion King*."

"Seriously?"

"Very. You?"

Jaz thought a moment. "The 'shoot the hostage' thing from *Speed*."

"That's more than a little disturbing," said Liam.

Jaz laughed. "No, it's two police guys talking about tactics. Keanu Reeves's character says that a wounded hostage is useless to a hostage taker on the move. His partner thinks it's nuts, but then in the next scene, it's how they escape."

"Why that scene?" Liam leaned forward, appearing genuinely interested.

"It reminds me how sometimes ideas that seem bad at one moment can be lifesavers the next. And sometimes it's true for people too."

"Yes," said Liam. "Sometimes it is."

It was dark by the time the weather finally settled. Having spent most of the day reworking the travel route to account for the shortened time on location, Jaz and Liam went to sleep intent on getting started at first light. Unlike Sebastian, Liam voiced no complaints about the early wake-ups or long hikes, and what he lacked in technical knowledge about climbing, he more than made up for in efficiency. For the next several days, they kept an unrelenting pace that Jaz doubted Sebastian would have managed. In fact, she was certain he couldn't have. Hell, it was a pace *she* couldn't have managed if Liam hadn't quietly taken over all chores and repacked her rope into his pack.

If only he didn't have that uncanny ability to know when she needed a comforting shoulder squeeze and when a few harshly said words would get her moving faster. Trying harder. Paying attention when fatigue was making her focus wane.

When they finished marking routes just before nightfall on the final day of the challenge, Jaz realized that she was glad Liam had taken Sebastian's place.

And that made her a terrible person.

"Was Sebastian's accident my fault?" Jaz asked Liam as they bedded down for their final night on the San Gabriel range. The sun was set for the night and the event would finish by eight in the morning, which would give them just enough time to hike out before the final bell. With all the route markers now set in stone, thoughts that had bubbled just below Jaz's consciousness for the past few days now rose unrestrained to the surface. She was here. She was happy. And it wasn't fair. "I mean, Devante was only in California because of me. And so was Sebastian. If it wasn't—"

"I no longer think Sebastian's accident was an accident, period."

A shiver ran along Jaz's skin. They hadn't discussed the collision since that morning at the police station, but Liam's tone had changed from considering to condemning. "You sound certain."

Liam, who'd been taping up a blister on the back of his heel, paused in midmotion, then carried on. "I am."

Jaz rubbed her face, fatigue weighing her down. "Clairvoyance courtesy of the mountains?"

Another hesitation. "Courtesy of Aiden McDane and the Trident Security team."

"McDane, Trident security, and what, telepathy?"

Instead of answering, Liam reached into the bottom of his pack and shamelessly pulled out a cell phone, battery pack, and some boxy gadget that was probably a signal magnifier. Also known as things Jaz wasn't allowed to have out here. "My work doesn't stop when yours starts." Liam punched in a code, unlocking his phone. "I received a full workup on Devante yesterday. Nothing remarkable except his childhood address."

Liam shifted and put his forearms on his knees, creating a more direct line of sight to Jaz.

Her shoulders tensed. Beyond the tent, the hooting of a Western screech owl rang out against the silent night, but inside the tent wall, a zinging tension suddenly filled the air.

"It's the same as Roman Robillard's."

"The champion Vector Ascent signed me on to replace," she whispered.

"They're cousins. The families lived together for a while when Devante and Roman were growing up."

Jaz's mind raced to catch up with the implications, her hand coming up to cover her mouth as Liam's initial assertion slipped into place. "So the detective was right. Devante hit the car on purpose because he thought I would be in the driver's seat and he wanted to take me out of the running. That's probably why he rented a large SUV too, to give himself an advantage."

Jaz drew up her knees, her forehead resting against them. Sebastian's injuries *were* her fault. Undeniably. Directly. Because there was some asshole with a vendetta against her.

"The mugging outside The Cellar, that probably wasn't a coincidence either," she said, closing her eyes. She was suddenly cold. And restless. Unable to stay in her own skin. "Not with Devante knowing where I would be."

"Probably not a coincidence, no." Liam pulled her into his chest, his arms closing around Jaz with iron security. "But we'll figure it out. I'm not going anywhere until we do."

"I'm glad you're here," Jaz whispered into his shoulder. "Does that make me a coward?"

"Absolutely."

Jaz looked up and saw a hint of a smile on Liam's lips. He brushed his thumb against her cheekbone, sending prickles of sensation all along her skin. At once, she could feel it happening again. Her body aching for his, despite her mind's protests. This was

Liam. Liam of all people. A once deep-held enemy, now an unexpected friend. A partner.

But still him. A man who enjoyed the kind of women that Jaz didn't want to be.

Liam's face moved closer. Stopped. His eyes shut as he drew a deep, purposeful breath. "Let's get some air."

They stood, and with a hand on the small of her back, Liam guided her outside the tent into the gentle evening chill. After the rain a few days ago, the mountains still had a damp, fresh smell, and the clear skies above were dancing with the moon and stars. The breeze tickled her skin and ruffled Liam's hair, the small strands that curled along the back of his neck swaying.

Jaz looked up at him. Liam stood with his legs firmly apart, his shoulders spread like a shield between her and the world. Every taut line of him was strong and certain. Like a rock against a storm. Except where a rock was cold and distant, Liam's gaze blazed with restrained fire that enveloped her without ever touching.

Her breaths quickened. Liam's sheer presence was taking control of her lungs. Her pounding heart. Jaz stepped toward him, her body reaching for his as if drawn by a great magnet toward a fateful collision. Her lips parted, need rushing through her blood.

JAZ

*L*iam's mouth descended upon hers, the intensity of the kiss stealing her breath. He pillaged her with ruthless claiming strokes that stole all sense and left footprints of hungry passion in their wake. Jaz felt Liam's hand wind tightly into her hair, his other one sliding along the angle of her hip. Her ribs. Dipping under her shirt for her breasts. Tiny pricks of pain where Liam held Jaz's hair spiderwebbed through her scalp, waking her nerves. Rousing the sensation. Making her thighs clench against the growing need that now pulsed between her legs.

Liam pulled his mouth away.

She felt empty, held together only by the feel of his hands still twined in her hair and splayed over her ribs.

Liam's lips pressed together as he studied her, his hazel eyes filled with such intensity that she felt as though he knew her every thought. Could sense the moisture that was filling her folds. The bulge in the front of his pants was large and twitching. "Should I stop?" Liam asked.

Jaz tried to shake her head no, but he wouldn't let her move. The reminder of who exactly she was playing with should have struck sense or at least fear into Jaz's brain. Instead, her need only roared louder. "Don't stop," she breathed into the inches of air between them.

"Are you scared?" he asked.

Her pulse raced. She didn't know where Liam could take her, only that it would be somewhere she hadn't gone before. Somewhere away from reality and Devante and being hunted. Somewhere intense. But safe. Because it was Liam. "Are you going to hurt me?"

Liam's grip on her hair tightened, the pull intensifying, his eyes continuing to drink in her every move. "Would you like me to?"

She swallowed. "No."

"Then I won't." The pressure on her hair eased back to firm tingling. Not painful, but still unyielding. Grounding.

Liam shifted his hand to run his fingers over Jaz's breast, which peaked to his touch despite the shirt. Her small breasts felt full. Aching for him. Jaz arched forward into his touch, her hand over his urging him to press harder.

Liam captured her wrist in his hand instead. A moment later, her other wrist followed until her arms were trapped together, held in his grip over her head. She pulled against the restraint, found it ungiving, and felt a rush of unexpected excitement racing along her spine. A heartbeat later, Liam took her mouth again, his tongue lashing with those claiming strokes that weakened her knees.

One hand still trapping her wrists, Liam walked Jaz backward until she felt the solid trunk of a tree against her back. Liam's mouth dropped to her breast, suckling through the fabric, his leg pressing between hers until she was riding his muscled thigh.

Jaz moaned against the sensation filling her breasts and spreading through her body to pool low in her belly. Her inner legs were tingling. Her hips were tight, undulating through the little sliver of space that she had. The security of Liam's hold gave Jaz no choice but to feel each sensation to its fullest; gave her body no chance to hide as he slid beneath her shirt and closed his mouth over her other breast. If feeling him through cloth had made Jaz's entire chest tingle, then the sensation of having his hot, hot mouth directly on her skin was like bathing in erotic lava.

She arched, her breaths so quick that the world was narrowing to nothing but sensation.

Liam pulled off Jaz's long-sleeve shirt. He made short work of wrapping it around her wrists and securing the ends to the tree behind her. Before Jaz could react to the change, Liam's mouth returned to her breast—but now he also slipped his finger into the waistband of her sleeping shorts. He felt along the inner crease of her leg.

She tensed on instinct, the part of her that was still capable of thought knowing the wetness he'd find there. Her face heated, but Liam continued without hesitation. He opened her tight thighs with his knee and purposefully, slowly, slid his hand through the wetness. Then his callused fingers stroked right along her folds.

Sensations assaulted Jaz from all sides. Her restrained wrists, the stretched, sensitive nipple in Liam's hot mouth, the raging need pulsating through her sex. All growing every second. She rose up on her toes in search of reprieve and found none. Only more stroking. More suckling. More everything.

Between her legs, his deft intrusion slid farther into the folds, now staking out their territory with unyielding insistence. And then there was something at her entrance.

Jaz's eyes widened, and she bucked.

"Behave, or I'll change my mind about spanking you," Liam's low, gravelly voice whispered into her ear. The erotic threat gripped her sex, her channel clamping over emptiness. A humiliating moan of pleasure escaped her.

Liam made an appreciative sound and brushed his finger right over her swollen clit.

The rising pressure of need exploded without warning, and Jaz shattered right there in his hold, her voice rising to the mountains. The release hit her in waves so harsh, they felt edged with pain and ecstasy, gripping her body over and over. Taking her breath until she lay slumped against the rough tree trunk behind her.

"You climax deliciously," Liam breathed against her neck. His breath tickled. His musky masculine scent mixed with the fresh mountain air. "I'd like to hear it again."

The full meaning of Liam's words only registered in Jaz's foggy mind when she felt him pull her shorts all the way off and kneel before her. Cool air touched her dripping sex, but with her arms restrained above her head and Liam pushing her thighs apart with his hands, she could do nothing to shield herself.

Her traitorous sex awoke to Liam's touch, arousal rebuilding itself in slow, needy leaps. Liam brushed her folds. Up and down, up and down, flicking the right and left side of her clit until she was writhing with need. Oh God.

"Liam." The word came out as half moan, half plea.

He put his finger at her entrance and slid inside her tightness, her channel clenching greedily around the intrusion. In and out, in and out. Despite the impossibility of it, the desire seizing every fiber of Jaz's exhausted body kept rising higher and higher until her own muscles no longer heeded her control. She arched and bucked and writhed, all at the mercy of Liam's hands. His mouth. His tongue, which now lapped away at the beading moisture around her clit. A little harder each time. Her heart raced, the inevitable abyss spreading wider and wider beneath her.

Then Liam put his lips right around her apex, and *sucked*.

Jaz fell into the gaping chasm, only to be caught, lifted, and sent off the edge again. Endorphins raced through her blood with dizzying speed, her unabashed screams filling the mountains themselves. There was no holding back. No restraint of sensation. Only world-spinning primal pleasure like she'd never experienced. Never even had known was possible.

17

LIAM

*L*iam pulled Jaz's small, exhaustedly limp body into his lap and cradled her against his chest. Bare skin against bare skin. Her flushed, sated warmth flowed into him through the coolness of the mountain evening. As Jaz's eyes closed in relaxation, Liam swallowed too many emotions to sort through. Strong, competitive, independent Jaz had given him the gift of her trust, and the delicious response of her body had touched a void Liam hadn't realized existed inside him.

He hadn't felt this satisfaction with a woman in years. Hell, if he were honest with himself, he hadn't felt like this ever. But this level of connection was also stripping him to the bone—because he shouldn't have let it happen. Jaz had been tired and vulnerable, assaulted with guilt and uncertainty and fear. She knew little about the sensual games he took for granted. But *he* knew, didn't he? Just as he knew that many powerful, independent women found erotic pleasure in giving up control. He knew it all, and he went for it anyway. Took advantage of her trust.

Because he hadn't been able to help himself.

Liam settled the sleeping Jaz into her sleeping bag, and stroked her hair. She looked peaceful. Content. He couldn't shut his eyes, though, not when he kept seeing her shatter with release each time he tried to. His cock was so hard and pulsing that it hurt to breathe from the pressure, yet he had to draw deep breaths just to ensure he didn't come right then and there from memories alone.

She'd enjoyed herself. He'd enjoyed himself. Liam had no idea where it left him. Where it left them. Because this thing between them could never be more than just sexual pleasure. Jaz deserved better than that. She deserved love and a real relationship, one with a man whose heart was as open and generous as hers.

Liam was the dark opposite of that.

"WAKE UP, SOLDIER." Jaz's voice penetrated through his deep haze some hours later, which was Liam's first indication that he had, in fact, fallen asleep. Not just fallen asleep, but stayed that way the whole night. That was new.

He blinked and rubbed his face. "Not a soldier. I was in the navy."

"Potato, potahto."

"No, not really." He sat up, studying her face critically. She'd probably want to talk about their extracurriculars last night, and he didn't know what to say to her. With someone else, he might have offered compliments and discussed what parts they enjoyed the most, so as to know what to build on in the future. But in this case, there wasn't going to be a repeat performance. "What time is it?"

"Seven."

That late? Shit. He scrambled up. "You want tent or breakfast duty?"

"Like I'm letting you anywhere near the gear."

"You just hate cooking." He unzipped the tent and stuck his head out into the fresh mountain air they'd enjoyed a little too much last night. Making short work of donning his hiking boots, Liam brought out the small stove and decided on coffee and oatmeal with raisins for their last meal, while Jaz secured all the technical gear.

"Can I ask you something?" she said into his back.

Here it came. Liam's shoulders tightened.

"Why were you such a jerk to me when you spent the summer with us?"

Liam twisted and stared at her incredulously. That was what she wanted to ask? Why he was a jerk all those ago, when tween Jaz wrote him a love letter? "Because I was a teenaged boy and an idiot. If it helps, I thought I was doing the right thing."

She put a hand on her hip. "How is humiliating a twelve-year-old with a crush the right thing? After you showed that letter to everyone, I couldn't look my brother in the eye for a year. Not to mention that my parents went berserk. They actually took my bedroom door off the hinges to make sure I wasn't secretly sneaking boys in."

Liam took out two bowls, poured in oatmeal, powdered milk, and raisins, and added hot water. "I was trying to protect you. You were growing up in Hollywood: best schools, extracurriculars, playdates, and tutors. When you live like that, it's easy to think guys who take advantage don't exist near you. But they do. I didn't want you to get hurt."

"So you hurt me instead."

"Yep." He turned, holding a conciliatory bowl of oatmeal toward her. "That about covers it. Would it help if I apologized now for how I went about it?"

She took the food. "Not really."

"That's what I figured too."

She snorted and crouched down beside him to eat. "Why did you spend the summers with us anyway?"

"Didn't get along with my mom and her boyfriends." He let a corner of his mouth twitch. "I hear I was an asshole at that age, so perhaps that's not so surprising?"

Jaz laughed, her bubbly, energetic voice filling the small clearing. She was so full of life, positive energy, and perpetual motion that it shifted the very fabric of a normal day. Jaz was the kind of woman who was the life of every gathering, while Liam was its warden.

They were already buckling on their packs when the topic Liam thought he'd safely escaped finally came up. And it started, unsurprisingly, with Jaz turning the shade of her neon-pink neckerchief.

"About last night," she said, starting into a walk on a narrow trail that made eye contact impossible. "Do you think we could *not* mention it to Kyan? Or, well, anyone?"

"Given that I like my nose unbroken, I support that idea fully."

THE END of the first challenge was much less glamorous than the opening, the photographers apparently having gotten all they came for the first time around. Once Jaz got her debrief, an admonishment about confidentiality, and a banana, they were released into the wild. Sebastian had already been flown back, which left Liam and Jaz to get some rest and catch their flight early the following day.

"Good evening, Mr. Rowen," the concierge at Liam's apartment building greeted him as they strolled into the marble decorated lobby. "Welcome back. I hope your houseguest has settled in well."

Liam stopped, pulling Jaz slightly behind him as if that would do anything just now. "What houseguest?"

The concierge, a middle-aged, balding man named Rodrigo who took great pride in his post, went to his computer at once. "I'm afraid it's not listed, sir. She had a key and thus wasn't required to register, as per your preferences." He looked up. "Would you like to change those now?"

"We're fine, Rodrigo," Liam assured him. The only people who had keys to his place were the Tridents and now Aiden, so a *she* could only be one of their wives.

"You've been living here less than two weeks," he told Jaz as they headed to the elevator. "And you already have visitors?"

She grinned up at him as they stepped into the elevator, her face lighting up the way it always did when she smiled. "Clearly, I'm the more popular one of us."

He made a sound in the back of his throat, his hand aching to rest on the curve of Jaz's hip, but hitting the elevator button instead.

"Given that at least one person is actively trying to hurt you, I'd really prefer if you'd become a bit less popular for a while."

"Fair point." Jaz's words came out in a whisper, her lips staying slightly parted. She stepped closer, and Liam's heart quickened at the invitation. Need and desire swam through him, though he'd promised himself he'd stay clear of Jaz Keasley. That they'd be nothing but friends. His head lowered toward her.

Jaz's hand reached toward the scruff along his jaw.

Ding.

The chime of the elevator reaching the uppermost story shattered the moment, bringing Liam back to his senses. He stepped back just as the door opened, extending his hand to allow Jaz to precede him. As they cleared the elevator bank and proceeded to his apartment, however, Liam noticed a sweet coconut smell trickling into the hallway. His memory stirred, his chest tightening as he unlocked his door.

"Liam. There you are," his *houseguest* said with an unabashed smile that made Liam's hand clench at his side. He'd forgotten that there was one other person he'd given his key to, to be used in case of emergency. Though no such event appeared to be in sight. The woman wiped her hands on her apron. "I didn't know you were seeing someone. Will you introduce me to the young lady?"

"I'm not *seeing*—never mind." Liam stuck his hand into his pocket. "What are you doing here?"

"Finishing up dinner. Should be ready by the time you two come in and wash up." She extended her weathered hand to Jaz. "It's wonderful to meet you. I'm Patti. I hope you don't mind beef Stroganoff? It's always been Liam's favorite."

"That sounds delicious." Jaz sounded equal parts polite and confused. Liam couldn't blame her there. He also couldn't keep them standing in the hallway much longer without this turning even more awkward. Squaring his shoulders, he motioned between the women. "Jaz, this is Patti Rowen, my mother. Mother, Jaz Keasley."

18

JAZ

"Um... Hello." Jaz shook hands with the middle-aged woman whose dark-brown hair and familiar features finally made sense. Liam's mother was tall for a woman, though still shorter than her son, and her gaze held a sadness behind a determined smile.

A beat of silence sizzled between them, then Patti clapped her hands together. "So, beef Stroganoff. I didn't know when you'd be here, but the sauce is all ready, and I'll just boil a bit of egg noodles. If you kids want to wash up and set the table, we can eat in about half an hour."

Liam helped Jaz take off her pack, then slid his own to the floor. "I'm not hungry. And you still haven't answered my question. Why are you here?"

Patti's smile faltered, then returned with renewed determination. "Well, you can just keep us company at the table, then." She turned, heading to the kitchen, and began filling a large pot with water. "I know, I know—you hate surprises and I came unannounced, but I wanted to see you. It couldn't wait."

Liam stalked after her, his shoulders tight. "What is it that couldn't wait?"

"Seeing you, of course." Patti turned to look over at Jaz. "Did you say your name was Jaz Keasley? Same as Kyan Keasley? Are you his sister?"

"I am." Jaz opened a pot lid to inhale the mouthwatering aroma of meat and mushrooms. "But please don't hold that against me. At least not until after dinner."

Patti laughed, which only invited more dark clouds to gather around Liam. He'd said he didn't get along with his mother, but from what Jaz could see unfolding before her, the conflict was one-sided. At least at the moment. And whatever else, she was not about to pass up a chance to learn more about Liam—whether he liked her sources or not.

"Is there anything I can help with?" Jaz asked.

Liam, who was still lingering a few paces behind, was on her in an eyeblink. His hand closed around her wrist. "Can I speak to you for a moment?"

Oh, this was too good. "Of course." Pulling out of his grip, Jaz stood on her toes to grab the dishes and started setting the table. "What about?"

She could almost hear Liam swallow a growl.

"It's so nice that Liam's keeping in touch with his childhood friends, or in your case, something more." Patti poured the egg noodles, which she must have brought along with the other ingredients, into the water. The more she spoke and traipsed around Liam's kitchen, the tenser his body became, until a small muscle ticked along his clenched jaw. Patti motioned at Liam with the pasta packaging before tossing it out. "You didn't tell me you had a girlfriend. A mother needs to know such things."

"Jaz isn't my girlfriend. And you don't need to know anything other than when my check is arriving." Liam's voice broke from controlled and distant to something that no longer hid his cold fury. "Now, I'm going to ask you again. Why. Are. You. Here?"

Patti seemed to finally deflate. She stopped moving about, her shoulders curling slightly inside her cardigan. Lowering the wooden spoon she'd used to stir the pasta, she let out a long breath and turned toward her son. "Liam." Her hand twitched toward him.

Liam stepped back.

Patti pulled her hand back against her body and sighed. "I just wanted to see if we could talk. To have a relationship. I miss you, Liam."

"You're about nineteen years too late on that front."

"I'm nineteen years smarter too. And so are you."

"I have work to do." His hazel eyes flat and his mouth cinching down into a horizontal line, Liam crossed the room and went back into the foyer. He flipped the dead bolt closed with a definitive *clonk*, strode past his mother, and vanished into the rear of the penthouse.

Patti watched him pass, then pressed her lips together and returned her attention to the pasta, which was now ready. "I'll... Why don't you fix plates for yourself and Liam. I've just remembered I have a few things to finish up at the hotel." She wiped her hands on a dish towel and conjured a smile that tried its damn best to hide the pain lurking behind aging hazel eyes. "The beef Stroganoff really tastes better when it's fresh and hot."

She was going to leave, Jaz realized. Her chest tightened. "Liam is being a jerk. If anyone is going to go without dinner, it will be Commander Broody. Do you drink wine? I'm sure I saw a bottle of something somewhere."

This time, Pattie's gentle smile was genuine, though still sad. "I appreciate that, Jaz, I really do. But Liam has every reason in the world to be furious with me."

Jaz looked back toward where Liam had disappeared into his office, their conversation from earlier tickling her memory.

"Why did you spend the summers with us anyway?"

"Didn't get along with my mom and her boyfriends."

Apparently, *didn't get along* had been an understatement. Still, this was ridiculous. Or just very sad. And Jaz wasn't about to stand for either scenario. "Well, I've spent many a waking moment dreaming up ways to make Liam furious, so we're in good company."

She rummaged through the wine cooler fridge that sat under Liam's gleaming countertop and pulled out a bottle of red. After filling two glasses, she handed one to Patti and towed the woman to the breakfast island. "Ferns are such cool plants to have indoors, don't you think?" Jaz pointed to Liam's plants, which had fortunately survived their trip away. "It's like living in a miniature rain forest. Though I'd have taken Liam as more of a cactus guy."

Patti laughed. "Definitely not a cactus guy. He likes taking care of things, and cacti are too self-sufficient."

Jaz echoed Patti's laugh and built off the conversation to discover that Patti and Liam's sister, Lisa, now lived in Ann Arbor, which was beautiful. Lisa liked to run, but wasn't a competitive athlete like Jaz. Patti leaned in to listen about all the details of Jaz's climbing, asking just the right probing questions and cheering along with successes. She actually enveloped Jaz in a spontaneous bear hug upon discovering that she was sponsored by Vector Ascent.

Patti was everything her parents weren't, and Liam had no idea how lucky he was to have her. And yet the man never came out of his study. Not even when it really was time for Patti to get back to her hotel.

"I'm sorry about..." Jaz waved her hand toward the empty hallway. "I don't know what has him acting like, well, like—"

"Sweetie, you wouldn't." Patti patted Jaz on the forearm. "But I wasn't what anyone would call a good mother when the kids were growing up, and Liam has every right to feel betrayed by me. At the time, I made the decisions I did because I was young, naive, and saw no other choice. But I can't go into all that. That was then, and this is now. And in this new now, Liam Rowan won't be rid of me even if he brings the whole SEAL Team Six in." Patti kissed Jaz's cheek and showed herself out, leaving Jaz staring at the ferns and parsing out the evening.

Yes, well, there was little question as to where Liam got all his drive from.

Liam never spoke much about family—but he was so closed about everything that the silence seemed a natural extension of his personality. Now, Jaz knew it was more than just a personality trait. Liam was waging a war Jaz had known nothing about. But she would find out.

19

LIAM

*L*iam circled Eli in the boxing ring, his weight balanced on the balls of his feet. He struck a left-right-left combo. Eli ducked and swerved, only taking a glancing hit from Liam's last slug, then returned the favor with a roundhouse into Liam's gut.

Liam grunted at the impact, then went after Eli. It felt good to hit someone he didn't worry about breaking. Good to have someone like Eli, who understood, without being told, that today was a no-holds-barred brawl.

Aiden looked on from the sidelines, his white shorts and shirt contrasting with bright blue mats. Wearing all white was a foolish move to Liam's thinking. Blood was difficult to remove from light fabrics. But for now, they were just starting—the mats smelled of cleaner instead of sweat, and all the gym equipment, from the gleaming free weights to the practice weapons to the reflective yellow vests by the door to the jogging trails, lay and hung in orderly rows.

Liam shifted around the sparring ring again, keeping his back to the climber's corner of the gym. The equipment made him think of

Jaz, and that was not where he wanted his head just now. Especially not with her brother, Kyan, due to arrive in the gym any moment.

Not only was making a move on a best friend's sister a violation of trust in general, but it being Liam specifically made everything a hundred times worse. Liam knew it. He got it. Hell, he even agreed. Sex, he could do. More than that? Everyone knew Liam wasn't relationship material, as proven by the fact that he never had a real one. Not with his family, and certainly not with any of the women he'd been with. He cared about them the same way sheepdogs cared for their charges—he'd put himself in harm's way to keep the wolves away, but there wouldn't be a partnership involved.

The Tridents were the closest thing Liam had to a close bond, and the pain of losing Bar—their best friend who'd been killed in Afghanistan—made Liam rethink the wisdom of having let the men in as close as he had. The fact that Cullen, Eli, and Kyan all had healthy marriages now while Liam couldn't even bring himself to enjoy women at play parties spoke to how different he was.

Liam was an exceedingly competent fighter, but a pissed-off Kyan could do unpleasant damage—and if Kyan ever caught wind of what happened between Liam and Jaz, he would most certainly be pissed off. Problem was that what happened didn't account for one tenth of what Liam wanted to do to the fierce sprite of a mountain climber. The types of things that would get him justifiably murdered.

Then there was that unholy alliance between Jaz and Patti, whose presence in Denton Valley was still an unexplained and unwelcome phenomenon. Liam had even called Lisa, who just said that Patti was being bitchy and hung up. It was all getting to be too much. Liam had just had his life figured out, his company expanding, his mind on business, when the women's intrusion sent cracks all along his plans.

"So you spend a week in Jazzy-girl's tent." Eli spoke over his volley of kicks, his voice breaking only slightly. "How did she not slit your throat while you slept?"

Liam blocked another roundhouse with his shin. "Took away her knives."

Eli ducked under Liam's hook. "Did you put the climbing rope to good use as well?"

Liam's gut tightened, his next cross heading right for Eli's damn mouth.

Eli grunted. Danced back. Dabbed his forearm against his bleeding lip. "What the bloody fuck, mate?" There was more curiosity than anger in the question. "Did I hit a nerve?"

"No, I did the hitting," Liam snapped at the Brit. "You did the letting down your guard like a pleb."

That was bullshit, and they both knew it. Before Eli could call him on it, Liam twisted to Aiden.

"Anything from our friends in the postal service?" Trident had called in some favors in hopes of IDing the origin of the threats, but it was a long shot.

"Nothing as yet," Aiden reported from outside the ring, his arms slung over the ropes. His voice sounded muted, almost as if his throat were sore, and his freckled complexion betrayed a deeper fatigue. "But I've been keeping an eye out in case he mails any more. The computer geeks are monitoring social media as well and tracing IP addresses of anything vile."

"Good." Liam threw his hands up in the universal sign of time-out, and once Eli came out of his fighting stance, Liam sized the Scot up. "Get in here, McDane."

Aiden climbed between the ropes and drew himself up into a fighting stance, his muscles taut and ready. Ghosts danced in his eyes today, as they did sometimes when nightmares gripped his sleep. Liam shifted to more secure footing in case Aiden lost it and decided to take his head off literally.

It was a good thing Liam was prepared, because Aiden's first haymaker rushed in so quickly that, despite dancing out of range, Liam felt the air from it along his cheek.

"Careful, mate," Eli murmured to Liam.

Yeah. No shit. Liam moved defensively around the ring, baiting Aiden into getting his energy out, then, when an opening finally came, swept the Scot's legs out from under him.

"Aich, fuck me," Aiden cursed, landing hard.

Liam extended his hand and was glad to see the other man take it. It wasn't one of his worst days, then. Good days were increasingly rare, though. It made Liam worried as hell—especially because of how helpless he felt. Aiden didn't want to talk to him. To anyone. And the last time someone pushed too hard, he'd gathered his stuff and moved to a different continent.

Aiden wasn't Liam's only worry, though, and the moment his mind had a millimeter of leeway to think, Liam was back to stewing over Jaz. And Patti. He and Jaz had been back from California for three days now. Sleeping in different rooms. Going about their business with every courtesy. Hell, he even trusted Jaz with the temp security team he put on her so he could come here and work out.

Liam hated every moment of it.

As if, somewhere in the mountains, he'd imprinted on Jaz's scent and warmth and couldn't sleep without her small body breathing softly against his. He'd slept so poorly these past few days, he wouldn't be surprised if he looked no better than Aiden did.

They exchanged another round of blows, then Liam rested while Aiden and Eli took a turn against each other before climbing into the ring with the Brit again. A very talkative Brit.

"So." Eli dropped low and went for a tackle this time, the two hitting the mat together as each vied for the stronger position. "You. Jaz. One tent. You know Kyan is going to kill you if things got creative out there, right?"

Liam rolled on top of Eli and straddled him. "Nothing creative. And if it had, it wouldn't be any of your—or Kyan's—business."

"What isn't any of my business?" Kyan asked from the doorway. He was dressed in street clothes, his gym bag hanging over his shoulder—and for a cowardly moment, Liam hoped he could use the logistics to slink away from a conversation. Running. That was another thing he'd never done in his life, but talking about Jaz with Kyan was going to tax every fiber of his self-control. The thought of lying to one of his best friends made bile rise in Liam's throat, but telling Kyan the truth would be much worse.

"Liam claims it's none of our business how he and Jaz spent a week together in close quarters," Eli, the asshole, called out despite his precarious position.

Liam's heart crashed against his ribs, his body bracing for the inevitable questions. The inevitable lies he'd have to tell. He hated Eli just then. And hated him even more when Eli's gaze caught his own and flinched suddenly, as if Eli had read the truth in Liam's eyes.

Kyan however, just barked a laugh. "Nice try, you wanker, but there is no one I'd trust with Jaz more. Rowen wouldn't take advantage of my sister." He pulled his gloves from the bag. "Plus, Jaz knows Liam's *preferences*, and she'd castrate him if he tried anything. Right, Rowen?"

Liam punched Eli before letting the man up.

"The sprite is too nosy for her own good, so yeah, she knows," Liam told Kyan. He was going to say something different, but realized at the last heartbeat that he couldn't lie to one of his best friends. Which didn't mean he was in a confessional mood either. "She also knows her own mind these days. Sebastian getting hurt hit her hard, though."

Kyan's face turned serious. "I appreciate what you did, Rowen, taking her partner's place for the challenge. It would have crushed her to forfeit. I know you two don't see eye to eye much, and what you did—I owe you."

At the side of the ring, Eli suddenly found the Velcro of his sparring gloves endlessly fascinating.

Liam's jaw tightened. "Speaking of work, McDane and I have some. Can you and Mason lock up when you're done?"

Trident Rescue and Security took up the whole fourth floor of an office building several blocks away from Liam's residence. The main operations center, which functioned as a twenty-four-hour monitoring station, had its screens tuned to different channels—everything from major network news to the more proprietary channels they had installed. Liam nodded to the pair of techs on duty and continued with Aiden to conference room Delta.

Monitors covered a wall of this room as well, muted footage of Al-Jazeera playing opposite CNN. From habit, Liam went over to the main computer and flipped through the log for a quick top-line update. Seeing nothing of immediate interest, he locked out the screen and turned to Aiden. "So, Roman Robillard and his sidekick Devante."

"The DA wants to charge Devante with assault," Aiden offered.

"Assault? How about attempted fucking murder?"

"They would, but the pesky thing about evidence is getting in the way." Aiden slid a file across the polished table. "I tracked down the drunks who went after Jaz—at least I think I did, since they dinna seem to clear on their own names, much less anyone else's. They got fifty bucks to rough up a girl matching Jaz's description. Were promised another fifty if they hurt her hand. But then they saw a purse and figured it had more than a fifty inside."

Liam had expected as much, but he still didn't like hearing it.

"Also found Roman," Aiden continues. "But he claims he knows nothing about Devante's antics."

Liam snorted. "Of course not."

"For whatever it's worth, I think Devante got in over his head. He's too petrified for his own future to cause any more trouble. A bit of good news there." Aiden took out another file from a cabinet, but instead of sliding it across the table, left it beside himself and tapped the top. "Been digging into the lass like you asked. But listen, mate, this steps over the line privacywise. You sure you wanna look at the file?"

"Safety trumps privacy."

"Aye." Aiden still kept his finger atop the file. "But if you two don't dislike each other quite as much as Kyan believes, you may wish to rethink your approach."

Liam's hand tightened on the table edge. "Don't play matchmaker with me, McDane. I don't do relationships. Now either give me the goddamn results, or else I'm going to see if there isn't some penguin in Antarctica who needs a new security system."

"All right." Aiden slid the file over, and raised his hands in surrender. "You're not gonna fancy what I found, though."

Liam pulled open the file jacket and flipped past the basic biodata until his attention got snagged by the numbers on Jaz's financials. Here, he found three separate bank accounts that the woman held—the total balances of which hovered just above zero.

"This can't be right." Liam frowned. Climbing sponsors provided gear and expenses more than spendable cash, but Liam knew for a fact that, like her brother, Jaz had inherited a trust fund from her affluent Hollywood family. Not only that, but she'd had money from childhood modeling and acting gigs. Even if her current contracts weren't paying as well as he'd thought, Jaz's savings should have set her up for life. "Where did all the money go?"

"Females of the Future fundraiser," Aiden said grimly and flipped to the next page in Liam's file.

"That bullshit scam from two years ago?" The Females of the Future had supposedly been a fund meant to provide a safe harbor to abused, athletically gifted girls from third-world countries. The nonprofit promised to pair the young athletes with US foster parents who'd help the girls reach their potential both athletically and socially. But that wasn't what had actually transpired. It'd been a scam that poured the supporters' interest-free loans into personal coffers and heart-tugging advertising. The organizer had been very publicly arrested, and the scandal held the headlines for several news cycles.

"Aye. The lass sank a decent portion of her money into it."

"And she probably kept it quiet for fear of her family's name somehow being dragged into the negative spotlight. Could have messed with her parents' business." Liam sighed. Jaz hadn't even told Kyan—though Liam was starting to understand that while the sprite loved her brother unconditionally, she wasn't quite as open with him as Kyan thought. "But what are these?" Liam pointed at several hefty withdrawals with vague descriptions. These, together with the scam charity payouts, were what had essentially bankrupted her. "Did she send good money after bad, or is this something else entirely?"

"That, I don't ken yet," Aiden admitted. "I've been attempting to track them down, but she dipped into virtual currency. I'm not sure she wants the destinations of these found."

20

JAZ

"For a guy on crutches, you still scurry about better than half of Denton Valley," Jaz said, carrying her and Sebastian's Frappuccinos to her favorite table. One of the green-aproned baristas waved to her, and Jaz grinned back, saluting the young man with her drink.

"For a girl who grew up with acting lessons, you should come up with better lies." Sebastian grimaced as he used two hands to elevate his leg on an extra chair. "Now, hand over the drink and the gossip. What's the latest on McBroody? I'm going to be living vicariously through you for the next few months, so don't you get stingy on me with the details."

Jaz wished she had details and gossip, but since returning from California, she'd felt a wall fall into place between her and Liam. While Patti's presence was certainly putting a strain on Liam, Jaz sensed that the wall had more to do with her brother than Liam's mother. Or maybe it had to do with Jaz herself. She moved closer, until the background music and low voice could make the conversation private.

"We got somewhat…intimate in Cali."

"I'd have been disappointed if you hadn't." Sebastian frowned. "Was it not very good?"

"The opposite, actually." Jaz fiddled with the label on her cup. "It was the best time I've ever had. I mean, I didn't even know those levels of sensation were possible. But…he is very…err, *controlling* in bed."

"And you didn't like that?"

"I loved it, actually. He um…tied my hands with my shirt." She raised a brow meaningfully.

"And that bothered you?" Sebastian clarified. "Or did he ruin your stuff? Are you pissed about the shirt?"

"What? No!" Jaz realized she'd raised her voice and lowered it, glaring at Sebastian. "The shirt was fine. I don't care about the shirt. And I already told you that I liked it."

He leaned in, his brows pulled together as if trying to decipher a foreign language. "I give up, Jazzy. What exactly is the problem?"

Heat rose to her cheeks. "I don't like that I liked it. How can I be yelling girl power from the mountaintops and then get off from having an overcontrolling SEAL tie me up?"

"Oh, my sweet summer child," Sebastian said sympathetically. "If you think getting tied up with a shirt is kinky, you need to have your horizons broadened. I'd take you for some education myself, but that might need to wait a bit. As for girl power, are you advocating that self-respecting girls limit themselves to missionary? Or that while men can get aroused by whatever the hell they please, girls should limit their pleasures to a list of preapproved topics?"

"Ew."

"My point exactly. What did you do with your previous boyfriends?"

"Liam isn't my boyfriend."

Sebastian rolled his eyes. "You know what I mean. Your previous partners. Did you enjoy them?"

She hadn't, not in bed. She'd acted like she did—hell, she should probably have won an Oscar for several of those bedroom performances—but not a single man had been able to bring her to real climax. Until Liam.

"It sounds to me like while you were busy saving the rest of the world, you forgot to explore your own," Sebastian said, with that rare hint of disapproval. "And you're literally living with an expert guide who you trust with your life. If you don't lean into that, Jazmine Keasley, you're a certified coward."

Jaz spooned some whipped cream onto her straw and gestured at Sebastian. "And you're a certified manipulator."

Sebastian leaned in, his eyes sparkling. "Jazmine Keasley. I double dog dare you to go to a kinky club or party with Liam Rowen. This week. Or I will never respect you again."

"You want me to do what?" Liam choked on his coffee, requiring a short coughing fit to clear his windpipe. Jaz considered smacking him on the back, but given their current discussion, that seemed too uncomfortable.

Yes, because choking to death is much more comfortable.

Fortunately, Liam reclaimed his own airway. He set his mug down on the kitchen island, the sunlight streaming through the window playing over the white porcelain. "Why do you want to go to a sex club?"

Despite having been asking herself that very same question, Jaz felt a pang of indignity when the words came from Liam. "Why shouldn't I?"

"Kinky play isn't your thing."

Her spine straightened. "How do you know what is and isn't my thing?"

"So kinky play *is* your thing?" he clarified.

"No!" *Shit.* Jaz realized the trap he'd laid only after she'd already walked straight into it. Liam raised a brow, and she glowered. "I mean, I've never been to anything like that. So I have no idea whether it is or is not my thing. And since when are you the judge of what I should and shouldn't want to find out more about?"

"Since that part a few minutes ago when you asked me to take you." Liam crossed his arms, which made his shoulders look even broader than they were. The strong angle of his jaw mirrored the ferocity of his gaze, which now bore into her. Everything about him, from his wide stance and straight back to the way his mouth pressed into a thin line suddenly screamed power—the kind that made heat grip Jaz's thighs no matter how much she shifted her feet. Liam tilted his head. "You had twenty-five years to scratch your curiosity itch. Why now?"

Jaz swallowed, the memory from that night in the mountains choosing this moment to ripple through her. The things Liam had done to her and her body. Her desperate, uncontrolled arousal. She felt her nipples stiffen, her pulse picking up the pace no matter how cool she tried to sound. "Sebastian double dog dared me, all right?"

Liam didn't move a muscle, yet the air seemed to chill around him. "Yeah. *No.* We're done with this discussion." He started to turn away.

"I enjoyed the shirt thing," Jaz blurted toward his turning back. She didn't know why she did, though it was the truth. The kind of truth no one sane shared with a man who was turning away. "I didn't think I would, but I did. A lot. I want to know what else exists."

Liam froze. Cursed under his breath. Then slowly turned back. There was no mockery in his gaze, but there was no pleasure either. He stared at her, his hazel eyes tight. Intense. "Do you know what Kyan will do to me if he finds out I took his baby sister to a sex club? That I touched her?"

Jaz flinched, ice slithering through her to douse all hints of arousal. Kyan. Of course. She'd been an idiot to think that something had changed between her and Liam. That they'd forged a bond that survived the night.

They hadn't. As he'd been in his teens, Liam was Kyan's friend first and foremost. The climax he'd given Jaz might have been the first of its kind for her, but to him, it was another night of play. *She* was another night of play. A fun diversion. A client. A favor to her brother. Irrelevant for her own sake.

But she'd set herself up for this, hadn't she? She knew who Liam was, and this time around, she had no one to blame but herself.

"Forget it," she said, pulling herself together with that same trained skill that let her walk onto a film set and beam smiles no matter what was happening inside her soul. "I was just playing Sebastian's dare." She started back to her room.

"Wait." Liam caught up with her, his hand closing around her elbow.

Jaz spun, breaking his grip. Her stomach was clenched in a knot already, and it took more self-control than she wished to keep the hurt and humiliation out of her voice. "I said, forget it. You're right —you didn't sign up to teach sex ed to your friend's baby sister. I'm sorry to have put you on the spot."

"It's not that clear-cut, Jaz," Liam snapped.

"Yes, it really is."

"No, it— Goddamn it." He slammed his palm on the kitchen counter, his eyes shutting for a moment. "I'm not relationship material, all right?" His eyes opened, his chest heaving as he found Jaz's gaze. "I can't have a relationship with you. With anyone. I'm just not built that way. Or maybe I was and got twisted around. But it's just not something that I'm capable of. I brought up Kyan because he knows that about me."

There was enough hurt and sincerity in Liam's face that Jaz froze where she stood, her attention shifting from her own tightness to the tension now saturating the air between them. She didn't believe Liam's stupid self-assessment for a moment—of course he was capable of a relationship—but the sudden vulnerability in his eyes, that was real. Not that she knew what to do with it.

Well, when all else fails, try the truth. "I wasn't fishing for a relationship. I'm not particularly in the market for one either." And if she was, she knew it wouldn't be with Liam. They weren't compatible in the long term. "Point is, what we did in the mountains, it was fun. That's what I was talking about. Fun. Pleasure. Sex. You're capable of sex, aren't you?"

He snorted, then shook his head, pointing a finger at Jaz's chest. "We are not having sex in a club."

"If the next words out of your mouth have anything to do with Kyan—"

"Forget Kyan. I simply don't usually enjoy having sex in public."

"Oh." A speck of heat touched Jaz's cheeks again, then her gaze narrowed. "Wait, you only objected to the sex part. Does that mean…"

"Yes. Fine. You win." Liam threw up his hands, then ran them through his short hair. "One night of everything you ever wanted to know about sexual play and were afraid to google."

LIAM

*F*riday night, Jaz sat in Liam's Land Rover, her hands rubbing along the seams of the tight black jeans she'd chosen to wear. Liam wished she'd picked something a little less flattering because he was going to have a difficult enough time keeping his hands to himself without that shapely body outlined to perfection and within fingers' reach for the whole evening. Why couldn't she have picked, say, a burlap sack? Though the damn woman would probably turn even that sexy.

Pulling out onto the interstate, Liam still couldn't believe he'd let himself get talked into this. He was already having a hell of a time getting the woman out of his mind, and a trip to Shadow Cove wasn't going to make it better. Despite Jaz's heady declarations about casual fun, he wasn't certain that things would be quite so simple. That she wouldn't get hurt once she discovered that he was damaged goods.

Seeing his hand tighten around the steering wheel, Liam made himself release a tight breath. He was getting ahead of himself. Jaz had responded with wild, wide-eyed wonder to gentle play, and if she wanted to explore her sensuality with him, it would be his absolute pleasure. Fun. Exploration. Discovery. *That's* what the night was supposed to be about, not Liam's personal hang-ups.

Provided that Jaz hadn't changed her mind. Liam checked his mirrors, then glanced sideways at Jaz. "It's not too late. We could go rock climbing instead."

"What?" She jumped a little at the sound of his voice. "No. We stick to the plan."

Liam made a noncommittal sound in the back of his throat, then looked pointedly at Jaz's thighs, which she was gripping for dear life.

She yanked her hands away.

Liam swallowed a chuckle.

"So where is this place?" Jaz asked, all business.

"Shadow Cove? About an hour and a half from here."

"That far?"

"Minimizes the chances of running into mutual acquaintances." Plus, Dior, who ran the place, was a friend and a former Green Beret. Shadow Cove was as clean and safe as the clubs got. "At least I presume you would rather this little field trip remained anonymous?"

"Good point." Jaz sat in silence for a while watching the mountains streaming along in their glory. Liam had seen her clinging to rock faces, dangle hundreds of feet in the air with only her body and her gear keeping her alive, and yet he was certain that this drive felt far more nerve-racking to her. Which wasn't altogether a bad thing.

"A few ground rules," he said, breaking the silence once they were off the highway and navigating the smaller roads. "Stay with me, don't interfere with anyone, and do not—under any circumstances—pull your phone out inside. Not even to check the time." Dior had zero tolerance for anything with a camera that might jeopardize the guests' privacy, and the penalties were severe.

Jaz pulled out her phone and set it on silent, fiddling with the controls until he parked near a low-profile building. With a clean beige brick exterior and dark, drawn-closed windows, Shadow Cove looked like a closed business, only the silver mailbox with the street number outside certifying that they were in the right place. Liam grabbed a bag from the back seat and put his palm against Jaz's back to guide her to the door. Through the thin fabric of her turquoise crop top, he could feel her muscles tighten with the mix of anxiety and anticipation that rolled off her in waves.

He would enjoy taking all that nervousness and channeling it into something more.

The small reception area was well lit and familiar, with wisps of music, thumps, and sounds of pleasure trickling in through the partially opened door on the other side. As a stranger, Jaz wouldn't usually be allowed entry, but Liam had made calls ahead of time.

"Liam!" A raven-haired woman in a Shadow Cove T-shirt came out from behind the counter, her smile bright as she twined her arms around him. "You're back. We've missed you."

"Good evening, Solana." Liam patted her back, but didn't return the embrace. Then he gently pushed Jaz forward. "This is my guest for the evening."

Solana's smile stayed in place as she checked her computer, then turned to greet Jaz, but the expression held more politeness than warmth. The receptionist was one of the women Liam had played with before. She'd enjoyed herself thoroughly—he'd made sure of that—but like everyone else, she'd mistaken their time together for something more. It was one of the reasons Liam tried not to tangle with the same woman more than once.

"Welcome," Solana told Jaz, the politeness slipping a bit. "The club safe word is *red*, and if you have any questions… Well, I imagine you have someone to help you along."

Jaz must have picked up on the sentiment, because as he guided her toward the main room, she gave him a suspicious gaze. "Let me guess. Ex-girlfriend?"

"I don't do girlfriends," Liam answered with the same quiet voice she'd used. "Now quit stalling and let's take a look." With a sweep of his arm, he pulled Jaz against him, wanting to feel her body's responses as they took in the room.

Shadow Cove was busy tonight, with most of the stations in use and lively chatter filling the seating area around the bar. On instinct,

Liam surveyed the whole room with his gaze. The light was low, the music playing an upbeat tune that at least three couples were using to set various rhythms. On the left side of the room, a pair of women were playing with hot wax, the one lying faceup on the table arching up in obvious ecstasy as pearly heated drops slid across her full breast. A few yards past that, a shibari rope master spoke softly to a woman he had expertly suspended in the air.

Jaz studied both the scenes with curiosity, but her body tensed at a harsh flogging scene playing out past the ropes. Liam recognized Noah, the naked young man being flogged, as one of Shadow's resident masochists—knew Noah was jerking against his restraints for a very different reason than Jaz imagined. Noah's weighted nipple clamps clanked as he moved.

Jaz twisted away, her hand crossing protectively over her breasts. "How can he like that?" she whispered.

Liam stepped behind Jaz, pulling her back against him. Gritting his teeth against his cock's sudden hardness, he ran his hands slowly over her arms, the curve of her hip, the tight swells of her breasts. He focused his thumbs on these, rolling the nipples into aroused bunches that hardened along with Jaz's intake of breath. She wriggled against the sensation, her breathing quickening when Liam put a restraining arm around her waist. "You have sensations you enjoy too, little sprite," he whispered against Jaz's ear. "Don't begrudge Noah his fun."

She said something under her breath that might have been a curse, and Liam slid his free hand down her back, letting his palm rest in warning against her taut backside. He could feel her thighs clenching at the erotic threat, her responsive body tightening.

Damn it, but was there anything more tempting than the open sincerity of Jaz's body? Ignoring the painful pulsing of his groin, Liam held his hand in place a few heartbeats longer, then released her completely.

Jaz shuddered, giving him a dark look as the arousal he'd brought her went unfulfilled. Rocking back on his heels, Liam put his hands in his pockets and stared down at her. Watched her shift her feet to ease the tension between her legs.

"Consider yourself punished," he murmured, still holding her gaze.

"You—" Jaz swallowed what she was about to say, and the blush already touching her cheeks deepened.

Liam chuckled. Then, putting his hand in the small of her back again, he steered her toward something he had an inkling Jaz would find more appealing. Several people waved and nodded to him as they passed, a few of the women—some utterly naked—giving him hopeful looks, but the growing buzzing in Liam's blood had nothing to do with them.

JAZ

*J*az stared at the naked woman bound against the wall. She wasn't naked, exactly, but given that her corset covered nothing of her bottom half and had been unlaced at the top enough to let her breasts spill free, she wasn't exactly dressed either. Her arms were raised over her head, the silk ribbons tying her wrists going to a mounted bracket on the wall behind her. A bar attached between her ankles kept her thighs spread for the man before her.

Tall and muscular, the man had short-cropped curly black hair, a golden tan to his skin, and the kind of bearing Jaz had learned to recognize as military training. Like Liam, he was dressed in dark slacks and a black shirt, though his was open halfway down his chest. As Jaz's gaze continued to take him in, she realized that the man held a riding crop in his hand—the kind Kyan had in the barn for horses, except this one was turquoise in color. With slow, deliberate motions, the man dragged the crop along his partner's arms. Breasts. Glistening inner thighs. Then higher.

The woman gasped as the small leather tip traced a line along her sex, back and forth across her folds. Her clit. She began to writhe, but the bar between her ankles kept her open. Pulling back the crop, the man wielding it slapped the moist leather against the fleshy part of her thigh, leaving a light pink mark. Again. Again. The woman bit her lip and panted, seemingly holding back her moans.

"Mmmm, very nice." The man with the crop had a deep voice, and Jaz couldn't stop herself from imagining Liam teasing her that way. Holding her that open and making good on the unspoken threat of his callused palm against her backside.

Jaz's channel clenched over its emptiness, though for the life of her, she couldn't fathom *why* the thought of being exposed made her wet. Why the whole thing made her needy and weak-kneed and so damn aroused.

Behind her, Liam gave a soft, all-too-knowing chuckle.

Flame rushed to Jaz's cheeks. She didn't like how easily he read her. Didn't like what image of her it painted. Recalling Liam's prediction that she'd enjoy this scene, Jaz turned to glare at him. "Just to be clear—if you come at me with a riding crop, I'm taking it and beating you over the head with it."

"Are you now?" Liam said mildly. Without taking his eyes off the scene, he stepped closer to Jaz. Ran his hands along her bare arms. And in a smooth, easy motion, gathered her wrists behind her back, trapping them in his large hand.

She pulled against the living handcuffs. Instead of loosening, the grip holding her cinched tighter in a strange reassurance.

Before Jaz could process the irony, the man before them exchanged the riding crop for a leather implement with a handle and dozens of suede thongs. He swung it against the woman's skin, the light slapping sounds mingling with her growing gasps. Once her nipples were each standing out pebbled, proud, and a bit inflamed, he switched to the area between her legs, swiping up and down her folds and clit until her whimpering became loud, high-pitched groans. Just as those groans reached a fever pitch, he took the tip of the handle and entered her with it, uttering a demand at the same time. The woman climaxed, wailing at the top of her lungs, her ecstasy filling the room.

Jaz's tingling thighs pressed together, her own panties moist with arousal. Her pulse raced, the room suddenly feeling too hot. Too everything. Sensation rose inside her, climbing higher and higher, a climax threatening to take over her senses. No. Not here. Not now. Jaz yanked against Liam's restraint.

This time, he let go immediately. "What are you feeling?"

"I need to use the restroom." Scurrying away as fast as she could, Jaz wove between the club patrons to the women's room on the other side of the floor. To her relief, the place was large and well lit, with stalls, showers, and lockers lining the space. Dropping onto a bench, Jaz closed her eyes and breathed through the arousal still coursing through her. She couldn't shake it. Couldn't make her body calm. Couldn't stop thinking about Liam's strong body and the clean male musk that she breathed in as he held her in place. As he'd whispered, *"Consider yourself punished."*

The night was supposed to be easygoing fun, not a hostile takeover of her senses.

"Are you all right?" Solana, the woman from the front desk, settled on the bench beside her. She'd changed her Shadow Cove T-shirt for a sexy low-cut number that made the most of her already large breasts and held a pair of high-heeled pumps in her hand. Setting the pumps aside, she focused her attention on Jaz. "What happened, sweetie?"

"I—" Jaz realized she had no idea what to say. *I got aroused when I wasn't expecting it, and now I'm freaked out even though that was the whole point of coming to a sex club*, didn't exactly sound rational. "It's my first time here. It's just a lot to take in."

Solana gave her a pity-filled look. "I bet. And I'm sure coming here with Liam Rowen isn't helping any."

"What does Liam have to do with it?" Jaz asked.

"Well, I mean, you look new to this whole thing, and—" She stopped, her brow furrowing. "Look, talking about other members isn't usually allowed, and I work here. So, I need your word that what's said in the women's room stays in the women's room."

"Of course. Cone of silence."

Solana nodded and leaned closer. "Well, what I wanted to tell you is that Liam is a hard-core sadist—that means he gets off on pain. Lots of pain. There are very few women who can take what he needs to give to feel satisfied. I personally think it's irresponsible to expect it of a newbie."

Jaz shook her head, which was slowly clearing. "That doesn't sound like him."

Solana snorted. "Of course it doesn't. If you haven't noticed, most of us don't exactly advertise our lifestyle outside the club. But listen, I like you and I'm telling you this because I don't want to see you hurt. Liam has been coming here a lot, and he goes through women like single-use dishes. And unless you can take what he wants to dish out, you aren't even going to last the meal."

"I don't—"

"You want proof?" Solana tipped her head. "You look like you want proof."

"Proof?" Jaz's arousal was fully gone now, and something unpleasant was filling the void.

"Yeah." Solana lowered her voice. "All right, did Liam tell you the club rules before you came?"

Jaz nodded. "No cell phones, no interfering with other people's play, that type of thing."

"Right. So you know what happens if you accidentally slip up?" Getting off the bench, Salena pulled down the waistband of her skirt to display an elongated puckered scar across the fleshy part of one butt cheek. "You get a choice—get thrown out of the club forever or take the punishment. And Dior—that's the owner—has Liam mete it out. Dior says he figures at least one of the two parties should enjoy it."

Jaz's chest tightened. "Liam did that? Beat you hard enough to leave scars?"

Solana pulled up her skirt and nodded solemnly. "And he loved the hell out of it. The only good part was that because I took it so well, he started respecting me. I'm actually the only one Liam does scenes with regularly."

"So you enjoyed it?"

"The punishment? Hell no. But otherwise, yeah, I'm a

masochist." She shrugged. "Anyway, unless you like pain, I would stay away from that one. Just my two cents."

As Solana finished changing, Jaz leaned back against the wall and studied the ceiling. She had trouble coalescing Solana's claims into what she knew of Liam Rowen, but she was also the first to admit that there was a great deal she *didn't* know about him—that much had been clear since meeting Patti. Was this why Liam had been so insistent that he didn't do relationships? Why didn't he want to bring Jaz to the club? And back there in the California mountains, why did he give her pleasure without taking his own? Was it because he knew he couldn't find it with Jaz? Was the best orgasm of her life his pity fuck?

Solana put away her lipstick and offered Jaz what was probably meant as an encouraging smile. "Do you want me to introduce you to some of the other guys?"

Jaz declined Solana's offer and found Liam waiting outside the door the moment she stepped out. His jaw was tight, his penetrating gaze boring into her. "What happened?"

Jaz forced an irrelevant shrug. "Nothing. Everything just got a little overwhelming, and I needed a moment."

"Hmm." Standing with his legs wide apart and shoulders spread, Liam emanated power from every gorgeous pore of his body. As he shifted himself slightly to block her view of everything but him, Jaz felt that hypnotic arousal spilling again into her blood. Making her toes curl.

With an effort of will, she shoved the feeling away. Jaz had promised Solana not to repeat their conversation, but one thing was clear—she needed more information. She needed to know who Liam was before she decided what she did and didn't want to explore with him.

"Liam. It's good to see you back, my friend." The man from the erotic scene they'd watched came up to them, his arm around the woman he'd been tormenting. Now dressed, she had a happy glow around her and leaned happily into the man's shoulder. The man nodded to Jaz. "And it's a pleasure to make your acquaintance. I'm Dior, and this is my wife, Tiffany."

Dior. The man Solana said owned Shadow Cove and—if the woman was telling the truth—knew about Liam's preferences. Well, wasn't this fortuitous ? A grin rose inside Jaz, which she caught and reined into something appropriately reserved just in time. "A pleasure to meet you both. I'm Jaz."

"Welcome to Shadow Cove," Dior said courteously before returning his attention to Liam. "I hope you both will find a chance to join us for a drink later."

"Not tonight—" Liam started to say.

"Absolutely," Jaz said over him. "In fact, why don't we all grab something now?"

23

JAZ

*L*iam said nothing during their drive home, each moment of silence thickening the air more and more. By Jaz's best guess, he was holding his tongue simply because he wanted to watch her face as he strangled her, and he couldn't strangle and watch the road at the same time. All bets would be off once they were back in his penthouse, however.

Jaz ran her hand over the Land Rover's leather armrest. Jaz couldn't exactly blame Liam for his simmering fury, but she wasn't sorry about what she'd done either. After what Solana had told her, Jaz needed to get more information—and interrogating Dior and Tiffany had been her best bet at the time. Not that it worked. Equally unfortunately, Liam was too smart to have missed what she'd been trying to do. By the time they finished drinks and walked out of the club, the storm brewing behind his eyes threatened to blow them both to the land of Oz.

Jaz's stomach tightened as Liam pulled into the garage and led the way to the elevator. Time to confront him was running out, and she still didn't have a plan for calming things.

Liam unlocked the door, let them both inside, and clicked the dead bolt into place.

"Thank you for the evening." Jaz stretched like a cat and let out a sleepy yawn. If she could delay until morning, the weather might change. "I'm off to bed."

"Like hell you are." Liam's arm shot out, blocking her way. He had those damn shoulders spread out again, and the taut muscles pressed against the silk of his shirt, sculpting the fabric. "*So, Dior, is Liam as good with a flogger as you are?*" Liam pitched his voice up in imitation of hers. "*What are his favorite scenes?* What the hell was that about?"

She put her hands on her hips and tipped her head up to look at him. The difference in their sizes was sometimes damn inconvenient. "So I asked your friends some questions. Not that Dior and Tiffany actually answered any of them. That's what normal people—that is, people who aren't you—do when they meet each other. It's called conversation."

A muscle in the side of Liam's jaw ticked. "We didn't go to Shadow Cove so you could explore my preferences. We went because you wished to explore yours."

Though Liam hadn't moved a muscle, it felt like he was closing in on her. Taking control of her body without laying a finger on her. The proximity, mixed with the memory of Liam's iron grip and his intoxicating male musk, was making Jaz's thighs clench all over again.

The man's ability to turn her on, to know more about her body than she did, was uncanny. And unfair. And all too powerful. Especially when measured against how little he divulged about himself.

Jaz swallowed. Shifted her weight. "Look, thank you for taking me to Shadow Cove." Her words rushed over each other. "I thought I'd be interested by that stuff. I wasn't. Sorry you didn't get laid."

"Don't lie to me." Liam's voice came in a low kind of growl that sent vibrations along her skin. "Why did you run from Dior's scene? What happened in that restroom to turn you into a budding journalist?"

"Let me pass." Jaz shoved against Liam's arm. "I'm not playing your games."

"My games?" He held his place. "You're the one playing games tonight, Jazmine. I just want to know why the damn rules changed."

"I discovered you're an asshole. And I don't play with assholes. Good enough?"

"Not nearly." Instead of backing away, Liam leaned his other palm against the wall, trapping Jaz between his outstretched arms. Her heart pounded against her ribs. His nostrils flared. "You knew I was an asshole before we went. An asshole that I *know* made you dripping wet in there."

Jaz's hand flew up, aiming for Liam's face. He caught her wrist in midmotion and pinned it to the wall behind her. Jaz struck again, and Liam pinned that hand as well. His face hovered before hers, their breaths mixing.

"You want to try that again?" Liam said.

Jaz's knee came up. Hard.

Liam twisted his leg, taking the blow with his thigh. With the next breath, Liam twisted her around and cracked his palm against the seat of her jeans.

The sound cracked through the hallway.

Jaz gasped. And then gasped again as the hot sting enveloping her ass became not altogether unpleasant. Which infuriated her even more.

"You—" She twisted back with a snarl, her heart pounding through her chest. Her backside. Her blood.

"Me what?" Liam's mouth was so close that the words tickled her skin. Gripping her shirt, Liam pressed Jaz against the wall behind her and kicked her ankles apart, taking her balance until it was only his hold keeping her upright.

And fuck it, she liked it. Even as she hated liking it.

"You asshole." She bared her teeth.

Closing what was left of the distance between them, Liam sealed his lips over hers. Jaz kissed him back hungrily, her head swimming. Somewhere deep in her core, a primal need roused to the invasion, making every sensation a thousand times more potent, especially Liam's dizzying taste.

Jaz couldn't think. The kiss deepened, pillaging her mouth, and

ALEX LIDELL

she raked her nails down Liam's back in vengeance for the assault on her senses. For turning her own body against her. Damn him. Damn him to hell.

Liam growled against her mouth. His hands cupping her still-tingling backside, he lifted her onto his hips, Jaz's legs wrapping around him on instinct. The man's hardness pressed against her, the pulsing of his cock evident even through clothes.

In a few swift steps, Liam carried her into the kitchen. Sitting her on the edge of the kitchen island, he pulled away, his breath ragged. With obvious, deliberate effort, Liam braced his hands on either side of her hips, his greater height letting him loom over her despite the perch.

"This would be a very good time to leave," Liam whispered, the words straining his throat. "Otherwise, your ass is mine—and I will let it know exactly how I feel about tonight."

Jaz's backside clenched, heat rushing along her sex and pooling low and desperate in her belly.

"I don't take orders." Tangling her hands in his hair, she took his mouth, her tongue assaulting his in defiance and challenge and deep, unbearable need.

With the next heartbeat, Liam snatched Jaz off the table and flipped her facedown onto the cool countertop. With a powerful hand pressing down on her back, he yanked off her shoes, jeans, and panties until she was bare from the waist down, bent over the counter, legs dangling in the air.

JAZ GASPED, the sudden vulnerability of the position sending her rearing back, only to discover that Liam's steel hold had pinned her down. Yet, the restraint somehow drove her arousal, making her breath come in sharp pants.

Moisture dripped from her sex, slithering along her heated skin.

Liam's knee roughly parted her legs, his hand sliding over Jaz's inner thighs. A little higher and he'd find the moisture coating her inner thighs. A moisture that left humiliatingly little to the

148

imagination about what turned her on. Jaz arched, fighting the inevitable.

Instead of retreating, Liam slid his hand between her folds, running it up and down her slickness with the same possessive authority as Dior had done earlier with Tiffany. Jaz's sex clenched, arousal rushing all the way down her legs. Curling her toes. Too much. Too strong.

Her cheeks flamed. "I hate you."

His hand lifted off her backside and came down with a hard smack.

"Fuck," Jaz yowled, fire exploding across her right cheek.

He slapped the other side. Again. Again. And then, just as the pain rose to a pinnacle, he flicked her clit, and the all-consuming sting morphed to molten pleasure. Oh God. Close. She was so impossibly close to a release she couldn't let happen. Not like this.

"Cut it out." The words came in short pants. "That hurts."

Liam slid two fingers into her, filling her even as her backside still burned and the threat of more to come drove up her arousal. "Good," he said. "It's punishment."

There was that word again, the one that made Jaz's channel clench.

Ignoring her whimper, Liam brought his hand down on her backside again, right on the spot where her cheeks met her thighs. Without pause, he issued another swat. And another.

Jaz shouted, gripping the edge of the counter.

Liam brushed over her clit, and the shout turned to a keen as a shattering release enveloped Jaz's body. Wave after wave tightened her muscles until she was lying like a rag doll, only the cold granite against her cheek reminding her where she was. She pulled her arms in to—

"Stay where you are," Liam ordered from behind. "We aren't done."

Wait, what?

Belatedly, Jaz realized that Liam's fingers were still inside her. That they were moving again. Waking her body. As her heartbeat quickened with new need, the intrusion withdrew, the sound of an opening zipper and foil packet letting her know exactly what was coming.

Liam sheathed himself inside her with a harsh thrust, the invasion so complete, all she could do was gasp for breath. With Liam inside her, she felt the tension of his own powerful body, his muscles quivering with restraint as he held still. Let her tight channel adjust to his size.

Except she didn't want the waiting. The adjusting. She wanted —needed—him to *thrust*.

She opened her mouth to curse him out, but Liam starting moving just then, thrusting in and out with harsh groans. Again. Again. In moments, he'd found a perfect punishing rhythm, pounding into her with sniper precision, every delicious stroke making her channel clench and pulse for more.

Jaz gasped for breath and curled her fingers around the other edge of the kitchen island, wet slaps of his sac striking her skin echoing shamelessly through the room.

24

ROMAN

*R*oman Robillard followed two men in military fatigues past a helipad and a formidable collection of Humvees to a large building that appeared to have started its life as a factory. The smell of soil and wet fallen leaves wafted through the air, proof of the rain he'd encountered on his way to New Jersey. Like any self-respecting climber, Roman was always aware of the weather. Cloud cover, temperature, wind—it all altered the chance of a successful climb. But sometimes, like now, obstacles came from man-made sources.

Or, in the case of Jazmine Keasley, the bitch who'd fucked her way into stealing his endorsement, woman-made sources. Roman's fingers closed into a fist. The upstart had played the *I have tits* game, stabbing him in the back with her affirmative action bullshit the moment he paused for breath. He was the better climber, and everyone and their dog knew it. This gender equality crap had gotten completely out of hand a while back, but this crossed the line. This ridiculous escapade was now destroying not only Roman's career, but the reputation of the entire sport.

Stopping by the front door, one of Roman's escorts exchanged a few words with the sentry standing guard. Like the others, this man too had a Rambo-wanna-be look about him, with bulging muscles in place of a lithe body.

"Does he have an appointment?" the sentry asked Roman's escorts.

Roman took a too-patient breath and repeated himself for the fourth time. "No. It was my understanding that your boss prefers to keep electronic communications to a minimum."

The dark web was very clear on that part. While Obsidian Ops Security Corporation had a proper corporate suite in Newark, Colonel Jeffrey Lucius held the equivalent of office hours every third Wednesday of the month at Obsidian's complex. That was where money could buy most any job that could be done by ex-special forces. Since Roman's needs were on the left side of legal, the third Wednesday of the month it was.

The sentry spoke into his earpiece, then cocked his head while someone with more brain cells answered back. He opened the door for Roman. "Right this way, sir."

The clang of metal on metal resounded through the space as the door slammed shut behind Roman and the escorts that still clung to either side of him like ticks. As if he were some kind of security threat. But then again, maybe Obsidian Ops' obsession with security was a good thing. It spoke of professionalism. And after the absolute mess his cousin Devante had made of everything, Roman was ready to invest the considerable resources required to hire pros. Which he should have done from the beginning—but who knew Jazfuck would prove to be as persistent as poison ivy?

Pausing by a nondescript metal door, the shorter of Roman's escort motioned for him to go inside. Roman did, finding himself in a spartan office with several computer monitors and a large man presiding behind a metal desk. Despite having seen Colonel Lucius's photographs online, Roman had underestimated his formidable presence.

"I understand you have a possible mission for my men," the commander said by way of greeting, his deep booming voice courteous but curt as he rose and came around to shake Roman's hand.

Despite the man's businesslike politeness, Roman felt a tightness around his chest. Maybe it was the direct way Lucius stared him right in the eye or the wide, too-confident stance, but Roman, even at his own six feet of height, felt dwarfed by the colonel.

"Yes, sir. I do. My name is—"

"Your name is Roman Robillard, and you're a champion-level rock climber on the sponsored circuits," Lucius cut him off. "Until you stopped passing your required drug testing and incurred a DUI or two."

Roman blinked in confusion.

The commander watched him carefully, his expression edging toward amusement. "You drove your own car here. My men ran the plate and Google filled in the rest." He perched himself on the edge of the desk. "I believe in doing my homework. It saves everyone's time."

"That's wise." Roman cleared his throat and clawed back his balance. There was too much at stake—for him and all the world's climbers—to let Lucius's parlor tricks distract him. "But you shouldn't believe everything you read on the internet, Colonel. The drug tests were bullshit, and as for the supposed DUI collision, that was entirely on the asshole in the other car. Unfortunately, the confusion created fertile ground for a certain Colorado bitch to blow enough dick to sabotage my agreement with Vector Ascent. If allowed to continue unchecked, she is going to make a mockery of the entire sport. The whole damn industry."

Vector Ascent was no doubt already regretting ever meeting Jazfuck, but in today's world, you couldn't fire a woman for incompetence without being accused of *sexism*. Since when did it become a sin to point out that half the population did not have a dick? Once she was gone, Vector Ascent would come begging—no, crawl begging—right back to Roman.

He'd make them stew a bit, but he'd accept eventually. Once they informed him on how much it was going to cost to clean up their mess. But he would come back. With great skill came great responsibility, and the climbing world needed Roman Robillard.

"I see." Lucius cocked his head. "And what are you hoping O2 can do about this situation?"

Clearly parlor tricks and large muscles did not translate to intelligence. "Remove the cheating bitch from the Clash of the Titans." Roman kept his voice even as he spelled it out for Lucius. "Accidently, of course."

"Does this woman pose a physical threat?"

Roman snorted. "She is five feet tall. The only physical threat she'd pose is to the soles of your men's boots."

"But you want her taken out?" Lucius clarified.

"Taken out of the pro climbing circuit she's destroying. I don't want her killed unless you can guarantee that there's no way it could get pinned on me. Simply injuring her would probably be preferable to having a body to deal with." Roman didn't want to come across as overly picky. "But you're the professional."

"Hmm."

Roman peered up at Lucius and was met with an iron gaze to go with the military flat-top haircut and the carefully maintained white facial hair. Between the colonel's demeanor and the stoic nature of his facial features, Roman couldn't gather what the other man was thinking. Surely he wasn't truly worried that Jazfuck would harm his special forces pets, so what was the delay? Was he waiting to discuss payment? This guy would be deadly across the table from him at his usual Tuesday poker night.

"Let me be frank, Mr. Robillard. What you've offered me isn't the sort of operation the O2 is interested in taking. We are a security agency. Our mission set encompasses protecting high-value property and mitigating threats to life and welfare. We don't rig sporting contests, insert ourselves in interpersonal squabbles, or clean up after DUIs. And we most certainly don't use our resources to injure defenseless young women whose accomplishments bigots like you find inconvenient. I'm sorry that you came all the way here only to waste your time."

The way he said it implied that Roman had wasted Lucius's time too. The colonel turned his back to Roman and walked back to his seat.

"Jazmine Keasley is as far from being a defenseless young woman as I am from Santa Claus. She has this guy Liam's army at her beck and call." Roman's jaw clenched, his frustration bubbling into his blood. "That's it, isn't it? I needed assistance from an organization that can go head-to-head with navy SEALs, but you don't want to go up against Trident Security. You're just as big a coward as anyone."

Lucius paused.

Roman took an involuntary step back. "I didn't mean coward, I meant—"

Lucius turned, but instead of anger, a flicker of interest fled across his chiseled face. "Liam Rowen and Trident Security got themselves involved in this?"

"Um. Yeah." Roman didn't know precisely why this appeared to be a vote in his favor, but he pressed his advantage anyway. "Liam has taken it upon himself to personally tail the Keasley woman. Never lets her out of his sight. I think her brother is his friend or something."

Colonel Jeffrey Lucius rubbed the goatee covering his square jaw. Pulling out a computer keyboard, he brought something up on screen and made a sound in the back of his throat. "Keasley is it. Brother Kyan Keasley."

It wasn't a question, and Roman didn't really know the answer, but he nodded anyway. "Yeah. Exactly." He shifted his weight. "Like I was saying from the beginning. Liam Rowen's Trident Security and the Keasley woman are trying to sabotage the Clash of the Titans."

Holding his breath, Roman watched Lucius deliberate with himself. Even still, he had no indication of what the man was thinking until Lucius finally spoke. "I'll see what I can do."

25

JAZ

*T*he first thing that struck Jaz upon their arrival in Denver for the Adventure World Outdoor Fair was the delicious aromas coming from the food vendor tents they passed near the entrance. Colorado in the fall was replete with the bright gold of looming aspen trees, but still held the edge of warm weather, despite the impending winter. The scents of funnel cakes, giant smoked turkey legs, and apple cider made her mouth water. Then she remembered why she was here, and all traces of appetite disappeared. "Do you think the Clash of the Titans plan to announce the first-round champion in Denver is a sign?"

Ivy shifted Bar over to her other hip. With Denver's proximity to Denton Valley, the whole gang had decided to come out and make a day of the event. In addition to Kyan, Ivy, and little Bar, Cullen and Sky had come along, as had Eli, a pregnant Dani, and their daughter, Ella. The little girl was "walking" Bumblebee, Ivy's giant German shepherd. The dog held the leash in his teeth and plainly considered himself the responsible party. "I mean, Jaz is the only one of the five climbers from Colorado, so that's got to be a sign."

"I wish, but it's all a money game. Adventure World attracts big outdoorsy crowds who like spending money on equipment." Jaz glanced over at Liam, who prowled along at her side with the same determination as Bumble. The others might be here for family fun, but he was working. Which was sexy and frustrating and a million other things that Jaz had trouble putting into words. Just like she was having trouble reassuring herself that none of their friends could actually see inside her head for a blow-by-blow visual of the sex they'd been having.

Feeling her cheeks heat, Jaz channeled her turmoil at Liam. "Can you at least try to look like a normal human being enjoying the day? Unless you think the funnel cake will attack me, I think we're all right here. There are like two thousand people, and a good third of them are still learning to read."

He didn't even look her way. "I'll start taking your advice on security about the same time you start taking mine on climbing gear."

"If you scare off all the patrons, we won't be invited back."

"I can live with that."

"Did I tell you I invited your mother to dinner?" She'd done no such thing, but she suddenly wanted to. Just to prod him. Given what he did to her in bed...and the couch...and on the kitchen counter, she needed some way to reclaim the upper hand.

Liam gave her a dark glare that promised he'd make her pay for that.

Jaz's traitorous body awakened in response. Damn it. Biology and physiology and all that was damn inconvenient. At least Jaz hoped that was all there was behind her actually being glad Liam was here with her.

She didn't realize she'd taken a step toward him until Liam edged away. It wasn't a large movement, but it was enough to make it clear that he had no intention of playing footsie in front of their friends. In front of Kyan.

Jaz had no such plans either, but the rejection still stung.

And continued stinging with every heartbeat. Jaz rubbed her arms, fighting to make sense of the emotions that had come unbidden. So what if Liam stepped away? They'd made an agreement. No commitments, no strings attached. Just pleasure and enjoyment. So why did this bother her?

Because "no commitment" wasn't the same as being Liam's dirty little secret. A toy to be brought out and played with only when no one was watching. Like a vibrator. Jaz's jaw tightened against the ache growing in her chest.

"Ice cweam! Ice cweeeeeeam!" A high-pitched yell shattered through Jaz's darkening mood. She got her bearings back just in time to watch little Ella let go of the dog's leash and make a dash for the frozen-treat vendor. Her former special forces father rushed after her; however, unlike his daughter, who had no qualms about running between people, Eli's large frame made slower progress.

Kyan and Cullen rallied to aid their brother-in-arms. The military's flanking maneuvers, however, seemed not to have accounted for clueless families and rushing children that made Ella's tiny form flicker in and out of view despite the SEALs' best efforts.

Which was when Bumblebee—distraught over losing his charge —decided to add his services to the tracking efforts and launched into the crowd.

Ivy gasped as slow-on-the-uptake tourists who didn't move for navy SEALs leaped out of the way for a German shepherd on a mission. Reaching Ella just as the toddler was about to run right through a knife-throwing game, Bumblebee leapt atop her, pinned the girl to the ground, and barked his victory.

Onlookers screamed.

Dani groaned.

Ella squealed in delight as the dog licked her face furiously. "Ice cweam, Wumble. Ice cweam."

"You still sure you want children?" Dani asked Sky, who smiled indulgently. They all knew she and Cullen both did and had been actively trying for some time.

At least Cullen, as bullheaded as he was, didn't ever pretend that he and Sky weren't having sex.

Leaving Cullen, Kyan, and Eli to deal with a dog, toddler, ice cream, and a bunch of frightened-out-of-their-minds fair visitors, the rest of them set course for the main stage, where Jaz was due in an hour for the results announcement. The closer they got, the fewer low rock-climbing walls, axe-throwing contests, and water-dunking booths they encountered, the vendors changing from family-friendly fun to the higher-end brands selling real equipment. Vector Ascent's booth boasted a large photo of Jaz in midclimb, along with a quote about trusting her life to only the best gear.

"Nice shot," Ivy said. "How did they get a camera up there?"

On another day, Jaz would have come up with something entertaining, but today she just shrugged. "They didn't. I was maybe three feet off the ground. The rest is Photoshop. Publicity is the name of the game."

Everything, wasn't it? Vector Ascent's promotion images, the whole pomp and circumstance around the competition, the way Liam maintained a constant distance from her in public. The reason Shadow Cove didn't allow cell phones. It wasn't about reality, it was about image. Perception. The need to put up a wartless front to the world.

"Speaking of publicity." Sky put her hands into her back pockets as she eyed Liam. "Did you put out a press release on the Trident group doing Jaz's security?"

Liam returned Sky's gaze with a dark one, the lack of surprise at Sky's question lending it gravity. "Of course I didn't."

"Hmm." Sky pursed her lips. "Yeah. I didn't think so."

Jaz narrowed her eyes at her friend. An investigative journalist and brilliant woman, Sky usually had five thoughts in her head for each one she said aloud. "Why exactly do you ask? Is there an issue?"

"Probably not," Sky hedged. "It's just Trident's security contract with Vector Ascent suddenly got picked up by several major news outlets, and I'm not sure why. The contract isn't a secret, but it would have taken some digging to find, and given other more prominent events going on, I'm not sure why someone bothered. And I don't like not knowing. Or at least not having a good guess."

"Maybe someone just needed an interesting twist on a straight climbing competition?" Ivy suggested. "People are vultures. Tell them athletes are defying gravity and scaling cliffs, and they don't care. Hint at something gruesome, and they'll buy popcorn and set out lawn chairs to watch. You want to know how many patients I get in the ER who walked themselves into traffic while trying to take photos of someone else's accident?"

"I don't doubt it." Sky nodded. "Like it or not, sensationalism sells. But if someone was going after cheap thrills and bothered to find the security contract, you'd think they'd have found Jaz's mugging too. Or maybe I'm overthinking this and Vector Ascent just pitched the story themselves for publicity's sake. Can you check with them?"

"No problem," Jaz said quickly. With her mood still gray from Liam's rejection, she welcomed the chance to get away from the others and brood in peace. "I need to check in with Vector Ascent anyway. Catch you guys at the announcement. You don't want to be standing around for an hour while they work out the logistics."

Giving the gang a wave over her shoulder, she started toward the main table, which was visible beyond the small forest of supply stalls. She'd just made it twenty yards, right to the middle of the labyrinth, when Liam—who dutifully changed direction to keep up with her—grabbed Jaz's upper arm.

Towing her into the relative privacy between two stalls, he squared off, his arms crossed over his muscled chest. "What's going on with you?" He glared down at her from his greater height, his gaze reproving. "You've been sulking for the past hour."

"Sulking?" Seriously? He had the gall to be upset with *her*?

"You're welcome to pick any word you like. So what's happened? And God help you if you say 'nothing.'"

"Nothing." She stepped around him. "Excuse me. I don't want to be late."

Liam shifted his weight, blocking her path. Something he was all too skilled at doing. Of course he was getting all close and powerful and sexy now, when there was little risk of anyone seeing.

Jaz inhaled his clean male musk and blew it out in a short breath. "I'm not playing."

"Good. That makes two of us." He stepped closer still, the heat from his body spilling into the small space between them. "So stop pretending I can read your mind, and tell me why you're suddenly pissed to high heaven."

"*Suddenly* is such an interesting word, don't you think? Let's take your *sudden* interest in my state of mind, for example. Nothing about it bothered you earlier, but now, *suddenly*, you can't bear for me to take another step without spilling my guts to you. Makes one wonder what changed exactly. Hmm… Oh! I think I got it." She snapped her fingers. "Your friends can no longer see you. You couldn't be seen sitting with the uncool kid in the cafeteria before, but now that no one is watching, it's game on."

"Did you *want* me to kiss you in front of your brother?" Liam demanded.

"I want my brother's presence to not get a fucking vote." She crossed her arms, her heart pounding against her ribs as the words spilled out of her. "Kiss me. Don't kiss me. Fuck me. Don't touch me. Do whatever the hell you want—but do it because of me, not because of whoever else happens to be around."

Liam lifted his chin, a muscle pulsing along the stubborn angle of his jaw. "And did you tell your girlfriends about our extracurriculars? Do Ivy and Dani and Sky know the many new ways you like to use rope? A blow-by-blow account of last night, perhaps?"

A blaze of fury heated Jaz's blood. "Not the same thing, and you know it."

"Do I?" He grabbed the back of her neck hard, the way they discovered she enjoyed in the heat of passion—though it felt different now. Intrusive and infuriating. "Don't you get it? When it comes to me, everyone will assume they know the blow by blow. Literally." Liam's words came in a quiet, forceful staccato, his chest heaving as if from a run. "Whatever it is they imagine, whatever they find dirty or distasteful or edgy, that is what you'll be assumed to have enjoyed. It was your reputation with the cool kids I was protecting. Not mine."

Jaz's pulse pounded in her ears, the sound overpowering the clatter of the fair beyond. The feel of Liam's grip on her, steady and possessive and claiming, was sinking into her bones. Her lips pulled into a snarl. "Worry about your own damn image. Try to—"

Liam's mouth clamped over hers, his rock-hard body pressing her into the plywood wall of the stall behind her. Need spilled into Jaz's veins, her nails raking Liam's arms as her tongue met his in a duel she was destined to lose. His kiss was claiming, punishing. The kind that washed away all doubt of his desire for her.

Bracing herself against Liam, Jaz wrapped her legs around his waist. She ground into the erection that pressed through their clothing into her thigh, her breath hitching as Liam captured her wrists. Pinned them to the wall above her. Her sex clenched, aching so badly with need that she moaned into his mouth and trusted him to swallow the sound. The intensity of the arousal pounded her like a merciless hail, taking over all thought. All logic. She needed relief. Release. She needed more than to grind against his clothes. God. She needed more.

There was a commotion nearby, and Liam smacked her hard but quietly on the ass to get her to lower her legs. Jaz's feet touched ground just in time for a group wearing the logo of one of the name-brand backpacks to lumber by on the other side of the stall. Her chest heaved with ragged breaths until the group's steps receded.

Instead of dousing her need, the rush of their near escape only added fuel to the flame. Jaz dug her fingers into him, her hand jetting toward the bulge—

"I knew it. You fucking slut."

Liam twisted toward the man who'd just stepped out from behind the opposite tent, the wind catching the reek of whiskey coming from him. Roman Robillard, the man Jaz had replaced on the climbing circuit, stumbled forward, his skin flushed.

"You make filth of our sport." Roman pointed a finger at her. "Fucking your way to what I earned. You think you can keep it quiet, don't you? But you can't. You won't. What's it about your pussy that makes men lose all common sense? Let's take a feel for—"

Roman broke off with a grunt of pain, only now seeming to

have realized that while he rambled, Liam had pinned his arms behind his back.

"I'd stop blabbering if I were you. If you want to keep this appendage." The look on Liam's face was nothing short of deadly. "Apologize. Now."

"It's that fucking slut who should be— Ow!" Roman yelped as Liam adjusted his hold enough to tweak the climber's ball-and-socket shoulder joint. "Lay off, man. That hurts."

"Does it now? Apologize." Liam wrenched his arm up again, eliciting a whimper from Roman.

Jaz rubbed her face. "He's drunk, Liam. Let him go. This asshole needs rehab and counseling, not a compound fracture."

Liam behaved as if he hadn't heard a word she said. *"Apologize."* He enunciated each syllable into Roman's ear.

"Ow. Fuck. S-sorry," Roman slurred. "Just let go."

A series of three tones sounded in the background, then the crackle of a loudspeaker. "All Clash of the Titans competitors report to the main stage," a disembodied female voice announced. "Clash of the Titans competitors to the main stage."

With a disgusted grunt, Liam released Roman. The drunk man tottered on his feet, then fell to the dirt. None of which stopped him from trying to spit at Jaz.

"Bitch."

Jaz grabbed Liam's arm before he could go for round two, which would no doubt land Roman in surgery and Liam in a jail cell. "He's not worth it."

Over the next forty minutes, Jaz and the other four challengers went over the stage logistics and gave quick interviews to the press, each person finding a way to work their brand into a statement. Jaz emphasized the durability and lightweight design of Vector Ascent's gear, playing to her smaller frame as an advertisement. The blond climber with a California-surfer look told the reporters that he only entrusted his life to a company with a hundred-year history of reliability. Carlos, a wiry climber of Mexican descent who was a gymnast before discovering a passion for the mountains, bragged about his gear's versatility. Carlos's sound bites were especially polished and elicited several follow-up questions that he answered with equal skill and articulation.

With the reporters' questions dying down and the arrows on Liam's Rolex creeping up toward the hour, Jaz felt her rising nerves strain her easygoing facade. Winning the first challenge wouldn't guarantee the final Clash of the Titans victory, but whoever's courses were chosen would have a major advantage over the other climbers because they would already be familiar with the routes. By the time everyone was seated and the judges launched into an explanation of the rules for the audience's benefit, Jaz could hardly think over the pounding in her chest and skull.

Twists of choice and fate had forced all her proverbial eggs into one final basket. If she won the Clash of the Titans, she'd have her bank account replenished, three years of guaranteed endorsements from Vector Ascent, and a career in professional climbing. If she didn't, she would have no choice but to slink back to her parents, her pockets filled with nothing but humiliation. Five climbers. One winner.

"Last month, our competitors had one week to mark five equitable climbing routes on the San Bernardino mountains," the woman on the stage announced energetically. "Since then, our judges have been hard at work to decide which set was the most equitable and challenging. Today, we are excited to announce the winner of the challenge. The climber whose routes will be used for the Clash of the Titans in two weeks' time. And now, the winner is—"

The announcement paused dramatically, a silence settling over the audience. Jaz's hands gripped her knees, her breath stilling. Liam put his arm around her. A bird of prey cawed somewhere in the distance.

"Ice cweam?" Ella asked hopefully into the tense silence.

"Jazmine Keasley, representing Vector Ascent!"

Jaz jerked. The crowd erupted in applause, the friends around her clapping the loudest. Only when Liam pushed her gently between the shoulder blades did Jaz realize she needed to start breathing again and get up on stage. Her acting training taking over, she bounded up the small steps to shake the announcer's hand and even accepted the microphone that was unexpectedly shoved into her hands.

The words came to her through the flow of endorphins. She thanked the judges. Talked up her sponsors. Praised the other competitors, whom she quickly invited to share the limelight. Judging by the several rounds of applause, whatever she was saying was well received. More clicks of the camera sounded, and then she was walking back, grinning, her head high and chest out and hair streaming in the wind.

Liam stepped up to meet her, the pride unmistakable in his hazel eyes. Without thinking about it, Jaz rose on her toes and covered his mouth with hers. She didn't care who saw. Who thought what. This was her moment, and she was happy. And she wanted Liam to share in her joy.

"Thank you," she told him once they finally separated, the points of their friends' surprised gazes poking into her back. "I couldn't have done this if you hadn't stood in for Sebastian."

"I'd argue you did this despite my company, not because of it." Liam brushed a thumb across Jaz's cheek. "The talent and hard work winning this competition took was all down to you."

They stayed there, their eyes locked, until Kyan cleared his throat and the moment was shattered.

"Congratulations, Jaz," Kyan said, though Jaz didn't miss the murderous look he threw at Liam before stepping up to kiss her cheek.

With the announcement over, the kids getting tired and cranky, and postexcitement fatigue starting to creep over the adults as well, there were no dissenting opinions over heading home. As they all reached the main parking area, Liam and Jaz split off from the rest of the group to head to the VIP parking lot in the back. Now that she'd gotten a glimpse of the bottlenecked main exit, she could say with certainty that the VIP's remote easy-on-easy-off access path was a major boon.

They were almost back at the truck, the noise of the crowds a distant rumble, when Liam stopped so abruptly that Jaz nearly bounced off his outstretched arm.

"What—"

He quieted her with a finger, his whole body taut, each muscle singing with alertness. "The dirt spatter around the truck's skirt. There's a clean streak breaking the mud. As if someone brushed a shoulder or an arm against the bottom part of the vehicle."

"Or a leg," said Jaz. "Or a dog ran by."

Liam crouched and tilted his head as if he were listening for something. Then he swore.

What's wrong? The words came to the tip of Jaz's tongue, but she didn't get to utter them. Instead, an expression of fierce determination rolled over Liam's face, and he threw his body over hers so suddenly that he knocked the wind out of her. Before Jaz could reinflate her lungs and gather a fresh inhale, Liam's Land Rover, the vehicle he'd driven over here from Denton Valley, emitted a creaking belch.

And exploded.

LIAM

*L*iam's awareness caught up to him by degrees. He heard the low background noise of small wheels on tile and the distant beeping of machines. Despite being on his stomach —an oddity in and of itself since he always slept on his side—light filled the space where he was, hurting his eyes. Forcing himself to pry his eyelids wider anyway, he took in his surroundings. A sterile white room. The smells of disinfectant and plastic tubing. A television up on one wall. A white board with information written in black dry erase marker.

He was in a hospital. He was in a hospital because... The memories hit him all at once. A mirror on his truck moved out of place. A break in the dried mud splatter that had clung to the bottom of his truck ever since he drove across a puddle. An ever-so-slight high-pitched noise that made him crouch. Looking under his car as his heart started to hammer.

The heat and booming shock wave of the explosion flashed before Liam's eyes. He shoved himself up, a sharp pain raking along his back as he did.

"Mr. Rowen!" a disembodied female voice chastised him as a hand clamped onto his forearm. Then, neon-green clogs and matching scrubs came into view, everything materializing into a slightly panicked young nurse. "Please lie back down. You've been injured and have some painkillers that can make you unsteady. I need you to—"

"Where's Jaz Keasley?"

"I'm sorry, I don't know who that is." The nurse, whose name tag claimed she'd respond to Mary Beth of Saint Joseph's Hospital in Denver, held her hands out in a calming gesture. "But if you could just lie down, I'm sure I can look into whatever it is you want to know."

Instead of obeying, Liam pushed himself up into a sitting position and swung his legs over the side of the bed. Mary Beth let out a squeak, and the room swam for a moment. Liam gripped the bedrail, gritting his teeth against the now-predictable onslaught of hurt. Jaz was there with him when the charge went off. He needed to find her.

"She is all right, Liam," a familiar, unsteady voice said from behind him. The last voice he'd expected to hear just now. His mother. "A few scrapes and bruises, but you shielded her from the worst of it."

Liam started to turn, but Patti came around to his side of the bed so he wouldn't have to. Her eyes were red, and the hands she was wringing shook slightly.

"The hospital wanted consent for treatment from next of kin, and I was in the system." She sounded apologetic. Defeated. "I couldn't not come. I knew you'd want me to leave as soon as you woke up, so I stayed while you were sleeping. Please don't be angry with me."

Liam tried to rub his face, realized that his IV tubing didn't extend that far, and used his other hand. "I'm not angry, Ma. I'm just surprised. You aren't usually..." He caught tears glistening in her eyes and changed what he was about to say. "Thank you for keeping track of Jaz for me."

"Mr. Rowen." Coming up to Liam's other side, Nurse Mary Beth turned her voice shrilly authoritative. "Mr. Rowen, lie back down right now. You're being unsafe. This is unacceptable."

Liam glared at her. "What exactly is unsafe and unacceptable, Nurse? Me being awake? Let's not confuse inconvenient and unacceptable."

"Mr. Rowen!—"

"Mary Beth." Patti smiled indulgently at the nurse. "Do you think you could tell the doctor that Liam is awake?"

The nurse closed her mouth, apparently realizing that in her quest for the upper hand, she'd forgotten a rather important tidbit of her job. As Mary Beth scurried out the door, Liam had to grudgingly admit that Patti handled that better than his own muddled brain.

Patti held up her phone. "I let Jaz know you're awake. She is on her way over with someone named Ivy. They told me you were near some kind of explosion." She shuddered. "So they took you in for surgery to remove shrap...shrapnel and—" The tears that had been clinging to Patti's eyes now spilled over onto her cheeks.

Liam frowned. He tried to reach toward her, but the IV stopped him again.

Wiping her cheeks, Patti fled the room.

Liam shook his head and immediately regretted it. What a fucking mess. Glaring at the offending IV line, he disconnected the main tubing tethering him to the bed, then pulled off the blood pressure cuff and EKG leads. The monitors began to wail red alert, but quieted mercifully at a press of a button. Right. Now to get out of the monkey dress.

Digging through a nearby cabinet, Liam found no trace of his clothes, but was thrilled to discover a set of clean scrubs. Good enough. Leaning against the wall more than he wished he needed to, he pulled on the bottoms, then tore off the hospital gown. The mirror above a sink showed him a torso covered in a mass of bandages, and the more he moved, the more he felt sharp needles of pain radiating up and down his spine.

"I hear you're already terrorizing the nurses?" Walking into the room, Ivy set her fists on her hips and regarded the monitors, discarded gown, and finally Liam with exasperation. "I'll take it as a sign you've returned to a baseline mental state."

Sliding around Ivy, Jaz rushed inside and wrapped an arm around Liam. Only one arm, the other being in a sling. "Hey, you. How do you feel? And what the hell are you doing out of bed?"

Relief rushed over Liam's skin, and he folded Jaz into him, savoring the coconut smell of her shampoo, the way her small body fit perfectly into the groove of his shoulder. His pulse quickened at the feel of her, then settled into a steady, satisfied rhythm that drowned out the pain in his back and the distant chirps of monitors.

Then memories of the explosion flashed through him again. The signs. The noise. The realization. The utter terror of knowing what was about to happen and the equal certainty that he had no way of getting Jaz away before it did. Pulling Jaz away to arm's length, he ran his palms over her face, her shoulders, over the arm in a sling. His breath caught. "How bad is it?"

"Not bad, considering some big oaf slammed me into the ground and nearly dislocated my shoulder," she said with a smile. "The sling is just for sympathy."

Liam's finger slid to Jaz's shoulder at once, catching her wince as he probed her collarbone and moved lower. His chest tightened. The damn sling wasn't for sympathy.

"She's all right. Some abrasions and a tweaked muscle, but she'll be able to compete." Ivy put her hand on Liam's chest and firmly pushed back a step. Ivy might be on the quieter side in the wild, but here in a hospital, the small emergency room doc was clearly a force to be reckoned with. The hard look she leveled at Liam now made him remember that as Kyan's wife, Ivy had practice taming belligerent SEALs.

"You, on the other hand, took some shrapnel and a hell of a concussion," Ivy informed him. "If one of the big pieces had hit elsewhere on your body, you could've been in serious trouble. Fortunately for you, nothing vital was hit, and it didn't dig in as deep as they'd originally feared. Still, the blow from the explosion knocked you unconscious, so they're going to keep you overnight for observation."

"I'm not staying here overnight," Liam said.

"I'm sorry." Ivy gave him a smile. "I think I might have given you the mistaken impression that this is a democracy and you get a vote."

"I do get a vote. I'm the patient." Liam crossed his arms over his chest, which was a mistake. But he'd be damned if he'd let the discomfort show on his face. "And since when do you have admission privileges in Denver, Dr. West-Keasley?"

Ivy snorted. Although she wasn't wearing a white medical coat, she looked every inch the in-charge physician. "I've got something more powerful than admission privileges. I have friends and a phone. Push me, and I'll check if you aren't due for a colonoscopy as long as you're here."

Liam narrowed his eyes and then decided she wasn't kidding. "You play dirty," he said, walking himself back to sit on the edge of the bed. But that was as much as he was willing to compromise. He was not changing back into a gown.

Ivy waved her slender hand at him. "Now reattach all the toys you pulled off while I go talk your nurse down from the ledge." She turned to Jaz. "If he tries to make a run for it, whack him right over that big bandage beneath the left shoulder blade. You won't do much damage, but he'll scream loudly enough for help to show."

Liam stared at the door for a few seconds after Ivy departed, then glanced over at Jaz, who was making a strong effort to keep a straight face.

"Don't worry, I'm waving a white flag," he said darkly as he reattached the IV and started on the EKG wires. "I know when I'm outgunned. That woman is…scary."

Jaz chuckled, the smile lighting up her face and eyes. Lighting up the room. "It's always the quiet ones." Smile fading, she pulled a chair over to sit near Liam. "The Denver police are looking into what happened, but they have no idea. Of course, the guys are running a parallel investigation. I'm sure they'll be barging in through the door any moment, but I wanted… I wanted to say thank you. For saving my life today. A few more steps and…" She swallowed, a small shudder running through her.

He shook his head firmly. "Let's not go down that road."

"Especially since it may not be accurate." Inviting himself into

173

the room, Cullen held the door open for his wife, Sky, his competent gaze surveying Liam from head to foot.

Liam straightened his back beneath the scrutiny.

Cullen snorted, but then let it go at that. None of them were strangers to seeing friends in hospital rooms, and there was an unspoken agreement to keep the *how are you feeling* discussions to a minimum. Especially since they were all medics who could read a medical chart. Cullen leaned against the wall.

"I took the liberty of dragging Aiden and Trident Security's tech geeks into this while you were napping," Cullen said. "Also, Eli is helping with the blast analysis. It was some sophisticated wiring. Military grade, not amateur crap. And best we can tell so far, it didn't kill you because it wasn't meant to."

"So a proverbial warning shot across the bow?" Liam turned his head toward the door that was once again opening. "Keasley. Welcome to the party."

Kyan nodded, his gaze, like Cullen's, scanning Liam from head to toe. Unlike Cullen, however, Kyan's visual interrogation continued on to Jaz and then to the proximity between her and Liam. Though Kyan said nothing, the temperature in the place seemed to drop several degrees.

Sky cleared her throat, breaking the uncomfortable silence. "So, about that shot across the bow—look what came off the wire a few minutes ago." She tapped the screen of the iPad she carried and held it out to Liam, who read the short article aloud.

LEAD FEMALE CLIMBER AND GIRLS AFLAME SUPPORTER NEARLY IN FLAMES

Jazmine Keasley, a female rock-climbing star and avid Girls Aflame supporter, was nearly caught in an explosion that destroyed a vehicle at the Adventure World Outdoor Fair in Denver, Colorado. Keasley's warp-speed flight to the top of the climbing world has caused many a skeptic to raise a brow, wondering whether some sort of backroom deal didn't help her achieve her position. Now, it appears someone has taken their verbal criticism one step further.

LIAM

*L*iam leaned over the ballistic reports scattered over the battleship-gray L-shaped desk in his home office, the rare night noise of a sleeping city seeping in through the windows. His watch claimed it was nearing two in the morning, but he wasn't ready to sleep yet, especially since whatever Ivy had snuck into his IV had knocked him out for hours in the hospital and didn't let up on the drive home either. Only now did he finally feel like he had his full wits about him, and those he intended to put to good use.

Shifting his coffee mug to his nondominant left hand, he inhaled the bold roast aroma and indulged in a slow sip. He'd dispensed with the heavy-duty pain meds the pharmacy had handed him, the extra-strength ibuprofen doing well enough to keep discomfort in check. Objectively speaking, he'd been in a great deal more pain going through Hell Week in SEAL training. The docs were right— he's been damn lucky. And he hated relying on luck.

With his right hand, Liam scrolled through the intel his security company had gathered about the many haters Jaz seemed to have gathered. As the now-familiar images flickered across the computer screen, Liam shook his head. It all didn't add up. There had been no signs of surveillance. No uptick in chatter. The threatening note to Jaz's parents did use the same "in flames" word play, but that was hardly original. From everything Trident had profiled about the note sender, it was an emotional, mentally unstable individual. The explosion was the work of a cool professional. It didn't add up.

Liam even had Roman Robillard checked out, but according to the latest report Aiden got from the PD, the asshole had been passed out drunk when the whole thing happened. Liam set his coffee mug down with a soft click, then frowned as another noise seemed to echo the sound.

Liam froze to listen. The noise came again. A soft mix between a moan and whimper that was trickling in from the hallway.

Pushing his chair back silently, Liam got to his feet and edged toward the soft calls. They came more often now, sneaking out of the bedroom where Jaz slept. Liam paused at the closed door, his hand flat against the wood.

"Jaz?"

No answer. No change in the noise either. She was sleeping.

Liam knocked. Softly, then with a bit more force. Then more than that.

No luck. Damn. He little liked the idea of barging in on Jaz unannounced, but given how deeply she was sleeping, his only other alternative was to bang some pots boot-camp style. He knew from firsthand experience that was a less than pleasant way to regain consciousness.

Jaz whimpered again.

Liam gave the wooden door one more futile knock, then pushed it open and let himself into the darkened room. As his eyes adjusted —and he instinctively peered into every corner just to make sure they were as alone as he expected—he focused his attention on where Jaz was now resting with her covers.

"*Get down,*" she called in a whispered shriek, whipping onto her back and flinging her arms across her pillows. "It's coming, Liam... It's... *No!*"

Whatever *it* was that was coming made Jaz arch her back, then

176

cover her head with her arms. Or try to. Her left hand was so tangled in the bedding that it wasn't getting far.

An invisible band tightened around Liam's chest. He knew what he was looking at. Had seen this before. Cullen, in particular, had struggled with the roughest memories of past events encroaching on his sleep. Aiden, Liam suspected, wasn't sleeping much period. And now Jaz. Who he was supposed to have kept safe.

"Easy there, Sprite." Stopping beside the mattress, Liam brushed a hand along her head, poised to jump back in case she kicked him for it. "You're having a nightmare. Wake up."

No reaction. No change.

"Hey," he said louder, shaking her bare calf where she'd slung off her covers. Jaz scrunched up her face and whimpered, but didn't quite break the surface into full awareness. Liam flicked on the bedside lamp, a little circle of light brightening up the room as he added a touch of command to his voice. "Come on, Sprite. Open your eyes."

Her eyes flicked open, wide in fright, as she scrambled away to the opposite side of her bed. In the dim light of the lamp, Liam could see the too-quick rise and fall of her chest, the way her small body huddled around her injured arm, the shadows sculpting the fear the dreams had etched into her features.

Of course she was having nightmares. She'd trusted him to protect her, and instead, a damn truck exploded not three steps away. Worse still, Liam had had no inkling of the danger before they were right on top of it. How the hell was she supposed to feel?

He lowered himself to sit on the side of her bed, careful not to touch her unless she made the first move. "Welcome back."

"Um, hello." She shifted her weight. "I didn't mean to wake you up. I'm sorry."

She was sorry? "I was awake." He paused, considering asking about the nightmare before changing tack. "Looks like your arm hurts a bit. Can I see?"

Jaz looked down at where she cradled the limb and let it go at once, as if the skin had turned into glowing coals. "No. It's nothing."

"Good," Liam agreed congenially, and patted the spot on the bed beside him. "Then you won't mind me taking a look."

To his relief, she started to move closer, but as Jaz shifted onto the better-lit part of the mattress, something new and determined flashed over her features. Her chin rose, her back stretching like a cat's. The tip of her tongue flicked out from between full lips.

"What exactly would you like to look at?" The purr in her words sent vibrations all the way to Liam's cock, which twitched involuntarily.

Jaz grinned. With a burst of new, wicked energy, she straddled Liam's lap, her hands sliding under his shirt.

Liam steadied her hips on instinct, which only made her shimmy against his hold. Shimmy against his other parts as well. Liam hardened at once, the sudden pressure so intense that it took a moment for him to find his voice. "Jaz—"

"Shh." She put a finger over his lips, then proceeded to push up his shirt. Lick the skin between his pectorals. Put her own hot mouth over his left nipple and suckle it with a pleased moan.

Liam slid his hands to her shoulders, fighting to get some common sense to coalesce in his quickly muddling brain. "Jaz. What are you doing?"

She rose onto her knees and nipped at his neck in reply. Her hand, which had been splayed over his abs a moment ago, dropped down into his waistband and slipped along his throbbing hardness. "I'm sure you'll figure it out sooner or later." Her words tickled his ear. Her fingers encircled his cock, sliding along the length of Liam's engorged shaft.

He couldn't quite suppress his gasp, his body reacting to hers with a primal need that pounded through his senses. His hands tightened over her shoulders, his whole body aching to pounce, to bury his cock in her hot tight channel, to breathe in her intoxicating coconut scent with every vicious pump. The effort to keep still raked through his body, a trickle of sweat snaking down the groove of his back to sting against the healing gash.

The sting. The hurt. *She* was hurt. Shaken up. Drunk on nightmares and memories and fear. Yes, that's what was off about all this. Liam blinked, drawing breath into his constricting lungs as Jaz pumped her hand along him. Fighting through the need that hammered at him, Liam focused on her face, on the anxious cast of her features that went beyond desire and dipped into desperation.

With a great deal more willpower than Liam thought he possessed, he shifted the woman away from him and held her at arm's length. "Jaz." He paused to swallow against the assault of sensations battering his body. No matter how much his body yearned otherwise, he couldn't do this. Couldn't take advantage of her this way. "Jaz, stop. You don't want this."

She reached toward his groin again. "When I want you to tell me what I want, I'll ask."

He caught her wrist. "No."

"A little explosion and you forget how to fuck?"

More like a little fucking to forget an explosion. "Yeah," he said softly, but not weakly. "Yeah, it seems I did." He released her wrist to tuck himself away.

She gestured to his still-twitching groin, her jaw tight. "Why?"

That was a damn good question. Especially given their no-strings-attached carnal-pleasures agreement. If Jaz wanted to bury her fears and anxiety away in a little nighttime recreation, who was Liam to say no? Hell, after the day he'd had, there was nothing he wanted more than to push the willing sprite into the mattress and give them both some mind-numbing satisfaction. And yet...

Before he could second-guess himself, Liam gathered Jaz into his arms and pulled her tightly against his chest.

"Let me go," she insisted, cinching her arms over her chest, but even as she said it, her voice hitched.

Liam held on, securing Jaz in his arms as her protests died away and the hitches in her breath became more frequent, devolving into sobs. Pressing his nose into her hair, he rocked them gently, holding them through the torrent of emotions that finally came.

"I'm sorry," Jaz said finally, wiping her cheeks with the back of her hand. "This is stupid. I'm—"

"Safe," Liam finished for her. "And yet it all flashes back before you when you least expect it."

She blinked, frowning at him. "How did you know?"

Liam shrugged one shoulder. "Not my first boom."

Jaz shook her head. "I feel so stupid. I'm not even the one who got hurt." She moved her arm experimentally. "You're the one who took the brunt, and yet I'm the one blubbering about it."

"Not stupid." He tucked some wayward dark tresses away from her forehead. "You're human."

"You're human too, even if you never act like it." She chuckled as she wiped her eyes, but it held no real humor. "Why can't I be as strong as you are?"

"You are," he countered. "It's just in a different way. Hell, in some ways—in many ways—I think you're even stronger."

Liam had meant to sound comforting, but as he said the words, he realized how damn true they were. Jaz was strong, stronger than him in all the ways that counted. As worthy an adversary as she was a partner. And he loved that about her. Loved many, many things about her.

The thought of losing her in that explosion made him tighten his arms around her, his heart seeking the comfort of her small form as much as giving it. He inhaled the coconut fragrance of her hair and savored the breath. Savored her. And not because she was Kyan's little sister, or a client, or anything else. But because she was Jaz. And he loved her.

And that, that was the scariest thing he'd ever experienced.

28

JAZ

*J*az awoke to the scent of clean male musk and the feel of a solid, muscular body against her back. The heavy arm draped over her felt like a weighted blanket, seductively beckoning her back into the folds of a deep, safe sleep. Jaz shifted just enough to glance at her watch. Eight in the morning.

"There is no way you're actually asleep," she murmured.

A soft snort tickled the back of her neck. "Not for a couple of hours now, no."

Jaz rolled over, looking up at Liam's face, the overnight stubble over his jaw underscoring the defined lines. She remembered last night. Her racing heart. The nightmares. The overwhelming irrational fear that she couldn't chase away with any amount of logic. And she remembered him. The way Liam had turned the tide. His words. His actions. His touch.

"It's eight," Jaz said. "Aren't you behind on twenty-five things by now?"

"I'm exactly where I want to be."

Letting her sleep. As if he'd known that it was only the safety of his arms and body that let Jaz finally settle into restful oblivion. Had anyone ever done that for her before? She knew the answer to that. Stretching out on her elbow, Jaz kissed Liam softly on the lips.

He scoffed, a small blush touching the top of his cheek. When he spoke, though, his voice was matter-of-fact, with a touch of military command. "Stop lazing about like a cat. There's training to do."

Jaz couldn't argue with that—and the reassurance that she could seek his strength at night and still be treated as an athlete in the morning meant more than Jaz had words to explain.

"Something occurred to me this morning," Jaz said as she finished lacing up her shoes moments later, Liam already waiting by the door. "You have this habit of staying one step behind me when we run. Afraid I'll see you huffing and puffing?"

He raised a brow. "Yes. Exactly."

Jaz put her hands on her hips. "Let's race."

Liam shook his head and opened the door, letting Jaz out ahead of him. "I need to have you in my line of sight and I've yet to grow a third eye."

"You don't need a third eye, you just need a circle. You. Me. The track. Eight miles."

"Eight miles on the track? Do you know how many laps that is? Too many for me to count, that's how many." Liam stepped outside the building ahead of Jaz, then stood aside to let him pick up her run. Though his injuries had to still be hurting, he moved with his usual predatory grace, his gaze always roving. Always surveying everything. As if that was the most natural thing in the world.

"Did you always want to be a SEAL?" Jaz asked.

"Did you always want to be a climber?"

"Stop answering a question with a question."

"Why?"

Jaz groaned. "Fine. I've wanted to be a climber since I went to Billy Harrison's birthday party in sixth grade. It was at a rock gym, and there was a tower that was so tall that by the time I was halfway up, I couldn't hear anyone on the ground anymore. I think it was the first moment of my life when there wasn't someone telling me what to do. No stage directions. No costumes. No lines.

Everything I did up there was my choice." She trailed off, watching a flock of birds move across the sky, wings flapping in a perfect V formation. Was their flight an ultimate choice or an ultimate script?

"You disliked acting?"

"I enjoyed many parts of it. The cameras, the attention, the chance to be different people. But it was everything in between that got to me. Every moment was scheduled. Acting classes. Auditions. My parents even took Kyan and me out of school for a while. When I discovered climbing, I discovered what being in charge of myself felt like. And I like it."

"You don't *always* like it," Liam murmured.

Jaz swatted at him.

Liam slid easily just out of reach and, though Jaz couldn't be sure, she thought she spotted a hint of a smile touching the corner of his mouth.

Bastard. "So. SEAL. Let me guess—it was your life dream to be yelled at, kept awake for days on end, and then spend a few years in third world countries being shot at." When Liam didn't answer right away, Jaz looked over to find his gaze distant, the soft scrape of their sneakers against the ground the only sound to be heard.

Just when she'd given up on getting an answer, Liam pulled up closer to her and pointed to the high school track they were passing. "I never wanted to go to military school," he said, changing course from trail to track. "It was something I was forced into and eventually learned to love." As they circled the lined red turf, he laid out the basics for her. Lisa's assault. Patti's payoff. His revenge. Except he didn't call it that.

So she served the word up for him.

"Revenge?" Liam glared at her, his pace getting faster. "How is supporting them and taking care about every part of their life *revenge?* For someone who's supposed to be in grad school, you have a pitiful understanding of the English language."

"Well, let's see." Jaz sped up to keep in step with him. "Ensuring someone is supported materially while cutting them off emotionally. Remind me again, who did that to who?"

"It's not the same. I was a child." He went faster still, his muscles slickening with sweat.

Jaz's thighs burned, but she kept the strain to herself. "But you aren't a child now. So why are you so determined to keep the status quo?" The words started to come with difficulty, her lungs aching for breath. "Your mom came to Colorado to fight for you. That has to count for something."

Instead of answering, Liam opened up his stride, taking them both into a full-out sprint that left no ability for either of them to continue with the conversation. It was a dick move, but one still had to admire the strategy, ruthless as it was.

After finishing the run, Jaz followed Liam to Trident Rescue and Security, where she used the gym while Liam caught up on work. She knew from experience that he would stay in the office until midnight if left unchecked, but they had one more appointment to keep—one that Ivy had extracted Jaz's and Liam's word about keeping before agreeing to spring them both from St. Joseph's.

LIAM HAD the stoic look of someone about to face the firing squad as he rang Kyan's square doorbell. In his signature black jeans and a dark silk shirt, he looked too formidable to be standing on a porch littered with action figures and a bright red tricycle, but Jaz figured it best to keep that bit of observation to herself.

"Come around back." Ivy's voice reached them from around the house, where Kyan and Bar appeared to be arguing about who should get to hold the open bottle of bubbles. Bumblebee watched the proceeding intently, ready to leap into the air and assault said bubbles as soon as the humans got around to producing them. Getting up from the patio table, the small doctor came around to greet them. "I'm glad you came. Kyan and I had a bet going on whether you'd show up."

"I keep my promises," said Liam.

Kyan's gaze cut over to him.

Liam lifted his chin.

Recognizing the signs of the male monkey dance, Jaz put her

fists on her hips. Clearly, Kyan was well aware that she and Liam were more than coworkers now, and just as plainly, Jaz's brother had thoughts on the matter. Ones that, as far as Jaz was concerned, Kyan could shove up his ass. "Is there something you want to say, Kyan? Perhaps you have an opinion on who I should be sleeping with? Because I have some comments about your life that I would absolutely love to share with you as well."

Kyan surrendered the bubbles to the toddler and came over to the patio table, turning one chair around and straddling it like a horse. He didn't wear baseball caps now like he used to, and the scars running along his face reminded Jaz of how many opinions on his life she'd, in fact, had. And shared incessantly. Hell, she'd once been the one to urge Ivy to use her medical position to stop Kyan from the daredevil stunts he'd been addicted to. But of course, that was different. Jaz had meddled in Kyan's life to protect him.

Yeah. Utterly different.

"Anything new from Jaz's mystery hater?" Kyan asked, which, in this company, was akin to a cease-fire accord.

Liam shook his head and took a seat as well, dutifully following Ivy's silent order to remove his shirt. "None that I can tie to the initial letters. Though the internet is full of opinions on how much Trident Security botched up Jaz's protection detail and whether Vector Ascent was right to sign her instead of Roman Robillard to begin with. By the way, remember that mugging? Devante confessed to having paid a couple of drunks to rough Jaz up a bit. He told them to go after her hands specifically... But it seems they saw a purse and got carried away."

Jaz cringed and rubbed her wrists. "Maybe Roman or Devante are somehow behind this mess too. I mean, Roman is getting his name in the press like he wanted, and it fits. He outsources hurting me to his cousin, who outsources it to a couple of drunks. When that fails, Devante tries to go after me himself. And when that fails too, Roman decides that if you want something done right, you have to do it yourself. Roman does fit the mentally unbalanced profile of the letter sender."

"Except that we saw Roman at Adventure World, and he was

185

too drunk to do much of anything," said Liam. "Also, the blast analysis suggests a more advanced knowledge of ballistics than anything in Roman's file indicates he has. He couldn't have built that device."

Ivy pulled back a bandage and applied something to the healing cuts that made Liam hiss.

Jaz cringed. "How's he doing?"

"*He* is fine," Liam answered for Ivy.

Ivy snorted. "Don't ask me how, but between being lucky, good, and damn stubborn, I don't see a reason Liam won't be able to belay at the competition in two weeks." She paused. "Provided you two are still going?"

Their ensuing silence was pregnant enough that Jaz suspected Kyan and Ivy had discussed the wisdom of Jaz bowing out of the competition. But to them, the Clash was just another climb. Hell, Kyan had thought it a good idea to step back from it even before things started to go boom. She didn't expect them to understand just how vital this was to her, but she did expect them to take her word for it when she explained that it was her Super Bowl.

When she turned to her brother, Kyan had the decency to look away. Yeah.

"Of course we're still going." Getting up from his seat, Liam pulled his shirt back on and did up the buttons with brutal efficiency. "Kyan, a word in private with you, please."

29

LIAM

*K*yan jerked his head toward the side of the house, where a new basketball hoop was now attached to the garage. A pile of lumber and instructions on the side of the driveway betrayed Kyan's plans for a tree house. Liam raised a brow. Kyan was skilled at many things, from demolition to hand-to-hand combat. So far as Liam was aware, however, carpentry was not on said list.

"I wanted to make some things for Bar," Kyan said with a touch of defensiveness. "For when he's old enough. There's a YouTube video for most anything now."

"True."

Kyan put his hands into his pocket. "Ivy wants to put up a swing set and maybe a sandbox there on the lawn."

That seemed more age appropriate. And less likely to collapse. Liam kept both those thoughts to himself. He and Kyan had other things to discuss, and he wanted to get it over with. "So, are we talking with gloves or without?"

Kyan crossed to an outdoor storage shed and fetched a basketball. Taking his time and pounding out the occasional dribble,

ALEX LIDELL

he lined up along the free throw line he'd painted on the driveway, raised his arm in a flawless bend, and shot the ball.

It swished right through, nothing but net. As the ball bounced, Kyan retrieved it and threw it—hard—into Liam's chest.

So, without gloves it was.

"I asked you to protect my sister, not sleep with her. Did you get confused?"

Liam drove the ball toward the net, grunting at the impact from Kyan's illegal check but still making the basket. "Things changed. Jaz's safety is still my number one priority, though."

With a disgusted grunt, Kyan smacked the ball from Liam's hands and headed toward the hoop. Liam blocked his way, stealing the ball. "You don't believe me?" Liam demanded.

"There's more to protecting Jaz than making sure shit doesn't blow up." Kyan went after the ball. "And you plow through women like flames through paper. I know you, Rowen. You like to play and you like to fuck. You know what you don't like? Coming back for seconds."

Liam pounded the ball against the asphalt, keeping it away from Kyan's attempts to gain possession. The man wasn't wrong, and Liam had no way of explaining why Jaz was different. Of confessing that for the past year, he'd found little interest in his usual fun. Not until Jaz.

"Jaz and I have an understanding." Pivoting around Kyan, Liam closed in on the hoop. "I've been upfront about my history and intentions." *Lie.* He'd never told her that his feelings had changed. How could he when he didn't understand it himself? How could he even know his love for Jaz was real when he'd never felt this intensely toward a woman before?

"Well, good for you." Kyan caught Liam's missed shot on the rebound. "Except, if I know my sister, she's too bighearted to believe that you really will walk away when the mood hits. Jaz thinks she can tame mountains and nature itself. That anything is possible. She's the ultimate fucking optimist." He threw the ball, scoring another point.

188

"What do you want me to say?" Liam took the basketball out to the edge of the driveway, but stayed in place.

Kyan drew a puffing breath. "Well, you can start by swearing to every deity known to man that you're keeping your domination kink to yourself. Because God help me, Rowen, if I find out you hit my sister, I will dismember you limb by limb."

The taut leash Liam had thus far managed to keep on his emotions finally snapped. He hurled the basketball at Kyan's head and, when the man raised his hands to catch the ball, rammed him to the ground. There was a thump of impact, then a soft pattering as the ball dropped from Kyan's hands and bounced away to disappear into the hedgerow between the lawn and the six-foot wooden privacy fence. Liam rose to his knees, straddling the other man.

"Did you just fucking ask whether I've assaulted Jaz?" He snarled, his heart pounding fury through his veins. "Or did you demand I tell you to get your sister off in bed? Because if you think either of those questions are appropriate, this little chat is going to end with you scraping blood off your driveway."

To Kyan's credit, the man lifted his palms in a gesture of surrender and stayed put until Liam got enough control of himself to keep from landing a punch that was already tingling in his knuckles. Stepping back with effort, Liam drew a slow, deliberate breath, then extended his hand to Kyan and pulled him up.

"I'm not going to harm Jaz in bed," Liam said, his gaze on the crack in an otherwise pristine asphalt top. "We both know the kind of things I play at, but it takes two to tango, Keasley. And I'm smart enough to recognize *no*, whether it's said aloud or not. I'm not asking you to like it, or bless or even condone it. I'm asking you to stay the hell out of it. We aren't a fucking threesome."

Kyan braced his palms on his thighs, his chest rising with heavy breaths that filled the silence between them. "I was out of line," he said finally. "What you do in bed..." He shook his head. "None of my business. But the fact that you're sleeping with her to begin with —that's the part that scares me shitless. I don't want her to get hurt. Physically or emotionally. So tell me you've thought about this. Tell me you're treating her well. That you've, I don't know, taken her to dinner or something."

Liam scoffed. Then stopped. He hadn't taken her to dinner, not in the way Kyan meant. Hadn't done anything normal people did to get to know each other.

"Yeah." Kyan's voice was dark. "That's what I thought."

Liam rubbed his face.

"Jaz might be smart all the time and hold herself like some iron-strong superwoman in front of the cameras, but she's always been tenderhearted beneath it all. You don't understand just how easy it is for you to hurt her. I need you—I'm *begging* you— to do whatever needs to be done to keep her from getting hurt."

Liam stood perfectly still, his heart in his throat, Kyan's censure hacking into him with more force than that shrapnel ever could've. Kyan knew him. Probably knew him better than he knew himself. Now, with Kyan staring him in the eye with a look that was both pleading and demanding, Liam felt the walls of reality and uncertainty close in around him.

He loved Jaz. He wanted to be with her. But was he capable of such a feat? With a lifetime of proof to the contrary, it was hard to deny Kyan's concern. Liam pivoted away, his hands going into his pockets.

"I will always put Jaz's welfare before my own," he told Kyan. He knew it wasn't the answer the other man was looking for, but it was an honest one. The best Liam could do. "I... I've got an appointment to get to. I'll leave Jaz with you for a bit."

Nodding silently, Kyan let him go, and Liam didn't know if he should feel relieved or disappointed.

30

JAZ

"*A* date?" Of all the things Jaz expected Liam to say when he knocked on her door three days before they were due to fly out to California for the championship Clash of the Titans round, a *date* ranked somewhere between a suggestion to get a poodle and an offer to plant lettuce. For all their time together, the only date they'd gone on included Sebastian and Devante—and that didn't exactly go as expected.

Liam crossed his arms over his chest. "From what I understand, it's what people who might like each other do together."

"But we don't like each other."

"Which is why I'm going to take you someplace you'll hate me for."

"Oh good." She swung off the bed, the alarm clock reading ten in the morning on a Saturday. Not that she'd actually slept in said bed last night, but she was lounging on it now. "At least I know the world hasn't totally twisted up on me. And where is this place?"

"If I tell you, you won't come," Liam said reasonably. "And you'll probably yell at me. Wear long pants and sleeves."

"Wait!" Jaz was off the bed before he could leave the room. "I never said yes!"

He grinned. "But you never said no either."

Unable to contradict that particular reasoning and too curious to know what passed for a date in Liam's mind, an hour later, Jaz found herself getting into the BMW Liam had acquired to replace his destroyed truck. From what she'd overheard Aiden and Liam saying, the thing was equipped with every sensor known to man and could probably take flight in a pinch. Which still didn't stop Liam from going over every inch of the car before allowing Jaz anywhere near it.

Neither the police nor Liam's people were any closer than before on drilling down on how the original explosives had gotten into Liam's truck, much less who put them there. The working theory from the authorities was that some resentful lone wolf took offense at Jaz's existence and decided to do something about it. Liam and Aiden felt certain that the act was more deliberate and less passionate than the police's theory maintained, but that didn't change the fact that there was no camera footage. No witnesses. No leads.

"Are you ever going to actually tell me where we're going?" Jaz asked, a newly suspicious wariness coming over her as Liam pulled up to a small, out-of-town airport. "And with who?" So far as she knew, the only pilots from Liam's close-friend circle were Eli and Aiden, and she saw neither one's car in the parking lot they were now circling. "Are we flying somewhere?"

"In a manner of speaking."

"Flying is an either-or type of activity, Liam. We either are flying or we aren't."

He considered this. "Define *flying*."

Jaz narrowed her eyes. "Moving through the air, without a tether to a stationary structure, for a greater distance than is possible by jumping."

Leaning across Jaz's lap, he opened her door from the inside before getting out of the vehicle. "Does the direction of movement matter? In your definition, I mean."

Jaz stepped out of the car, the wind whipping her face. It was oddly still here for an airport. No tourists bustling around with baggage, no tired children, no walls and arrows herding passengers through check-in. Instead, the place looked more like an oversized and very well-ordered parking lot, with small planes lined up in perfect rows. Beside the occasional sound of an engine, the place was quiet. Serene in its own way.

"Direction of movement?" Jaz echoed Liam's words. "Like north, south, east, and west? No. Doesn't matter."

"There are a few more directions than those out there." Liam led her to a white-painted building, its roof high enough to house more equipment.

"More directions than those on a compass?"

Liam shrugged a shoulder and pointed up and down with his finger. Before Jaz could process what he meant by that, Liam led them inside the hangar and to a woman with short purple hair who sat behind a computer desk in the corner. "Kristi, good afternoon. Are you ready for us?"

"We are. Henry will be your pilot today. Are you still planning a tandem jump?"

Jaz's thoughts froze, her stomach clenching into a ball of lead. Grabbing Liam's triceps, she pulled him away from the desk and glared up at him. "Jump?" Saying the word made her already taut insides cinch down harder around her diaphragm. "What the hell does she mean by tandem *jump?*"

"Means that you will be attached to my harness," Liam said with absolutely zero contrition. Taking a liability waiver from Kristi, he slid it and a pen to Jaz, the words *skydiving* and *risk of death* popping out from the page in bold ink. "No time to send you through airborne school."

Jaz's fingers, which were still on Liam's triceps, dug into his flesh. "So I'm crystal clear… For our date, you want to jump out of a perfectly good plane three days before the most important climbing competition of my life?" She didn't realize how loudly she was talking until she heard her voice reverberating through the hangar.

Taking Jaz's face in both his hands, Liam kissed her with a passionate thoroughness that made Jaz's pounding heart hammer for a new reason altogether. When he pulled back, his face was still inches from hers and her lips tingled from the connection. Liam grinned like a cat with a bowl of cream, the mischief playing in his eyes so at odds with his usual signature severity. "It will be fun, Jaz. Pure, exhilarating fun."

"This is insane." Jaz swallowed, glancing back at Kristi, who was already pulling out jumpsuits and laying them out on the table. "You're insane."

"Agreed. Let's do this."

"This is Jaz, I take it? Nice to meet you, sweetie."

An hour and safety brief later, Jaz was dressed in an orange jumpsuit, the twin-engine plane soaring 14,000 feet above the earth. Liam strapped his equipment on with the competent ease of someone who'd done this more times than he could count, then double-checked Jaz's harness. She liked the feel of the webbing against her, the solidness of Liam's body behind her back. It felt safe. Secure.

Right up until the part where Liam walked them to the open plane door and Jaz looked down at the impossible expanse of sky that opened beneath them. She gasped. The air tasted chillier up here. Goose bumps ran along her skin. Her breath stopped, then started again, adrenaline filling each molecule of her blood as the *lub-dub lub-dub lub-dub* of her heart pounded on her rib cage.

Liam said they were going flying. But he'd never meant the plane. He meant for real. Now.

He meant free-fall.

Jaz grabbed his hand.

"Clear!" Henry yelled from the cockpit.

Without the slightest hesitation, Liam stepped off the edge and plunged them into the sky.

Jaz screamed, but the air caught in her lungs and the sound morphed into something...joyful. Free. With the initial shock now only an echo in her bones, the sensation of weightlessness overtook her. The wind whipped her hair, and her cheeks flapped from the rushing air that filled her ears. She was cold and hot. Scared and safe. She was falling. She was *flying*.

Spreading her arms wide, Jaz whooped her joy to the

mischievous skies and heard Liam's low answering chuckle tickle her ear.

Liam finally pulled the ripcord. With a sharp jerk, the harness dug into Jaz's body until she and Liam seemed to pause in midair before starting to glide along. The streaking world shifted to something new and majestic.

They floated down together, meandering like autumn leaves through the heavens until the patch of open greenery opened up amid the canopy of the forest. Liam shifted the ropes, directing them with perfect ease to the landing spot.

After Jaz's feet settled on the ground, Liam detached the parachute and harness, and all Jaz could think of was how high she was on life itself. Twisting toward the man who'd given her this gift, Jaz curled her hands into Liam's short hair and pulled their mouths together.

Instead of bending down, Liam hoisted Jaz up onto his hips. His hardness pressed into her through their clothes, and she pressed her own sex against it. Blood rushed in her veins, carrying a toxic mix of need and excitement through her. "Today was the most amazing—"

Liam's radio crackled.

Jaz groaned.

Pulling away from the kiss for a moment, Liam pressed the radio button on the shoulder of his jumpsuit. "Ground control Alpha Charlie, this is Falcon Five," he said evenly, despite Jaz continuing to press herself against him. "No need for a pickup. We'll be hiking out when ready."

"Acknowledged, no pickup," a disembodied voice crackled back over the receiver. "Stay safe, Falcon Five." Despite the radio discipline, Jaz swore she could hear the smirk come back. And she didn't care.

AFTER TAKING their time at the clearing, they returned to Liam's apartment, where a dessert of crostata with blackberries, strawberries, and blueberries was waiting by the door. It wasn't fancily wrapped or decorated with anything but a set of plastic utensils, but the berries were so fresh that each one exploded with flavor in Jaz's mouth.

"That was the most reckless and amazing thing I've ever done," Jaz told Liam. "If Vector Ascent ever found out I went skydiving, I'd be in so much trouble."

Somehow, the threat of trouble didn't bother her as much as it should have just then.

Liam grinned. "Naughty climber. What are we going to do about that?"

Jaz threw a berry at him. "Hey, it's your fault I went astray. Before meeting you, I didn't even play a game of friendly basketball when on sponsorship."

"Oh, so the devil made you do it?"

"Well, yes, technically speaking." She stuck her tongue out at him.

Putting down his finished dessert, Liam flickered his fingers over his knee.

"Maybe you need your backside warmed to get you back on the straight and narrow."

Molten eroticism shot straight from Jaz's sex to her head, the threat turning her on a great deal more than she wished it had. She wasn't the kind of person who enjoyed...*that*. She wasn't. No matter how hot it was. And it was hot at hell. Taking the offensive before Liam could catch the scent of her thoughts, Jaz picked up a strawberry with her teeth and straddled his lap. She leaned down to share the wild fruit.

Liam went hard beneath her even before his teeth nipped into the berry, his palms cupping her backside.

Jaz ran her hand along Liam's cheekbone, stroking along his chiseled clean-shaven jaw. There was so much strength that lived behind Liam's hazel eyes. So much responsibility. And, deep down, so much passion and life that it called to something inside Jaz's soul. "What am I going to do with you?" she whispered, not meaning to say the words aloud, but doing it anyway.

Liam cocked an eyebrow at her, his gaze to intimate that she felt her core grow damp all over again.

"The question, Jaz, is what *I'm* going to do with *you*."

With that, he moved smoothly from the couch and carried her into the bedroom, making short work of her clothes until she was naked and spread-eagle over the sheets, each limb secured to a bedpost with whatever piece of cloth found itself closest to Liam's hand. Towering over Jaz, Liam rubbed his thumbs over her pebbling nipples before running his callused hands along the full expanse of her skin. "Let's see if I can make you fly all over again," he murmured into Jaz's ear.

And then he did just that.

In the morning, Jaz found herself draped over Liam's naked body, his chest rising and falling in an even rhythm beneath her. Realizing it was the first time she'd ever beaten him to consciousness, Jaz carefully slid herself down toward his cock, her mind reeling with the various choices of vengeful torment that had suddenly opened themselves up to her. Just as she got to his hips, however, her mouth watering with the thoughts of mischief, the buzzing vibration of Liam's cell phone clattered along the polished bedside table.

Liam's muscular thighs tightened as he shifted, coming awake in an instant. A second later, he had the phone in one hand and Jaz's hair in the other. "Whatever it is, now is a bad time for it, Aiden."

Jaz grinned and licked the head of her target.

On the other end of the phone line, a male voice spoke rapidly, probably trying to get a word in edgewise before the line went dead.

Liam shifted again, but now, instead of throwing his phone down as she'd expected, he released his hold on Jaz instead. "Understood," he said, swinging his legs off the side of the bed. "Have everyone meet in the delta conference room. We're on our way."

LIAM

*C*onference room Delta was already full by the time Liam and Jaz arrived at the office—which didn't bode well for the news. It meant Aiden had already vetted the information, and, from the stony expression on his face, it wasn't good.

Liam pulled a chair out for Jaz, then took his own seat, the large leather chair at the head of the table rocking gently beneath him. Looking around the table, Liam took silent attendance. Aiden was there, of course; that was expected. Lucy from the PR department. Nell Hewitt, a twenty-something computer genius with an insatiable love of hacking who they'd snagged for IT. Eli. Kyan. Cullen and Sky. Liam's gaze lingered on Sky the longest. With her strawberry-blonde hair pulled back into a ponytail and a laptop open on the table, she looked ready for battle. And Liam knew better than to do battle with Sky.

"All right," he said by way of opening. "What do we have?"

Sky looked to Aiden, who flipped a switch, bringing a large-screen television monitor on the side of the room to life. The screen flickered once, then focused on a news anchor wearing a suit and a serious expression while the Trident Rescue and Security logo digitally decorated the backdrop behind him.

"Trident Rescue and Security, a company run by Liam Rowen out of Denton Valley, Colorado, is under fire today due to reports of failing in their duty to insulate pro world-champion mountain climber Jazmine Keasley from a terrorist attack. Ms. Keasley was nearly killed in an explosion a little over a week ago despite being under the protection of the security firm. Sources close to the events reveal that Vector Ascent, the company that originally hired Mr. Rowen's operation, has now recalled the contract, citing inadequate services. Channel Seven has reached out to Trident Security for comment, but the company didn't respond. We will update this story as more of it becomes available."

Aiden shut off the footage.

"This is bullshit," Jaz said. "Since when are terrorists involved? And Vector didn't recall the contract—they'd have told me."

"Any deliberate explosion can be called an extremism attack," said Aiden. "More to the point, truth rarely stands in the way of sensationalism. Regardless, I started getting calls after this aired to discuss the matter. And before you ask, Channel Seven isn't the only one reporting. It's going all the way up to national news."

Liam lifted a brow. It wasn't pleasant, but it wasn't exactly earth-shattering news either. He looked at Sky. "I imagine you're going to tell me why this is worse than I think it is, misinformation about the contract notwithstanding."

"That depends on what you think *this* is," Sky answered with brutal frankness. "On the surface, this looks like a bit of bad press about a security company's misstep. Unfortunate and unfair, but par for the course for a company of Trident's size. What caught my attention was the syntax. The way some of the wording came off and how the information was being pieced together." She brought up another file, this one a montage of various talking news heads all saying the same thing in almost the same way.

"I'm still not following the pucker factor," said Liam.

"When different reporters cover the same incident, they naturally report the details in slightly different manners. Different words, different highlights, different depth of analysis. On the other hand, when companies issue press releases with convenient quotes, summaries, and descriptions, we often see a slew of very similar articles. This is especially true when reporters don't have a lot of independent information, so they rely on written documents provided by somebody else. This whole thing looks like one giant press release. Down to the whole terrorist leap and fact-checking error about the contract."

"But no one issued a press release on this," said Jaz. "Not the police or Vector Ascent. Certainly not Trident Security or me."

"Exactly." Sky nodded. "We had the same issue with the original news about Trident's contract being made public. It wasn't any of us and it wasn't Vector. So I went back to look at all the reporting that touches you. The coverage of Trident taking Jaz's contract, news of the explosion that repeated wording from the threat letter, and now this bit of drivel about Trident's ineffectiveness—they *all* have the same feel to them. As if the same person wrote all the stories. So I did some digging with my journalistic contacts and confirmed that all the stories were seeded in major papers, which generally calls for serious favors."

"Seeded by who?" asked Liam.

"That's exactly what I asked." Nell pulled down on the hem of her oversized anime T-shirt before moving to the next screenshot. A string of numbers that probably made sense only to her filled the screen. "Sky and Aiden asked me to see if I could source the info sent to the various news channels. I isolated the protocols and… never mind. Bottom line—all data streams came from the same IP."

Three parts of the screen merged together.

"It gets more interesting." Eli snagged Nell's keyboard for himself. "The polymer used in the explosion is pretty common in itself, which is why I paid little attention to it in the postblast analysis. That said, there are only three major suppliers. Again, not useful information until—"

"Until you have an actual delivery location to check out," Nell jumped in. "So once we had an IP address and the physical location it came back to, we could run that against the recent shipping orders. Overlap again. Right to here. Boom." She punched the air, then seemed to remember where she was and cringed. "Sorry. I just like it when calculations work out."

Eli pressed some buttons, unearthing a map that started to slowly zoom in on the East Coast of the United States. As the geo-location circle tightened mile by mile, Liam felt a familiar dread similarly tightening up his diaphragm. He knew where they'd end up even before the map came to a halt.

"Obsidian Ops." Liam's voice sounded too stoic even to his own ears. "Their main complex in New Jersey."

"The evil security company that nearly got Kyan killed last year?" said Jaz. "They've been behind all this from the beginning? Why would they care about me?"

"Not evil, but certainly Machiavellian," said Kyan, his gaze piercing Liam's. "And I have a feeling Jaz was never the real target. Though I imagine her last name being the same as mine was icing on the cake for Lucius."

"Aye. That's my analysis as well." Aiden looked grim. "Jaz wasn't the real target of the explosion. Trident Security was. Or rather, our reputation. We encroached on Obsidian's international turf, and this was their response."

Liam nodded. "They tried lawyers first, and when paper didn't work, they fired a literal shot—or blast—across my bow." This also explained why he saw no threat indicators in internet chatter surrounding Jaz. There weren't any.

Jaz rubbed her hands over her arms, and Liam wondered whether being relegated from presumed target to collateral damage was making her feel better or worse. "Doesn't it seem a little, well, careless, for someone as good as Obsidian Ops not to obscure their IP address and have the explosives order shipped right to their office?"

Liam exchanged glances with Aiden and knew the man's thoughts reflected his own. Sighing, he turned his attention to Jaz. "They left a crumb trail on purpose, Jaz. They wanted us to figure things out eventually so that we'd get the message."

Though he let none of his emotions show, the next words Liam had to say ripped him apart. "Aiden, sever the contract with Vector

Ascent. Lucy." He turned toward the PR director. "Issue a public statement declaring that Trident Rescue and Security is fully disassociating itself from Vector, the Clash of the Titans competition, and Jaz Keasley. I don't care what reason you give, just make it sound good. We aren't risking any more bystanders in this cockfight."

"No, wait." Jaz's hand closed around Liam's wrist. Her fingers were warm and strong, and he wondered if she could feel how her touch made his pulse bound. "Let's do the opposite. Ignore the story altogether. Obsidian is a bully, and bullies hate to be ignored. Plus, the Clash is in three days. If you put a press release out now, it will only generate confusion when you show up with me. You're the face of Trident Security, and the nuance of whether you're there in a protection role or just as a climbing partner is going to be lost on people."

Liam swallowed. "Jaz…"

Silence settled around the table.

"Why are you looking at me like that?"

He blew out a breath. "Jaz, we aren't just putting out a story that Trident Security is pulling out of the event," Liam said gently. "We're putting out the truth. I won't be going with you."

Her face paled. "But you're my partner. I can't do this without you."

He pulled his hand out of her grasp. "You're going to have to. In fact, the more distance we have between each other right now, the better."

3 2

JAZ

*J*az knew she hadn't heard Liam correctly. Or just that she'd misunderstood what he meant. Her competition, *the* competition, was two days after tomorrow. Whatever else Liam might be, he was reliable. A rock. Someone she could lean on even when the road got hard.

Liam met her gaze, his own eyes deep and regretful.

No. Jaz's fingers tightened on the edge of the table, her heart pounding. No, he would never just walk away. They'd find a solution. Trident Security could pull out as publicly as Liam wanted, but not him. Not from her. Not on this.

Liam raised a hand. "May we have the room, please," he said to the others, without ever looking away from Jaz. In her peripheral vision, she saw the others push away from the conference table and quietly step out. Aiden left last, his expression unreadable as he studied her and Liam for a long moment before finally pulling the door closed himself.

"I'm sorry," said Liam. "I wish there—"

"This is a joint decision. Let's talk about this. We have options— there are always options. We could put you in a disguise, for example." She let a corner of her mouth rise in a defiant, quirky smile. "Personally, I think you would look delicious in drag. But I'm open to other ideas, if you insist."

"Jaz. Stop." A muscle ticked along Liam's clenched jaw. "There is just no safe way for you to be associated with me right now, not with me squarely in Obsidian's crosshairs. The explosion is a case in point. Obsidian wasn't actively trying to kill you when they blew up my car, but they knew it could happen. They were all right with it. You're acceptable collateral damage to them, and every second I stay beside you, the danger factor to you increases. Goddammit." He slapped his palm on the table. "All this time I thought I was protecting you, I was actually the one putting you in danger. That stops now. It has to."

Jaz shook her head, just like she had been the entire time Liam was speaking. "Let's talk through this. There has to be a way to stay safe without utterly destroying my chances at the Clash of the Titans."

"I'm sure there is. But it will be a way that doesn't involve me."

"So that's it? You think you get to make a unilateral decision?" Her voice rose. "Even if that decision will likely destroy my career?"

"You can have a new career. You can have a new life."

Jaz's hands clenched into fists, her hopes and reason shattering beneath a sudden deluge of fury that spilled into her blood. Wrong. Everything about this was so damn wrong. Placing her palms flat onto the tabletop, Jaz rose out of her chair to get a few inches on Liam. "I never asked you to get involved. Hell, I was the one who told you to fuck off right from the beginning. *You* insisted. *You* inserted yourself into my life, my career, my world. *You* barreled over my wishes, going over my head all the way to my sponsor, because you wanted things done your way. All under the banner of safety. Well, congratulations. You got your way. But there are consequences to what you did. Problems that your bullheadedness creates. All I'm asking now is that you follow through with what you started instead of pulling the pin from a grenade and tossing both into my lap to fix."

"I am following through with what I started." Liam stated with infuriating calm. "And what I started was a campaign to keep you alive, not one to help you win a competition."

"This isn't just a competition." Jaz's hands, braced atop the table, started to tremble, the words pushing through all barriers. "This is my last chance. If I don't get the damn Clash of the Titans prize money and title, my life in Denton Valley is over." She swallowed, the words—the truth—choking her.

Except for Sebastian, no one knew what had happened to the money Jaz had. But she needed Liam to understand the stakes. She trusted him to understand the stakes. And she hoped to hell she wasn't making a mistake in letting him in on the most vulnerable secret of her adult life.

Just as she'd done in the airplane, Jaz drew a breath and plunged in. "A few years ago, I took a wrong turn. I trusted a charlatan and loaned a lot of money to a fundraising venture called Females of the Future. The organization was supposed to pool our funds together and invest them, with the dividends going to help girls overseas. The idea was that we'd get a better return on investment with a large sum. After the initial interest-free term, we'd be paid on future loans at higher percentage than newcomers. Anyway, it was all a scam. The leader went to prison. Many of us barely proved that we knew nothing about it."

Sinking into her chair, Jaz continued the story, detailing the days when her financial security and independence had been pulled out from under her.

"There were signs all along that something wasn't right. The money we invested grew too fast, but that seemed like a good thing so I didn't ask questions. I had thank-you letters and photos from all these girls whose lives I was going to change. I was going to be their hero and, eventually, come out ahead while I was at it. That obviously didn't happen. I came away with nothing. I'm behind on rent now, and on tuition. Winning this competition, the prize money and endorsements that would go with the victory, is my last chance to hang on to a climbing life. So I'm asking...no, I'm begging you— don't turn your back on me."

Though she hadn't moved, Jaz felt as though she'd been running for miles. Blowing out a long breath, she tried to read Liam's thoughts in his beautiful, stoic face. Except there was little to read there, his shift of weight being the only indication that he'd heard her at all.

Jaz frowned. "You don't seem surprised."

Liam lifted one shoulder.

"Wait, you knew?" She blinked. "The grad school loans, the empty bank account, everything?"

"I had a full workup done on your financials. I needed to know what vulnerabilities you had."

Jaz stared at him, the feeling of betrayal stinging all the way to her core. Bile rose up her throat, which was threatening to close. "No, you didn't. You didn't *need* to know my financial background to provide physical protection against a physical threat. You chose to invade my privacy."

Liam had the grace to look away. "In full disclosure, we never figured out what happened to the other half of your money. Whatever you didn't invest in the scam. It seemed to have gone through a number of accounts on its way out of yours and never returned."

"You want to know where it went?" Jaz spat the words. "It went to those girls, the ones my contributions were supposed to help. The ones who'd crafted their lives, made their choices, and risked their futures because of a promise I made to them. They thought they could rely on me, and I wasn't going to destroy their dream just because I was stupid enough to fall for a scam."

She let that sink in because it was exactly what Liam was doing as well. Turning his back on Jaz's dream because he got caught up in his competitor's net.

"I'm sorry," Liam said.

Yeah. Jaz spread her fingers on the tabletop, the polished wood peeking out between the gaps. "So what now? You disappear from my life and come back when the whole thing blows over and you're horny for a good fuck?"

Liam pushed back his chair and opened a drawer beneath the desk. "Maybe," he said as if it didn't matter all that much. "Maybe not. I guess we'll have to figure it out if our paths cross again." Pulling a checkbook out of the drawer, he signed a blank check and slid it to Jaz across the table. "Write in whatever amount the prize money was going to cover and keep it."

It felt like a blow, hitting her just beneath the diaphragm. Just when she'd thought things between them couldn't fall further than they had, Liam had struck her again. Then dropped the floor out from beneath her.

"I don't want your fucking money."

Liam shrugged and pulled out his phone as if to say that the conversation—just like the one-night stand that had lasted too long —was over.

"We—" Jaz started to say.

"There is no *we*," Liam said. "I'd say we're over, but the reality is there was never a *we* to begin with. I'm not relationship material— I've told you that from the beginning. I've sent a few emails. My people are moving your things back to your place. The rent is being covered." He stood, shaking his head, and pushed his rolling chair back under the table. "Enough, Jaz. It's done, so accept it and stop moping like a lost puppy. It didn't suit you when you were a twelve-year-old, and it suits you even less at twenty-five. I'm not the man you need, and you're certainly not the woman I want."

Jaz got to her feet, her heart pounding in her ears. Beyond the window, a dark cloud gathered against the sun, threatening thunder and rain. "No kidding. A word of advice for the future? The woman you're looking for? She doesn't have a brain. Or opinions. I'd suggest a Barbie from Toys "R" Us, but they're out of business."

Liam looked down at her, his shoulders spread to show every inch of his height and muscle. "Well, you certainly have a brain. But your failure to use it when you first realized something wasn't right with that so-called charity, that was entirely on you. You made your bed there. Don't make it out like it's my fault that things turned out as they did. As for the Clash of the Titans—win it. Lose it. Don't go at all. Not my problem. I gave my best friend my word that I'd protect you, and that's exactly what I'm doing."

33

LIAM

*L*iam barely made it from the conference room to his office before his bravado gave out on him. Shutting the door, he pressed his back against the wood and struggled for breath that refused to come. He felt as if he'd just taken the worst pounding of his life, every muscle inside him screaming from the impact. Looking down at his hands, he realized they were shaking. That his entire body was shaking.

He had no idea how in the world Jaz believed him, but the hurt in her eyes told him that he'd done his job well. That his poisonous words had hit their mark. And if they hadn't, the check had.

Liam wished like hell there had been some other way, but once he realized Jaz wouldn't go down without a fight, he knew there wasn't. Her being alive and unharmed trumped whatever he wanted for himself. Jaz deserved to be happy. She deserved so many things, and for one selfish, utterly delusional moment, he'd thought that maybe he might be the man who could give them to her.

And then reality came crashing down.

There was a knock at the door, the sound hard and insistent, as if whoever it was—and Liam was fairly certain it was Aiden—was more giving warning of impending entry than asking permission for it. The knock sounded again, and Liam stepped away from the door he'd been blocking just in time to see the handle turn.

The door opened. Aiden strode in.

Closing the door with one hand, Aiden weighed up Liam with his gaze. "For what it's worth, you did the right thing, mate."

"I don't remember asking for opinions."

"You keep me around because you don't have to ask."

Liam walked to the window that overlooked the bustle of the Denton Valley downtown that sprawled below. The dense cloud that had been gathering minutes ago now aggregated into a downpour, and the air felt charged even from indoors. "I need a work-up on Lucius, the colonel in charge of Obsidian's New Jersey center. Personal skeletons. Weaknesses. If his mama missed her weekly church service recently, I want to know. Cross the line."

"Aye." Aiden didn't sound surprised. "Are you armed for war, then?"

"More of a scalpel insurgency." Liam broke off as someone knocked on his office door again, though, unlike Aiden's signal, this one was fast and furious. Before the pounding escalated to a full drumbeat, the door handle turned, and the last person Liam had expected to see in his office strode inside, her hands on her hips.

"Tell me, Liam—because I'm extremely curious—did you just wake up one morning and decide to ruin my life, or was it more of a planned operation?" she demanded.

"Is there something I can help you with, ma'am?" Aiden edged his body between Liam and the woman.

Liam had a sense that getting rid of this particular visitor would not be quite so easy. Pulling himself together with herculean effort, Liam swallowed his emotions behind a stoic mask. "Aiden, allow me to introduce Lisa Rowen, my sister. Lisa, this is Aiden, my second-in-command."

"Should I be impressed?" Lisa asked. She looked much as she

did on the Zoom screen. Too-tight designer clothes, slightly unkempt brown hair, and a sour expression.

"That's entirely up to you," said Liam.

Aiden gave him a mock salute and let himself out of the office. Right.

Pulling out a chair, Liam settled behind his desk, glad to have an extra barrier between himself and his sibling. "Lisa, this really isn't a good time for a visit."

"Yes, well, it's never really a good time for you, is it?"

That was fair. "No. I guess it never really is. But this time, I'm serious. Something's happened, and I need to attend to it."

"I know the song and dance, Liam. Something's always just happened for you. Conveniently enough, that something always seems to morph into you amassing more and more while Mom and I have less and less." She looked around Liam's office with an assessing gaze. "This is a nice building. What's it worth? A million dollars? Two? Three?"

Trident Rescue and Security was worth a great deal more than three million. Hell, the equipment alone was worth more than that, without even starting to consider the professionals working within the company's walls. "What does my business have to do with anything?" Liam asked. "Are you looking for a job?"

"You'd love that, wouldn't you? Maybe you can arrange for me to scrub floors on my hands and knees, just so that you could walk by me every day on the way to your penthouse suite and feel superior. You think your rich, educated ass is so much better than mine, but the reality is that you're the same poor trash you've always been. You just happen to be poor trash with money now."

Liam looked at his watch, wondering how long this was going to take before Lisa got to whatever point brought her here. Which was probably money. He wondered if he could just give her his checkbook and call it a day. Unlike Jaz, Lisa would take it.

"Can we skip to the part where you tell me why you're here?" Liam asked. "And please, tell me that picking up Mom is at least part of this quest."

"I knew you'd say that. Anything to get your embarrassing little family back into their dark cupboard."

"I thought you liked Ann Arbor."

"You sent me and Mom into exile, with just enough money to ensure we don't starve. A monthly drip to keep us appeased while ensuring we never get ahead and become a threat. I accepted it from you, all the petty humiliations, but this last straw is too much. If you think I'm going to stand by and quietly watch you give away my fair share to some cunt, you've got another think coming."

It took most of his energy reserves to realize Lisa was referring to Jaz, and then the rest to keep from bodily throwing the woman out of his office.

"This thing you have with the Keasley slut, it's not going to last. I'm sorry to be brutal, Liam, I really am, but someone needs to lay the truth out for you before she takes you for every penny you have."

"Let me see if I have this right," he said slowly. "I'm in a relationship with a woman you've never met, but now she's in it for the money?"

On any other day, he would have caught on to Lisa's direction earlier, but today, with his mind and heart in knots, it took too long. As the full picture of Lisa's assault finally settled in, he didn't know whether—given the events of the past hour—he found her description simply twisted or morosely hilarious.

"Of course she's in it for the money," Lisa said. "What else would she be in it for? You and I both know you have the emotional range of a carrier pigeon and can't care less for anyone without a dick, M16, and military insignia. The only long-term relationships you have are the ones you pay for." She swept her hand over the office, presumably indicating Liam's employees. "It's not your fault. You were born this way. Why do you think Mom had to send you away? But you're an adult now, and I can't let you get tangled up with this girl and leave us with nothing."

Yeah. Lisa was still Lisa, and this was par for the course with her. She had her priorities, and most days, Liam could roll with the punches. But today,...today she'd pulled Jaz into it, and that made blood rush through his veins, his face heating with fury he had no strength to contain.

"Do not ever, *ever* speak of Jaz." The words pushed between Liam's clenched teeth. "And for your information, she and I aren't together anymore."

Relief washed over Lisa's face.

Liam's gut twisted. Standing, he braced his hands on the tabletop and leaned in toward her. "But you know what I did before she walked out? I offered her a blank check. Told her she could take anything."

Lisa's relaxing features twisted into something so venomous that her skin seemed to take on a greenish hue. Swinging back her arm, she cracked it hard over Liam's cheek, the sound echoing through the room. "You fucking asshole."

Liam caught her wrist, holding it in a tight grip. "She threw it back in my face."

Jaz's expression drew itself in Liam's mind, her eyes flashing with utter betrayal at the offer of money. Now, holding Lisa's wrist in his grip, Liam tried to understand why his sister was so different. Where was her pride, her drive, her passion? And for that matter, where was the appropriate reaction to light in her pupils?

His gaze dropped to the hand he was holding, which Lisa—wild as a banshee—struggled to pull out of his grip. Struggled so much, Liam didn't think she even heard the vital part of the story.

"Let me go," Lisa hissed.

Liam turned her arm over and pulled up the sleeve of her Gucci shirt all the way to the elbow. He ran his fingers over the skin at the bend of the arm. No tracks. None on the back of her hand either.

"Let me go, you asshole!"

Her hand curled into a fist. Liam forced it open and pried the fingers apart. His stomach clenched as he stared at the telltale marks of injections. Shit.

He released her hand, and Lisa yanked it back.

"Does Mom know?" Liam demanded.

"It's not what you think. It's from a doctor."

Holy fucking shit. Stupid. How had he been so fucking stupid.

"How long?" He sank back into his chair, a void opening beneath him. "More than a year? More than five?"

"Mind your own damn business. No wonder that cunt walked away from you. Who'd want someone so fucking controlling in their life?" With a swish of satin skirts, Lisa strode out of Liam's office.

JAZ

"*H*ey, hey, hey, climbing girl." Sebastian wrapped his arms around Jaz, pressing her into his shoulder. "It's going to be all right. We're going to get you unpacked and wash the ass-that-shall-not-be-named out of your clothes. Leave it to me, girl. You focus on the climb, and by the time you're back, your apartment will look like you never left. Though you should have taken the asshole's check."

"Bastian—"

"And then used it to order a cockroach farm to be delivered to his penthouse."

Jaz squeezed Sebastian back, a small smile managing to sneak through the heaviness weighing down on her soul. She'd bared everything to Liam, and he'd walked all over it in combat boots. But she couldn't focus on that now. She had to move forward. "I'm not unpacking any of these." She waved her hand around the things Liam's people had carefully packaged and brought over at lightning speed. "Whatever happens day after tomorrow at the Clash of the Titans, I'm not coming back to Denton Valley."

Sebastian pushed Jaz away from him and held her at arm's length. He was looking better now, almost back to his old self again, except for the limp, which the doctors couldn't promise would ever go away. "I wish I could go with you."

"Me too," Jaz whispered. But that was impossible. Sebastian wasn't strong enough for the competition now.

"How did Vector Ascent take the news?"

Jaz cringed. "Badly. They're fed up with all the issues. Between the car accident and then the explosion and Trident Security pulling out, it's a lot more press juggling than they signed up for. I was told to just show up and they'll have a partner for me. Period. No consultation and certainly no opinions on my part. I think if I wasn't already ahead in having won the first round, they'd have pulled out altogether."

"But you did win the first round," said Sebastian. "Your routes will be used. That gives you an edge on the others."

"An edge that will be totally offset by the fact I'll be climbing with someone I've never met before. We're going to waste time on signals and explanations and the lack of experience working together."

"Uh-huh." Sebastian walked over to the fridge and pulled out two pints of Phish Food ice cream that he'd brought over and a couple of spoons. Tossing a pint and a spoon to Jaz, he leaned his tall frame against one of the boxes. "So are we going to talk about the elephant in the room, or should I keep pretending this is all just a professional inconvenience?"

Putting down the ice cream, Jaz wrapped her arms around herself. "Can we just keep pretending it's professional?"

"Not a chance."

Jaz sighed. "I guess the worst part of everything is that it's a repeat performance. Fool me once, shame on you, fool me twice, shame on me kind of thing. Gullible, starstruck Jaz trusts a man who every shred of common sense tells her she shouldn't, and then acts surprised when said man has his own agenda. How can I be so damn stupid?"

"Don't tell me you're lumping Liam Rowen into the same category as that Females of the Future git?"

"Doesn't look so different from where I'm standing. I believed in a lie both times, relied on someone else with my heart and soul. But that's over now. I'm doing what I should have been doing from the start—relying on myself." She opened the ice cream and took a confident scoop, gesturing with the spoon as she spoke. "No more self-pity. I'm flying out to California tomorrow, and I'm winning this thing. And when it's all done—however it's done—I'm heading to Seattle."

"Seattle?" Sebastian's brows climbed. "What's in Seattle?"

"Mount Rainier. Rain. No state income tax. There's an outpost near Diablo Lake where I can work for room and board. I did get the security deposit from the apartment back, and it's going to pay the packers and movers. Can you do me the biggest favor in the world and make sure my stuff gets picked up for storage?"

"WHAT DO you mean my bag isn't lost? It isn't here." Holding the phone between her shoulder and ear, Jaz navigated the passengers flocking around the rotating baggage carousel and eyed the line stretching toward in-person customer care. An hour wait for counter service at minimum. At least somebody had answered the phone when she called the airline. "I'm standing at baggage claim at Los Angeles Airport right now. The bag carousel doesn't have my bag. Hence lost. Can you help?"

"Okay. I understand." On the other end, the representative sounded like he was typing something into a computer. "Please, don't worry. I'm very sorry for the inconvenience that you're experiencing. I'm here to help and will get this resolved for you. Can you please spell your full name and address for me?"

She did.

"And are you a frequent flier with American Airlines?"

"How does that help locate my bag? No. Never mind." Jaz looked up her number and quickly provided it.

"Thank you so much for that information, Ms. Keasley. Am I pronouncing your name correctly?"

"Yes. Great job." Jaz looked at her watch. Someone from the

Clash of the Titans competition committee was due to pick her up from the airport in an hour, and her gear—her climbing gear—had gone missing. "Is it possible some of the luggage was diverted to a different baggage carousel? Or is it still in Denver, where I had a layover?"

"Please tell me the flight you come in on?"

She gave him the number, explaining there'd been a layover in Denver.

"I see. And where are you now?"

Seriously? "The LA airport. Baggage claim. Should I get in line for in-person assistance?"

"Okay, I understand. I know getting your luggage on time is very important and it's a great inconvenience to have it unavailable at your destination. But please don't worry. You have the right place. You don't need to divert to in-person customer service as I am here to assist you with this important matter. Can I put you on a brief hold while I process this information?"

Silence came over the line. Jaz drew a deep breath and fiddled with her zipper. With the climb starting tomorrow, she needed to keep her mind focused—a feat that the universe seemed determined to make difficult. She'd opted for an earlier flight out of Denton Valley than originally planned—only to run into weather and a layover that required her to sit in the Denver airport for hours. Then she got motion sick. And now, on top of everything, her gear bag was missing. The one she'd packed perfectly for the climb, adjusting all the straps and arranging her things the way she liked it.

"Ms. Keasley, thank you so much for waiting," the representative said, coming back onto the line. "I truly appreciate your patience while I check on a few things. I have good news for you. Your flight arrived at the Los Angeles airport thirty-four minutes ago. All the bags from the flight are being routed to baggage claim C. Please go ahead and pick up your bags there. Would you like me to look up the directions of the carousel for you?"

Jaz ground her teeth. "I know the flight arrived at the airport. I was on the flight. And I *am* standing at baggage claim C. However, my bag is not here."

"Yes. I understand. In that case, I recommend that you wait by the carousel. Although we strive to bring luggage out as soon as the plane arrives, sometimes there are delays. If your bags do not come out within twenty minutes, please give us a call back at the main number, and a representative will be happy to assist you."

"Sir, please listen to me. All the bags from my flight have already come out on baggage claim C. The bags arriving now are from a totally different airline. I don't see any logical reason why my bag would suddenly appear mixed with Delta Airlines' baggage."

"We don't mix bags between flights and airlines, ma'am. If you flew on Delta airline, I suggest you contact their customer service for assistance."

Jaz threw her face up toward the ceiling and let out a silent scream.

"Is there anything else I can help you with today?" the representative asked.

"Look, can I just give you the number from my claim ticket and you tell me the last place someone actually laid eyes on my bag?" Jaz waited until the rep agreed, then read off the number, repeating it several times before the man on the other end understood.

"Yes, thank you so much for that. Allow me a moment to look into the matter."

The line went silent, the man returning ten minutes later to thank Jaz for her patience and understanding. "I looked into this important matter for you. I see that you checked one oversized bag —a backpack—in at Denton Valley Airport, for that flight with service to Los Angeles. Your bag was scanned in Denver at your layover location and loaded onto the plane to Los Angeles. Please pick up your luggage at baggage carousel C—"

"For the fourth damn time, I *am* at baggage claim C, and my bag is not!"

"I am so sorry for the inconvenience. But that is the most I can do from here. Since your bag does show tracking to Los Angeles, it should be in Los Angeles. If you're still having trouble, our friendly representatives at the in-person service counter will be more than happy to assist you."

Jaz hung up. Immediately, her phone chirped with three missed messages. The driver from the competition noticed that her flight had landed and she wasn't waiting outside.

She explained the missing-bag-of-gear situation.

The answer came immediately. *Don't worry about it. Happens all the time here—I'll come back for the bag later. If we don't get you checked in to the roster, the gear will be a moot point.*

After the idiot in the customer service center, Jaz was ready to hug whoever it was on the other end of the text. Following his instructions to go to ground transportation, she scanned the waiting vehicles until she located the red Toyota Camry and headed for the passenger's seat. Her hand was already on the handle, halfway through opening the door, when she realized that she knew the man in the driver's seat.

Roman Robillard.

LIAM

*L*iam sat by the window at the Taoism café, watching the sun play off the glass. It was eight in the morning of the day Jaz would be flying out to California, and Liam's heart was shredding from the memory of his own words. He tried not to think of how she was packing. Checking all her gear and putting little colorful zip ties on her bag. Tried not to think of who her partner would be, of the fact that he'd turned over the duty of holding her safety line to some stranger.

He was being responsible. Being in Obsidian Ops' crosshairs made him dangerous to be around, and he couldn't pass that risk on to Jaz. Which didn't make it all hurt any less.

And then there was Lisa. Liam was little looking forward to revealing his sister's drug habit to Patti this morning, but even with all her problems, Lisa did get one thing right.

You and I both know you have the emotional range of a carrier pigeon… The only long-term relationships you have are the ones you pay for.

The front door of the café opened with a chime, and Liam felt his back stiffen as his mother walked in, looking around until she spotted him sitting in the back and headed his way. "Liam." Patti's smile was hesitant, as if a part of her feared being here. Or feared being turned away again. Unlike the usual jeans and T-shirt he was used to seeing her in on Zoom, today she wore a long skirt and blouse, as if she wanted to dress the part of a parent. With a start, Liam realized that Patti had a fragility about her he hadn't noticed previously.

Feeling a ripple of discomfort snake down his back, Liam rose and pulled the chair out for her before reclaiming his own chair.

"I'm glad you called." Patti reached toward him, her hand hovering a few inches from his cheek before pulling back. "I imagine I don't get to do that right now. So to what do I owe the invitation to breakfast?"

Liam wrapped his fingers around his glass of cold drinking water, while the waitress appeared to set a pot of hot water, a basket of teas, and an assortment of pastries he'd ordered on the table. "Lisa accosted me in my office the other day."

Patti winced. "I didn't know she was coming. What did she want?" A frown etched her face. "If it was about money, we need to talk—"

"She's using, Mom. Did you know?"

Patti covered her face with her hands. "I knew *something* was off. The moods, the constant money needs. I felt her slipping away. It was one of the reasons I came up here. Between the changes in Lisa and your pushing me further away with every stipend check and cold conversation, I woke up one day knowing that I was on the verge of losing both my children. I'm not giving up without a fight this time, Liam. On either of you." She swallowed. "Are you sure about the drugs? Her forearms—"

"The tracks are between her fingers. I'm going to find a rehab program, and we'll go from there." He let that line of discussion end there. He and Patti were equally to blame for having missed the signs and would somehow need to find a way of cooperating to dig Lisa out. But if they were to be forced to talk more often, they had to get one other thing settled. "What did you tell her about Jaz?"

Patti raised a brow at him. "About Jaz? The truth. That I thought you found a partner for yourself. That you were in love. Why?"

"Don't play games, Mother. Never, and especially, especially not today."

"Games?" Patti opened her mouth to say something, then closed it and focused on selecting a tea from the basket and putting it into the pot, the scent of chamomile filling the air at once. "I came all the way from Michigan to repair our relationship, only to be forced to watch you nearly get ripped to shreds by shrapnel from your own truck. This is the first conversation you've willingly initiated with me in years. So believe me, whatever other faults you can assign to me, playing games isn't on the menu."

"Then why lie about Jaz?"

This time, Patti looked at him with an utterly confused expression. "I didn't."

Liam sighed, laying his hands on the table. Running an insurgency operation in Afghanistan was downright easier than discussing his love life—or lack thereof—with his mother. "For someone who has made her opinion on my inability to maintain a meaningful relationship clear to me on multiple occasions, this sudden romanticism is unbecoming. To say the least."

"How can I have done that when you've never told me about a single girlfriend?" Patti demanded.

Liam's hand curled into a fist. "So you didn't tell me I was and always would be a useless burden to have around? That I was one of those rare people born incapable of—"

"You're going to hold my words from twenty years ago against me now?" Patti's voice shook as she interrupted. "I was trying to raise two children without enough money for rent and barely enough for food. I wasn't perfect. I wasn't even adequate. But I've always loved you. How could you think otherwise?"

"Oh, I don't know. Maybe it was the part where you decided to exile me from the family. And then tell me not to come back. To put your boyfriend on the phone to tell me that you didn't want me and that no smart person ever would." Words that Liam had never intended to say aloud to Patti now poured from him, and he couldn't quite understand why, except that ever since meeting Jaz, he needed to know.

Blood drained from Patti's face. Her hands trembled around the glass so badly that the water spilled over the edge and trickled down her wrist. "I didn't think you remembered that. I prayed that you didn't. I said and did a lot of things back then that I'm not proud of, but that certainly doesn't make all the drivel true. How can you even think any of it could be true with the man you've become?"

Patti took a sip of her water, not meeting Liam's eyes, her own ringed with moisture.

"You don't know how bad things were back then, Liam. How little I had to give you. If things had kept going as they were, you'd have had to drop out of school to get a job. And then when Lisa was attacked on top of everything—"

"When I let her be attacked." If Liam wasn't going to pull punches with Patti, he certainly wouldn't with himself either.

"You fought like a gladiator. Bobby Johnson was eighteen years old and on the football team. You were a malnourished eleven-year-old boy. But you didn't stop until he knocked you so hard that you were bleeding on the floor. And not even then." Patti traced the small scar above Liam's eyes, her touch feather soft. "Hell, why do you think Bobby's father offered to pay for your military schooling?"

"To get me to shut up," said Liam.

"Yes," Patti admitted without blinking, "but it wasn't just that. Even when you were eleven, we all realized you were a force to be reckoned with. It was Bobby's father who saw it first, and not just because he wanted to protect his son. He took me aside and told me that you were more of a man than his Bobby ever would be. He was the one who suggested Trident Military Academy, because he'd gone there himself. He told me he hoped paying your tuition was a tiny way toward balancing the wrong of the world."

"You never told me that."

"No." A tear streaked down Patti's cheek. "Because Mr. Johnson wanted to protect Bobby, and so his offer came with strings attached. You get the best schooling and a chance at a future that I could never give you, but in exchange, you wouldn't be around to exact the vengeance we knew you'd want. I don't know if it matters, but Lisa agreed with the plan."

"So you let me think that you didn't love me," Liam whispered. "That I wasn't lovable."

"It was the only way to get you to stay away. You don't understand—being with us wasn't safe for you. One return home, with you all spit and vinegar, and your tuition would have been pulled. I didn't want to push you away, Liam. I hated pushing you away. But it was the only way to keep your future safe."

"Why didn't you tell me?" Liam whispered.

"For the obvious reasons at first. You hated taking anything from anyone, and you were so righteous. And right. Then because I was humiliated about what I'd done."

Liam stared out the window, his heart bleeding. How could he blame his mother for pushing him away to keep him safe when he'd just done as much to Jaz? How could he know she was wrong without admitting the error of what he'd done? He hadn't given Jaz a choice. And unlike the impoverished, overwhelmed Patti, he had every reason to know better.

"Liam. What is it?"

He realized Patti had his hand between hers at the same time he saw a tear fall down from his cheek onto their clasped hands.

"I think I just took a page from your playbook," he said softly. "And I know from firsthand experience the effect that has. Except I don't have the excuse of being alone and overwhelmed."

"True," said Patti. "But that also means you don't have to wait until you get older and wiser before you start fixing things."

LIAM SELECTED Jaz's number from his phone, his car speaker filling with the sound of the dialing digits.

Jaz's phone rang once, twice, five times, then disconnected without even going to voicemail. The same as it had the last three times he'd attempted to reach her. Right. Liam turned off the phone and pulled into a spot near Jaz's apartment building, taking the stairs up two at a time to her door.

He rang the doorbell and followed it up with a knock even as the *ding dong dong* still echoed from the chime. Yes, he knew he was acting like an anxious teenager. And he didn't care. He wanted to talk to her. Needed to talk to her.

Liam's shoulders tensed as he heard the footsteps approaching the door on the other side. The lock snapped open. Liam's stomach clenched. For a moment, his whole body tightened and he nearly took off right back down the stairs he'd just climbed—but he caught himself in time to be standing still as the door finally opened.

And Sebastian filled the doorway.

"Where's Jaz?" Liam asked.

Sebastian lifted a brow. Behind the tall young man, Liam could see boxes filling Jaz's apartment. Not just the couple that were brought over from his place, but many, many more. Rolls of packing tape and brown paper littered what Liam could see of the furniture. *What the hell?* It looked for all the world like she was moving, but why and where? He'd paid the rent on the apartment and knew for a fact that Jaz had nearly no money left in her bank account.

Realizing that Sebastian was still blocking the door, Liam switched his attention to the man's face. "I'm looking for Jaz," he repeated.

"So you said. She isn't here."

"Well, where is she? I need to talk to her. It's important."

Sebastian, who'd been leaning with a hand against the doorframe, straightened. He was about the same height as Liam, but lankier and—despite being a rock climber—somewhat awkward on the flat ground. Even if Sebastian wasn't still recovering from his injury, Liam could lay the younger man out without breaking a sweat. Liam knew it. Sebastian knew it. And yet that didn't stop Sebastian from squaring off, his arms crossed over his chest.

"You want to know what's important? What's important is that Jaz is able to channel what little mental bandwidth she has left into concentrating on tomorrow's competition. In case you missed the memo, this Clash of the Titans is her version of the NFL. What you did to her—how and when you did it—is nothing short of criminal. So, *no*, I'm not letting you in. Or telling you where she is. Or mentioning that you were even here. And before you ask, the reason she isn't picking up any of your calls—presuming you made any—is because I blocked your number from her phone."

Liam rocked back on his heels. He appreciated that Jaz had loyal friends, but Sebastian didn't know what he was talking about. Not fully. "Listen." Liam held his hands out in a calming gesture despite feeling anything but calm. "I know you think you're doing what's best, but—"

"Do you care about her?" he demanded. "Did you ever care about her?"

The question hit him like a blow. Liam was used to challenges, but this was personal, and the question somehow made him feel naked. But he answered it anyway. "Yes," he said without flinching. "And when I told her I didn't, it was an utter lie. A cowardly one. I care about her very much, Sebastian, and I would very much like to tell her this myself. So can you please help?"

Sebastian regarded him for several heartbeats, his face unreadable. "If that's true," he said finally. "If you truly do care, then you'll give her the courtesy of waiting until the competition is over. For the next forty-eight hours, Jaz needs to keep her head in the game, not be mulling over the changes of your mercurial heart."

Liam's jaw tightened. Sebastian raised his chin at the challenge and didn't back off a single inch.

"All right," Liam said, switching tactics. "What about all the boxes? Where's she moving to?"

Sebastian shrugged. "Down the block. Maybe. Or maybe down the coast. I guess you'll have to wait to find that out until you talk to her. *After* the climb."

"You do know I run a pretty decent security company? It wouldn't take all that much work to track this down, whether you tell me or not."

Sebastian shrugged again and slipped his hands into his pockets. "True," he said. "I imagine you can do that. But I guess it all comes down to the question of whether you actually care about her. And if you do, you'll respect her privacy. And her space."

Liam drew a long breath and blew it out. As much as he fucking hated to admit it, on this point, Sebastian was right.

JAZ

*R*oman Robillard? What in the ever-loving hell was he doing here? The last time she saw the man, Roman was drunk out of his mind and threatening her and Liam at the Adventure World fair. Jaz's hand tightened on the handle of her rolling bag as she took a step back from the car and checked her phone messages to ensure she hadn't missed something. She hadn't. And yet, here he was, picking her up on behalf of Vector Ascent and the Clash of the Titans.

Roman reached across the seat and opened the passenger's door. "I know, I know. I probably should have warned you it was me picking you up. But honestly, I was kind of worried you wouldn't show up and I'd lose my job."

"You're working for the challenge?" Taking out her phone, Jaz texted both the main competition administration and Vector Ascent about the pickup.

The car behind Roman's Camry gave an annoyed honk. "Hey, lovebirds, can you take this reunion elsewhere?" the driver shouted through the open window. "Some of us need to get on with it." When Jaz failed to move immediately, the man honked again, this time laying into his horn until others joined in.

Jaz flipped the drivers off, waiting for confirmation that Roman was indeed supposed to be there before considering getting into his car. Unfortunately, said confirmation from Vector Ascent showed up a moment later. With a frustrated grunt, Jaz put her bag into the back and got in beside Roman. "What's your job exactly?"

"Hello, Jaz, it's good to see you again too," Roman said good-naturedly. Without the reek of alcohol coming off him, he was much more the articulate athlete who had once dominated Vector Ascent's marketing campaigns.

"You can't be *too* glad to see me when I said no such thing about you."

"And here I was hoping for something along the lines of *I'm glad you don't have any hard feelings about my having Vector Ascent's championship slot, and I look forward to working with you this week.*"

"How about this one: *You outright threatened me, and your cousin tried to kill me with his car, so you'll forgive my lack of enthusiasm.*"

Roman scratched the stubble growing along his jawline. "First things first. Devante is Devante, and I'm me. I love him because he's family, but he's always been...obsessive. Unstable. I can't even begin to tell you what might have been going through his mind when he got into that car. All I can say is that obviously it was nothing healthy. I went to his place to clean up, and he had letter cutouts from newspapers and magazines as if to make those weird anonymous notes from the movies. The man needs help. Period. And I hope that when he's behind bars, he'll get it. I *am* sorry you got hung up in his psychosis, but his mental illness is neither my doing nor my fault.

"As for what I said to you at Adventure World... That one is on me. I'm not proud of cornering you and your lover. I got drunk and stupid. And for what it's worth, I'm sorry."

He took a turn onto the freeway and studied Jaz out of the corner of his eye. "Also, while we're on Confession Island, I should also tell you I'm not just the guy Vector Ascent sent to pick you up. I'm also, kind of, the guy they selected to be your climbing partner."

Jaz leaned her head back against the seat, letting Roman's words process for a minute. Given that Roman was Vector's former poster boy, it wasn't altogether impossible that Vector decided to bring him back. Especially given their recent conversation with her. It actually made sense. But still. Roman?

"All right, let's have it out," Roman said with a sigh. "Yes, I'm more than a little devastated that it's not me leading the pack, but I've accepted the reality of the situation, and I do appreciate Vector Ascent giving me the chance to be involved again. And yeah, I imagine if I were in your shoes, not being allowed to pick my own climbing partner, I'd be pretty pissed as well. But again, reality. To Vector, we're both PR. Nothing more. And we do all have the same goal of winning. So can we call a truce for the next thirty hours?"

Jaz winced. Sober Roman sounded damn reasonable. And in the man's defense, everything she thought she knew about him was speculation, third-hand info, and internet rumors—their one drunken encounter at Adventure World notwithstanding. More to the point, he was right about their current common goal. There was only one mature thing to do. "Fine. Truth. Thank you." She stretched and looked back at her bag. "Though I regret to remind you that we have a gear problem."

"That seems like the kind of thing for a partner to help out with, so I've been working on it since you texted me. According to Reddit, it's a common issue around here, and there are some tricks to getting things found sooner rather than later," he said. "Between the check-ins and going over the routes and everything else, you're going to have your hands full the rest of the day. I'll drop you off with the other competitors, then grab your claim stub and swing back to the airport."

"That's actually…" That was actually the first bit of good news she'd heard that day. "Thank you," Jaz said, and meant it.

"So what happened with that guy I saw you with the other day?" he asked.

"Long story. Short ending. I'm here, he's not."

"I'm sorry."

"No, you're not."

"Okay, I'm not actually sorry that I'm here instead of him. But while I don't know whether you broke up with your boyfriend or not, I do care that your head is in the game. Even if I'm not the one leading this pack, I have every intention of us winning."

"Fair," said Jaz. With Roman's reasonableness, it was getting increasingly difficult to keep hating the man. Plus, he had a point about the whole event—at day's end—being about PR. Whatever void in Jaz's soul Liam had left, it was her job to pretend all was well. Just like in any acting gig. Forcing a genuine-looking smile onto her face, Jaz turned toward Roman. "All right. Since you got here first and I'm sure have been scouting the terrain, tell me *everything*."

ROMAN DROPPED Jaz off at the hotel and, as promised, disappeared to follow up on the bag situation. It was already getting close to dinnertime, and the evening flew by in a flurry of signing forms, taking photographs, and offering sound bites as to the quality of their sponsors' gear. Jaz fielded a few specific questions about the advantage she had by having won the first challenge round and thus having her routes showcased in the final. She was just finishing up the last of the press interviews when her phone vibrated.

Roman: *Good news and bad news. They found the bag, but at a different airport. It'll be here by morning, though. Promise.*

Shit. That was cutting it a lot closer than Jaz wanted. But there wasn't much alternative. There was a set of backup gear available, but using someone else's things always carried a disadvantage.

Thanks, she texted back. *I'll drive over in the morning to take it.*

Roman: *I got it. If I'm a little late, they'll let it slide. If you're a little late, they'll throw a fit. I'm heading back to get some sleep for now, and you should too.*

∿

"MAY I HAVE YOUR ATTENTION, PLEASE!" The official opening ceremony gathered all the competitors together in the same place they'd started the original challenge. Sitting on the raised podium, Jaz knew she gave off an air of confident nonchalance she did not feel. The bag had been late again, but Roman finally texted her with pictures of him holding the damn thing, which should have made Jaz feel better but didn't. Having spent the night reliving the explosion, Jaz was the exact opposite of the image she gave the camera.

Exhausted. Heartbroken. Alone.

Sebastian had wisely blocked Liam's number from Jaz's phone before she left. Not because either of them expected the asshole to reach out, but because removing the possibility of it made it easier to not wonder. To not plan the venomous comebacks she wanted to throw in Liam's face.

The wind blew, carrying with it the scent of mountain freshness. A freedom that called to Jaz's bones. She breathed in the smell, focusing on the occasional call of the stray birds while the official's voice filled the microphone.

"As you know, we'll be using the routes marked for us by Vector Ascent champion's Jazmine Kingsley. The five passages are equitable climbs of about five hours each, and will be assigned by random lot draw. All located within a mile of each other, the routes have an initial approach of moderate difficulty followed by a section requiring supreme technical knowledge and expert gear handling.

"Of course, climbing is never a solitary sport. In addition to the emergency radio, each of our champions has a partner following along to hold their safety line. However, the challengers must take lead on all climbs and must be the only ones to attach any anchor into stone. Now then, it is now eight thirty in the morning. The climb starts at nine thirty sharp. Let's get our Titans onto the mountain."

A gong sounded, and Jaz walked off the podium to where Roman was already waiting atop the ATV, her climbing backpack happily strapped to the back. Like Jaz, he was dressed head to toe in Vector Ascent gear, his climbing shoes, helmet, and chalk bag strapped to his pack. Jaz's eyes narrowed. "My zip ties are gone. I use them to make sure that no one tampers with my gear after it's packed."

Roman turned to follow her gaze, his voice gaining a note of irritation. "Yeah. The TSA informed me that zip ties aren't an approved locking device for bags. Can we please focus less on luggage and more on the climb? Whatever your mental block with this is, it needs to get unblocked."

Getting to the starting point, Jaz secured her harness and double-checked Roman's, who scowled but let it happen. The official behind them signed Jaz's readiness to central ops, and a few staticky moments later received an all-clear call. As she'd done many times before, Jaz cleared her mind and stepped up to the stone that held her future. "On belay," she called to Roman.

"Belay on."

"Climbing."

"Climb away," Roman said.

As Jaz started up the mountain with all speed, she spared one look toward the earth disappearing beneath her. There, fallen to the ground by Roman's feet, was a small colored piece of plastic. Although she couldn't be sure, the speck looked to be the color of one of her zip ties.

37

LIAM

*O*n the early morning of the Clash of the Titans final climb, Liam landed in Las Vegas, Nevada. While he couldn't be beside Jaz, keeping her safe as she climbed today, he could still protect her future. Liam was done playing cordially with Obsidian Ops. Today, he would make it personal and ensure Colonel Lucius would never again go after people Liam cared about.

Straightening the lapels of his suit, Liam strode into The Other Cosmopolitan—the upscale piano bar where, per deep-dug intelligence, Lucius was secretly visiting his illegitimate daughter this morning. So far as Liam knew, the colonel had gone to great lengths to ensure no one in Obsidian Ops knew of the child. To Lucius, this secret was a matter of life and death. Which would make Liam's presence here a message stronger than bullets and bombs.

On the surface of it, The Other Cosmopolitan was just another glamorous Sin City establishment. Bejeweled walls sparkled, and cleverly lit square columns played video reels that made it look as if people danced inside them. On the far left, a raised dais held a glossy baby grand, which sang beautifully beneath the pianist's dexterous fingers. On the right, the equally glossy bar currently served breakfast coffee and expensive pastries.

Beneath the glamorous surface package, the place was run and operated by the Tomitano crime family. Liam had spotted imprints of sidearms on at least six official security guards and as many unofficial ones, who found a reason to mill around him ever since Liam had stepped into the place. Whether he would be coming out of it alive remained to be seen.

Aiden and Nell, Trident's genius hacker, had outdone themselves in following Lucius's digital footprint on the dark web to discover the colonel's monthly clockwork patronage of the place. Or specifically, of young Miss Stephanie Tomitano who, at the tender age of eleven, appeared unable to avoid social media.

Stopping just inside the door, Liam adjusted the French cuffs peeking out from beneath his jacket. Even this early in the morning, The Other Cosmopolitan maintained its formal dress code—which was why both Lucius and his illegitimate daughter appeared to be wearing their Sunday best as they shared their breakfast.

Liam's stomach tightened. He was crossing the line coming here, and he knew it. But Lucius needed to be jerked up short for thinking he could pull Liam's personal life into their business dispute.

"How many for breakfast today, sir?" A waiter appeared with the menu already in hand.

"Thank you, but my party is already here." With a confident nod to the staff, Liam strode over to the table Lucius and his daughter currently occupied and settled into an empty chair. "A cappuccino for me, please," he said over his shoulder to the tensely hovering waiter, while ignoring the several men in suits casually moving closer. Reaching into his inside jacket pocket, Liam pulled out a small wrapped box. "Lucius, I'm so sorry I'm late. But I swung by and picked up Stephanie's birthday present like you asked. Did I get the right box?"

Translation: Yes, I've found your weakness. I know you have a daughter with the mob and the last thing you want is for anyone at Obsidian Ops to know about her. The mob on one side, and Obsidian Ops on the other. It's a hard place to be. One wrong move, and I'll blow your secret wide open.

On the other side of the table, the child's innocent eyes opened in wide delight, her curled ponytails swinging over her ears.

Lucius's eyes hardened to stone. Quickly opening the gift box, he pulled out the brand-new iPhone—still in its factory-sealed packaging—that Liam had put in there.

"Oh my God!" Stephanie squealed loudly enough to drown out the piano. "You got me an iPhone, Daddy? Really? Thank you, thank you, thank you."

"You can only keep it if you show me you can be responsible with it," Lucius answered with only the slightest of hesitations. "Now, let me see you go sit at the bar and set it up with proper security settings while I have a small chat with Mr. Rowen."

Stephanie grinned and skipped off with the iPhone. The men who had *accidently* surrounded the table took a step back with her. Lucius looked ready to throw thunderbolts from his eyes.

Liam could hardly blame him for that. He had, after all, pulled Lucius's daughter into their turf war. But Lucius had gone after Jaz. That made them even.

"If you do anything to hurt her—" Lucius started to say.

Liam held up his palms. "Never. But I can't speak for the company you keep and how they'd react to various facts coming out. On either side." Taking a sip from the cappuccino the waiter unobtrusively placed at Liam's elbow, he gestured with his chin to where Stephanie was cooing over her new toy.

"Have the phone checked. There's nothing on it," Liam continued. "Friendly word of advice, though. I know Obsidian Ops planted the explosives on my truck. Go near Jaz or anyone from my Denton Valley family again, and I will personally shove an M4 so far up your ass that you'll be able to shoot it just by farting. And then I'll send out a few press releases of my own. I imagine Obsidian Ops will be as happy to know your vulnerability as the Tomitano crime family will be upset over having their reputation sullied. I presume they *don't* want it known that Stephanie's sire is a mutt like you?"

"You are a suicidal idiot," the head of Obsidian Ops' East Coast operations hissed quietly. "One word from me and my friends over there will be carrying out your body."

Liam smiled, showing his teeth. One of the security suits to his right looked to have a twitchy trigger finger, his hand hovering close to the bulge on the side of his jacket. Liam marked the man's location while keeping his attention on Lucius. "Maybe. Or maybe they'll decide you're at more fault than I am. You know how these mob guys are." He leaned back in his chair to give his adversary a bit of breathing room. "Listen, Lucius—you and I, we're just business competitors. All I want is for us to keep business conflicts from becoming personal. The sooner we can agree on the rules of engagement, the sooner you can go back to enjoying breakfast with your daughter. A few more minutes and I imagine little Steph will discover the lack of parental controls on that thing and will be downloading TikTok."

A vein on the side of Lucius's temple pulsed, but the rest of his body stayed well controlled. "You have it all wrong, Rowen. I never *went after* that Keasley woman. Don't get me wrong, the name does have a certain black spot in my heart, but I don't mix business and pleasure, and I didn't this time either." He raised his hand to signal the waiter. "A whiskey sour for me and my friend, please, Alfonso."

The waiter nodded.

The goons in suits retreated farther.

Liam leaned forward. "The explosion—"

"Oh, that was me," Lucius agreed without a trace of shame. "But that was a simple publicity op against Trident Security's reputation. No one was hurt. If I wanted your Jaz dead, she would have been."

True. But there was more than just dead and alive to consider. "And if I'd been a second slower spotting the charge? Or she'd run ahead of me? You know she could have gotten hurt. And I'm telling you, she isn't acceptable collateral damage. No one fucking is."

Lucius sighed, and took a sip of the newly delivered whiskey. "Point made. And for what it's worth, I agree that the way the Adventure World fiasco went down was less than ideal. My guy was a young, overeager operative. He should have waited to ignite the charge later, when you were alone, but he realized his detonator was spotted and panicked. He figured everyone was far enough away. To his credit, he was right."

"You can then also credit him with my presence here," Liam said.

Lucius's hand tightened on his glass. "Oh, believe me, I will. Think about it logically. I need an actual domestic murder investigation hanging over me about as about as much as I need a prostate exam. But meanwhile, just as a show of good faith, I'll make the rookie's error up to you. Would you like the lunatic who *actually* wants your sidepiece in pieces? Because he's still out there and not under my control."

Liam froze.

Lucius smiled. "I help you clear this up, and you never bring up Stephanie ever again. Do we have a deal?"

Liam nodded.

"Roman Robillard."

"Robillard? We ruled him out from the explosion."

"Clean your ears out, Rowen. I just told you that mess was mine. But why do you imagine I started this whole publicity stunt to begin with? Much as I dislike you, I have better things to do than dig through minor client files. But when Roman waltzed into my office thinking he could order a contract hit as if it were McDonald's, it got my attention."

Liam's stomach tightened. It did explain the strange delay about the start of the smear campaign. "What did you tell him?"

"To pound sand. But then I heard you were involved, and I milked the details. Last I spoke to him, he believed we actually tried to take the girl out and failed."

"This is your notion of a good faith gesture?"

"No, but this is. Roman is taking matters into his own insane hands. And if my latest intel is right, he's your little girl's new climbing partner." The colonel looked at his watch. "It's nine thirty a.m. Which means they're on the mountain right about now."

Blood drained from Liam's face.

Lucius smiled and took a lazy sip of his drink. "I'll do you one better. I keep a pilot and a hot chopper while I'm here, but as your needs appear greater than mine, I'll let you make use of them." His gaze hardened. "I expect to call this incident closed after that."

JAZ

*J*az hauled herself up onto a luxurious two-foot ledge, taking a few moments to catch her breath. They were two hours, three minutes into the climb and had just come to the transition point where the route dynamics changed from speed movements to the much more technical and gear-intensive approach. It would take time to rearrange her gear before continuing to the more difficult portions of the ascent, but she'd planned for that.

The initial adrenaline of the climb had calmed now, but her body felt awake and alive, her lungs drawing large gulps of delicious air with every inhale. Fatigued muscles reported in with a not unpleasant heat. To her surprise, Roman had so far proved to be a very decent partner. He wasn't Sebastian or Liam—Jaz tried and failed not to flinch at the thought—but he was the next best thing, moving quickly and taking direction well. While the competitors were the ones who set up the climb and handled the equipment, the partners needed to keep up and keep alert to avoid losing precious time. Whatever else Jaz could say about Roman, he moved like a monkey when he was sober. The possibility of true victory, which had seemed so impossible a day ago, now lay squarely within reach.

"We're going to crush this, Roman." Jaz swung her pack off her back while Roman hoisted himself onto the ledge beside her. She grinned, extending a hand to help him the rest of the way. "Especially if you can move your ass a little faster."

Roman grinned back, his brown eyes alert as he reclipped himself into a safety line beside her. "Yes," he agreed. "There will absolutely be crushing. And winning." A trick of the light made the man's eyes seem to flash as he said the latter, but just as a small tightness touched the back of Jaz's neck, Roman broke eye contact and pulled a water bottle from his pack. Taking a few grateful gulps, he sighed with contentment. "Want some?"

"Sure." Jaz held out her hand.

Roman tossed the water-filled canteen to her.

Jaz went to catch it, but instead of heading into her awaiting grip, the plastic container flew toward her face. Jaz jerked away, managing to only get clipped on the chin before the bottle tumbled over the side of the mountain. Her breath caught.

"Man, you almost had that." Roman shook his head. "That was your water bottle too."

"What the fuck was that?"

"A fallen water bottle," Roman answered with no trace of remorse. As if the whole fiasco hadn't been an accident at all. "Doesn't it suck when something that's yours smacks you in the face and falls away for no good reason at all?"

Jaz swallowed, her perspective on Roman readjusting itself to a new reality. Plainly, Roman wasn't nearly as all right with the situation as he'd been pretending, and she needed to stuff this new pissed-off side of him back into the genie bottle before this turned from bad to worse. Shoving down the words she actually wanted to say, Jaz made her tone agreeable. Sympathetic.

"Yeah, it does." Despite roaring fury, she gave Roman a rueful smile that would have made her acting teachers proud. "Vector Ascent really didn't handle this well. Let's win this thing and set them straight."

"I don't see it being quite that easy," said Roman.

"No?" Jaz reached into her pack, taking out the extra quickdraw

carabiners she'd need for the rest of the route. "Once we win we——"
She cut off as her fingers, which had been running over the gear by
long habit, felt something unusual along the webbing. Her gaze
dropped to her hands. To the small rip in the nylon webbing
connecting the two parts of the quickdraw together. No, not a rip,
a cut.

Reaching to the bottom of her pack again, Jaz pulled out the
rest of the equipment she hadn't yet touched and felt blood drain
from her face. A third had something wrong with it. The damage
was different on each piece of gear. Different damage, but the same
end result waiting in the wings: a plummet to the ground.

Jaz lifted her head toward Roman's gaze, the memory of the
colorful plastic zip tie that she thought she saw by his feet flashing
through her mind.

The corners of Roman's mouth curled toward a smile.
"Something wrong?"

"What did you do?" she whispered.

Roman stretched his back. "Let's just say I made the
competition more about heart and skill, and less about who you
spread your legs for."

"What are you talking about?"

For the first time since she'd met him yesterday, anger filled
Roman's voice. "I'm talking about you fucking your way into my
slot. Did you think I wouldn't figure it out?"

Jaz's hands ran over the gear again. The sabotage was limited to
the gear she'd need for the second portion of the climb. The things
at the very bottom of her pack, which she hadn't had a chance to
check due to its last-minute arrival.

The pack. Roman had been the one to pick her lost pack up
from the airport. Except the airline representative kept insisting
the bag was never missing. "Did you snatch my pack off the
carousel?"

"Don't be ridiculous." Roman snorted. "I tipped the handler to
bring it out to me early."

Insane. He was insane.

"You really thought I was going to roll over and let you destroy my life, didn't you?" Roman's face darkened. "Tell me, Jazmine, how is that working out for you?"

Heart pounding, Jaz held out her palms. "Roman. Listen to me. You saw the route plan. You know how dangerous and technical the next part is. If we go with this gear, we're going to die. Both of us. Do you understand me? We need to climb down."

"Now, now. Climbing down is no way to win." He walked toward her. "No. What we're going to do is make this real. Climbing is about skill. Strength. Body and mountain. You know what it's *not* about? Toys."

"You mean safety gear?"

"I mean cheating. Faking. But that's not going to happen now. No more gear hauling your ass up the mountain for you. The Clash of the Titans is now officially a free-climb event."

"But the others—" Jaz cut herself off. If Roman had tampered with her stuff, he could have found a way to sabotage the other climbers' gear as well. Was he trying to get people killed, or had he figured the climbers would catch on in time?

"There can be only one champion," Roman continued. "And soon, there'll be no question as to who that really is. Whose face belongs on the posters and billboards and endorsement checks."

"Fair point." Moving as unconsciously as she could, Jaz unzipped the side pocket of her pack where the emergency radio was stored. She needed to keep him talking. Keep him distracted. "So how do you want to go about this now?" she asked, her fingers seeking the cool plastic—and meeting only cloth.

"Looking for this?" Roman pulled the radio from his pack.

Jaz lunged for it.

Roman held the radio up out of her reach, like an older brother toying with a younger sibling.

Jaz kicked his knee.

Roman turned just in time to take the brunt of the kick on his thigh, his face contorting into something vicious. Something not altogether sane. Lifting his hand, the man slapped Jaz across the face hard enough to knock her into the rock wall.

Pain exploded along Jaz's temple, a bit of blood dripping down the side of her face. She licked her lips, tasting blood as her mind raced. She was still anchored into the stone, the safety line keeping her from falling to her death also constricting her movements. Not that the two-foot-wide ledge had much room to begin with. She couldn't run away from him. That meant she needed him to go away from her.

"You win." Jaz lifted her hands in surrender. "You're right. I'm too much of a coward to climb without gear. I'm not like you. I forfeit. You can go ahead. Summit and take the victory that belongs to you by rights."

"Don't patronize me. You think I don't know what you're doing?" Roman slapped Jaz again, bringing her to her knees. "You think I'm going to just leave you to rappel down to all those judges whose cocks you've blown? To fuck them into a new arrangement while I climb?"

Jaz's pulse raced, terror drowning out the pain in her cheek. "What do you want, then? Just tell me what you want."

"What do I want?" he parroted, bits of saliva spraying from the sides of his mouth. "How about fairness with a side of justice? How about an even playing field? How about no little bitch fucking her way into my hard-earned job?" With a growl, Roman grabbed the front of Jaz's harness and lifted her off her feet until they were eye level. Before Jaz could react, he threw her off the cliff.

Jaz gasped as her body went airborne, managing to stick her legs out in front of her a moment before the safety line went taut—thus avoiding slamming face-first into the stone. Now hanging parallel to the ground, Jaz stared up at Roman, who crouched on the ledge above her.

"See?" Roman said in a tone that was absurdly conversational. "Climbing comes down to skill. And I'm afraid that—besides morals—is the thing you're lacking." Taking out a knife, Roman made a small slice in the rope keeping Jaz from falling into the abyss below, severing the line a quarter of the way through.

LIAM

*L*iam sat with his legs hanging out the side of the helicopter, studying the mountain through a set of binoculars while the propeller whirled noisily. He remembered the terrain from when he'd been out here with Jaz, but the view from the skies was nothing like that from the ground. He touched his headset, talking to the pilot. "Can you take us around again, Kurt?"

"Yes, sir."

The chopper banked, Obsidian's well-trained pilot keeping them far enough from the action to avoid attracting undue attention and interfering with the competition. Though Lucius's information about Roman Robillard being Jaz's climbing partner checked out, everyone on the ground reported no predeparture problems. At Liam's insistence—and more than a little arm bending—the judges even agreed to do a test of the emergency radios with all climbing pairs. When all climbers checked in with an *all's well*, Liam had no choice but to bite his tongue and leave. At least far enough to get out of sight.

Liam pressed the binoculars back to his eyes, finally catching sight of small figures moving along the side of the cliff. Just five pairs at first, then details. A blond climber in neon-orange scampering up the westmost course. Then the small, nimble competitor whose name escaped Liam. Then—Jaz. Liam released a sigh of relief as he watched the woman he loved pull herself safely onto a wide ledge and extend her hand to help Roman up beside her. Despite their history, Jaz looked at ease with her climbing partner. She also looked beautiful and athletic and at the top of her game, the wind whipping her long hair into a wildness that matched her spirit.

Maybe Lucius was wrong about Roman's intentions. Or maybe the colonel had simply been playing on Liam's fears. Either way, Jaz was fine and would no doubt skin Liam alive if she ever learned of his presence here. He reached up to the mic again. "Let's pull back. No need to ruin anyone's concentration with a chopper flying around." He was already starting to lower the binoculars when Roman's face filled the viewport, a menacing presence almost palpable in the magnifier's image. Liam's hand stilled. There was something strange behind Roman's eyes, something that looked to be utterly without emotion. Like a Rottweiler who was ready to go for the jugular.

And then he did.

Liam called for Kurt to reverse course back to the mountain just as Roman threw a canteen at Jaz's head. In the bustle of activity that followed, Liam could only watch as Roman pulled back his arm and struck Jaz so hard that she bounced against the stone.

"Jaz!" Liam shouted, though he knew the distance and propeller noise would swallow the sound.

"Sir?" the pilot's voice sounded in the microphone.

With an effort of will, Liam reined in the fear that Roman's strike sent coursing through his blood. Reaching into his training, he shrugged on the professionalism that SEALs had disciplined into him, his heartbeat slowing to fall in line with the clear, detached mind a ready state required. "Confrontation within climbing team Charlie," he reported back to the pilot. "Call it into base camp and bring me close enough for extraction."

"Reporting confrontation in climbing team Charlie," the pilot echoed immediately, the sound of the engines shifting as the chopper sought better air. "Coming in."

As the pilot brought them closer, Liam attached a rappel line to his harness. By the time he could see unaided, Jaz was already hanging off the side of the cliff. Roman crouched next to her. Taking something out of his pocket.

Jaz's rope jerked.

Jaz screamed.

"He's cutting her safety line," Liam informed the pilot through the open mic. "Get to within arm's reach."

"Negative, sir. The propeller will hit the stone." A pause. "There is a platform twenty feet above I can drop you on."

Shit. Fucking shit. "Understood," Liam said into the mic, fighting to keep his heart and breath steady as Kurt maneuvered the bird, precious moments ticking by with every rotation of the propeller blades. Moments that could cost Jaz her life. It felt like years until Kurt signaled an all clear and Liam unclipped himself from the chopper's safety tether and rappelled down to the stone.

Scampering down the twenty-foot wall, Liam hopped lightly onto the ledge where Roman crouched. Though the wind carried away most of the words, Liam could tell that the asshole and Jaz were talking. Despite the serrated blade Roman held against her rope, Jaz was still alive.

"Step away, Roman," Liam ordered, his voice booming over the mountain.

Jaz let out a short, unintelligible noise.

Roman stiffened. Turned. But he didn't get up from his crouch or pull the knife away to safety.

"The game is up," Liam said with a calm he didn't feel. "It's time to go. No one needs to get hurt."

Roman's face rose to meet Liam's gaze. The man's brown eyes looked darker than Liam remembered. Emotionless except for a deep-seated hatred that bordered on insanity.

"Mr. Liam Rowen. I admit to being surprised to see you here." Roman slid the blade over Jaz's rope, nicking apart another fiber. "You should leave, though. This is a private sort of party."

"Is it?" Liam's gaze surveyed everything at once. The madman standing in front of him. The fraying rope. The way Jaz's iron discipline kept her from moving about despite the terror that must be surging through her veins. Despite everything, Liam couldn't suppress a rush of pride. How many trained soldiers would have started flailing by now, putting strain on a rope that couldn't bear any more insult? Returning his attention to Roman, Liam reached into the inside pocket of his jacket—the same one he'd worn to the Cosmopolitan—and pulled out his sidearm. "Change of plans. Get the hell away from her."

Roman's upper lip pulled back, his teeth glistening in the sunlight.

Liam pulled back the Sig's hammer, the front sight now lined up squarely with Roman's chest. The gun's familiar weight felt right in his hand, and his heart tapped an even, rhythmic pulse. One wrong step and Liam would pull the trigger. It was as simple and clear as that. "Drop the knife."

Roman's hand tightened around the blade, his knuckles white.

Liam started to squeeze the trigger.

"Stop!" The knife fell away from Roman's hand and clattered to the stone. "Fine. Fuck. Whatever. You're an insane man." Roman straightened as he spoke, raising his hands. "If you want this bitch so badly, she's all yours. I've got a competition to finish."

Beside Roman, Jaz was already pulling herself back up onto the ledge. *Good girl.*

"Kick the knife toward me," Liam told Roman.

Roman's foot swung obediently, sliding the knife toward Liam and—

Gaining momentum, Roman twisted and struck Jaz square in the chest just as her knees cleared the lip of the ledge.

Jaz screamed and fell back over, jerking the rope. The rope fibers gave an ominous creak.

Holstering his weapon, Liam sprinted a few steps to the edge where Jaz had partially caught herself on the stone, taking some of the pressure off the ripping line. Liam grabbed hold of Jaz's harness just as her safety line gave out completely. Hauling Jaz up, Liam pressed her against his chest and drew desperate gulps of air as the reality of what had almost happened hit. Behind him, he could hear

Roman scampering away along the mountain, the chopper still hovering overhead. Though the radio earpiece was still firmly settled into Liam's left ear, the chatter of Kurt updating base camp control seemed both distant and irrelevant. "Jaz," he whispered.

She pulled away from his chest, her dirt-and-blood-smudged face as beautiful as ever. "Liam?"

Unable to stop himself, Liam covered her mouth with his. She parted her lips for him, and he plunged inside, tasting her sweetness with a kiss that channeled all his desperation and hope and fear. And she kissed him back. It was over in seconds, and Jaz's breath was as ragged as Liam's own when they pulled apart and stared at each other. Liam knew this wasn't forgiveness or absolution of the past, but an acknowledgment of the now. The joy of being alive. And that was the most he could ask for.

"What are you doing here?" Jaz asked.

"Long story." He swallowed, not caring about the open mic. "One that ends with me saying I'm sorry for being an absolute idiot who tried to push you away." Tucking a lock of her hair behind Jaz's ear, Liam traced his thumb gently along her cheek. It was the most he'd let himself do, and he savored every touch of her skin. The way her scent and presence filled a void in his soul.

Jaz's throat bobbed as she swallowed.

"I'll climb with you if you still think you have a chance," Liam offered. He didn't care that he was dressed in a business suit with some safety gear from the chopper quickly thrown on over the Armani tailoring. Didn't care how unprepared he was. If Jaz needed him to climb, he would. Even though he wanted nothing more than to bundle her to the nearest ER to be checked out instead.

Jaz let out a small chuckle. "I'm fairly certain that at this point…" The humor faded from her face with thundering suddenness, her hand tightening around Liam's biceps. "Roman. Where is he?"

Liam frowned. "Ran off. What—"

"He's obsessed with winning this thing. And he kept talking about leveling the playing field. I don't know if he has a weapon in his pack somewhere. He sabotaged my safety gear, Liam. I don't know what access he had to the others' packs, or even if that was his way of *leveling* the field, but—"

"Got it." Liam held up a hand, halting Jaz midsentence, and raised his voice. "Rowen to Kurt."

"Kurt," the pilot's response came quickly through the earpiece.

"Survey the area. Do any climbers appear to be having gear issues?"

A pause. "Negative."

"Have base camp call in the possibility of gear tampering to every team."

"Understood."

Liam nodded to Jaz. "Also, do you have eyes on Roman Robillard?" he asked Kurt.

This time, the pause was longer. "Negative. I can't see him."

"His pack is gone too," Jaz said, reading Liam's expression and looking around the ledge. "I don't know what he's capable of just now, but he isn't in his right mind. We need to find him."

She was right, and Liam knew better than to argue the *we* part. Taking a carabiner off his harness, Liam slid it over a loop in Jaz's, attaching them both together. "Then let's take a flight and look," he said, tying them into the helicopter's tether cord. "Hang tight."

Pulling Jaz tightly against him, Liam signaled Kurt to take the slack up from the line. The helicopter obediently moved away from the mountain, plucking the pair of them together into the air. With her arms around Liam, Jaz whooped in pleasure, her joyful holler cut short as an explosion shook the mountain below.

LIAM

*L*iam's arms tightened around Jaz as stones rained down onto the platform they'd lifted off moments ago. Four pairs of climbers, eight living bodies, all came off the mountain face at once, dangling above the ground from the safety lines. Screams and curses filled the air, the chaos a contrast to the monotone reporting Kurt sent through the earpiece. The pilot still had no eyes on Roman, and the sky would soon be filled with helicopters from the national news, all flocking like vultures toward the sounds of carnage.

Strapped into his rig, Jaz clung to Liam with a death grip that made moving about difficult. Liam's heart went out to her. First, the truck explosion and the nightmares it brought, and now the realization that the partner she'd been climbing with had explosives right in his pack. Explosives that could have gone off at any time. How was he to tell Jaz that he had to leave her now to go find Roman, lest the asshole had a deadlier arsenal up his sleeve?

"Liam." Jaz shifted in his hold, but instead of seeking comfort, she pointed back toward the mountain. Liam twisted to look at what had caught her attention.

One of the climbers, the lanky surfer-looking kid with blond hair and playful eyes, wasn't flailing around like the others. Instead of fighting for purchase, the kid now hung limply on the rope. Blood trickled down his face and saturated his shirt while his partner clung with desperate paralysis to a piece of stone he'd managed to snag.

Of all things to bring Jaz out of her own terror, it was the sight of someone else who needed help. This was why he loved her.

"That's Corey. Can we grab him?"

Liam shook his head. "Can't get the helicopter that close without hitting the propellers. That's why we swung so far away. Kurt called in search and rescue."

"They can fly closer?"

"No."

Despite hanging off a helicopter tether hundreds of feet above the ground, Jaz managed to give him a reproachful look.

"They should be able to land over there." Liam pointed to a large flat portion of the mountain. "Then climb down the rest of the way."

"That's over an hour's climb," said Jaz. The slight trembling of her muscles was calming now as her attention was focused on a hurt opponent. "I don't think Corey has that long. What about the Ballerina's Skirt?"

Liam considered the treacherous ledge that encircled the mountain like a tutu, intersecting with all the climbing routes Jaz had originally set up. In fact, he'd already marked the place as a starting point to patrol for Roman—but while it had good top clearance for a chopper and was a fun technical climb from down up, climbing it from top down, especially without the right equipment, was an exercise in suicide.

As if reading his mind, Jaz gestured toward the skirt. "I can do it. I can make the climb. Fifteen minutes and I'll be at Corey's side."

"Absolutely not. Are you insane?" He hadn't meant for the words to come out as roughly as they did and wished he could take them back the moment he'd heard what he said. But it was too late. Jaz had already stiffened in his arms, pulling away from him without moving a muscle. "Jaz... I just don't want to see you hurt. I just meant——"

"I'm clear on what you meant."

Liam's stomach tightened at the very thought of Jaz on that stone wall, one wrong move away from disaster. "Dead rescuers help no one. It's too dangerous." He took a breath. "I'm not even trying it. And believe me, I would if I thought it was possible."

"You can't make that climb," Jaz said matter-of-factly, her attention on the mountain. There was no boasting or panic in her voice. No excitement. Just professional calculation. "You don't have the skill, Liam. I do. I'm not asking for your permission. I'm asking for your trust and a ride. Will you give it to me or not?"

This was it. The line in the sand and the soul. Fear closed Liam's throat, but he'd made the mistake of forcing Jaz down the path of his choice once, and he knew better than to do it again. Especially because Jaz was right about one thing—she was infinitely more qualified to make this decision than he was.

Liam reached up to his headset. "Kurt. We have a change of plan. Update rescue that we're sending a climber down."

To his credit, the pilot only gave a brief curse under his breath before changing course and setting the pair of them down on the suicide ledge. Reaching into himself for the operational calm he and Jaz both needed, Liam gave her a crash course in helicopter rescue operations. "Kurt is going to hold the bird as still as he can, but you need to be aware that you can still be jerked off the rock face. Make sure there's nothing in the way for you to slam into." Taking off his radio and earpiece, he attached them to Jaz. "The mic is live, so just speak normally and——" Liam cut off as a movement along the side of his vision caught his attention. He spun around, his weapon out.

Nothing was there. Just loose stones.

"Liam," said Jaz, her voice higher than usual.

He turned back. And found Roman holding a blade to her neck.

"I was wondering how long it would take you to get here," Roman said, his gaze surveying Liam, the gun, and finally, the sky. Instead of fear, the scene appeared to inject energy into the man.

He spoke more quickly than before, his words tripping over each other. "The last time, you misunderstood. How it all is. Will be. But we're going to correct that."

Liam held still. With the initial shock of surprise behind him, he could now see a remote control device in Roman's free hand. Given that the man had already caused one explosion, there was no reason to doubt he would set off the next. Worse still, Roman's pupils were now so dilated that Liam suspected he'd taken drugs for courage before sending the last explosion breaking up the stone. "What do you want?" Liam asked, keeping his voice even.

"I've already explained it." Roman's face darkened. "A fair competition. Which is what we have now, provided you don't interfere. No gear. No buddy system. Just a race of skill to the top."

In Roman's hold, Jaz let her hands drop to her harness and fingered the gear attached to the various loops. She wasn't usually given to fidgeting, and Liam had to trust that if she was doing so now, she had a plan in mind. That meant his job was to buy her time. To follow her lead. Even if he was following it blind. "No interference intended," Liam said. "We just came to try and get the injured climber out. The surfer boy down there. He's unconscious."

"He'll be fine," Roman barked. "And we both know you can't make the climb down from here, so don't bother lying. I know you came here to hunt me down. You thought you were so smart. Knowing that I'd have to climb the Ballerina's Skirt. Thinking of snatching me here. But that's not how things are going to go." He waved the detonator for emphasis, his words tripping over each other. "You will do what I say. Exactly what I say. Or there will be bodies falling."

Jaz gave a small show of struggling against the knife at her throat, while quietly pulling an anchor from her belt. The small device in hand, she slipped it into a stone crack by her hip, one so hidden that Liam hadn't even noticed it was there. But Jaz had.

Liam lifted his hands in surrender, the gun now pointing toward the sky. "All right," he said, keeping eye contact with Roman. Keeping the man talking while Jaz finished anchoring herself into the mountain with an expertise Liam hadn't given her enough credit for. "What do you want?"

"Everyone climbs. Even you. Everyone on the mountain is going up to the top. That's where the media is waiting. No gear. No toys. No partners." Roman's hands shook as he spoke. "Everyone goes up! The press covers it. Or I detonate the other charge. Have your pilot relay that to everyone."

"Where should we all go?" Liam asked. "The original routes ended in different places."

Roman hesitated.

"How about the summit?" Liam suggested before the man could get agitated from the indecision. "We could all go there. A clear winner. What do you think?"

As Roman considered the suggestion, Jaz detached the helicopter tether from her harness and clipped it to Roman's. Now she was connected to the mountain and Roman to the chopper, but the detonator and knife were still in Roman's hold. Her gaze found Liam's. Darted to the gun. *Shoot him,* she mouthed.

Liam didn't hesitate. Twisting the weapon back into his grip, he found the front sight and depressed the trigger in a single smooth motion. The Sig Sauer went bump in his hand, the sound of the discharge echoing over the mountaintops as blood spilled from Roman's wrist and covered his fingers.

The detonator fell first. Then Roman staggered backward, the knife falling from his hand. As he went over the edge, however, he still took Jaz with him—until the two tethers pulled their bodies apart from each other.

Liam rushed to the edge, grabbing Jaz's rope to haul her back up. His pulse pounded as he ran his hands over her, the number of things that could have gone wrong now replaying themselves in his mind. In his blood. "You *are* insane," he breathed.

"And you're a decent shot." She let out a staggered breath. "I didn't think you'd be able to get his hand without at least grazing me."

Liam swallowed, brushing her hair from her face, though the wind kept swinging the locks right back onto her sun-kissed skin.

"Well, going through you would have been an easier shot, but I just figured we still need to rescue Corey, and I'm certainly not climbing down this thing. So, you know…"

Jaz laughed. He'd just offered that she risk her life again, and she laughed, because she was Jaz, and he finally understood her.

JAZ

*J*az shivered in Liam's arms as all the climbers were evacuated to the base point, where the Clash of the Titans had started only hours ago. The majestic mountains in the background no longer gave off a peaceful feel, and despite her app's assurance that the temperature was holding steady, she felt cold to the bone. Fortunately, the shivering hadn't started until Corey was safely airlifted to the trauma center, but now that it had taken hold, it refused to leave her in peace.

She'd started this morning, with one goal: to win a climbing competition. And then, before the sun had fully reached its zenith, she'd just wanted to end the day alive. To ensure that others did too. Even Roman, who, so far as she knew, was now being kept on a psych observation hold. But now that it was over, now that it hit her just how easily things could have gone in the other direction, she was...cold.

Getting ahold of herself, she twisted up to see Liam's face. They were sitting on the ground, a blanket beneath them, while the climbers with greater injuries were herded toward the waiting ambulance. Checking in with her body, Jaz knew she too was hurt, but it wasn't terrible. And she didn't want to deal with it just now.

Especially since, in all the excitement, she was yet to find out what the hell Liam had been doing in a chopper to begin with.

"So, want to give me some background to this cinematic rescue?" she asked. "And since when do you wear business suits when jumping out of helicopters?"

"Since I was wearing one while having a chat with Lucius." Liam picked at the ruined Armani. "The good colonel confirmed that Obsidian Ops blew up my truck, but everything pointed to Roman posing the real danger. So when Lucius told me Roman was your climbing partner, I decided a wardrobe change wasn't worth the time."

"So you're saying you came because Lucius told you to."

Liam snorted. "Maybe I should put him back on my Christmas card list." The hint of humor faded from his face. "You have no idea how scared I was that you might get hurt. Hell, I had no idea I could be that scared."

She bit her lip as everything fell back into place. Liam had pushed her away when he thought it best and then reversed course when new intelligence came in. Despite everything that had happened, nothing had changed between them, even if—for that brief time on the mountain—she'd imagined it had.

Stop moping like a lost puppy... Liam's voice called in her memories. *I'm not the man you need, and you're certainly not the woman I want.*

She pulled away from him, returning herself to reality. To common sense. Liam was doing exactly what he'd promised Kyan he would—trying to protect her. He hadn't come here for her, he'd come to neutralize a threat. And absent Roman's antics, he'd still be in Denton Valley.

So if Jaz didn't want another stab in the heart like she'd received in Liam's conference room, she needed to put some distance between them.

Fool me once, shame on you. Fool me twice, shame on me.

"I'm glad you got the word in time," she said as she stood, straightened her dirt-and-blood-smeared climbing jacket. "Without you, the day would have ended differently. I'm going to go see whether they need anything else from me today and then head back to the hotel."

Liam rose to stand beside her. "I'll go with you."

"You should stay here." She held out a hand to stop him. "Someone will certainly have more questions for you, and I imagine whose-ever chopper you borrowed will want their toy back."

"Jaz——" He reached for her, his arms dropping to his sides when she stepped out of reach. "I'm sorry for what I said before. I really am. I thought being near me would put you in danger, so I said whatever I could to make you leave. It wasn't true. I want to be with you. Like I've never wanted to be with anyone."

"No." She took another step back from him, gently shaking her head. "What you want is a damsel in distress."

A devastated look crossed Liam's face, but Jaz knew better than to fall for that beautiful heart-wrenching gaze again. Liam was who he was. And she was grown up enough now to accept it.

"Do you mind telling Kyan that I'm all right?" she asked briskly. All business. It was the only way of keeping the stinging in her eyes from spilling free. "I know he's worried, but I'm just not up for reliving everything with him over the phone—and you know he won't stop pressing until he's evaluated every detail."

"Of course."

"Great." Jaz made herself smile and held her hand out to shake his, trying not to savor the steady, reliable feel of his palm. "I'll see you later, then. Thank you again for all you did. Truly. If there's a way I can repay you, just... Just have someone from Trident Security reach out."

JAZ ACCEPTED the Vector Ascent rep's offer of fresh clothes and a ride to urgent care, promised the nurse practitioner who saw her to follow up with a doctor if anything felt worse, and called an Uber to take her back to the hotel. It was easier to be with a stranger than alone with herself just now, and she asked him to take an extra lap around the city before dropping her off. Even then, she veered off to a coffee shop, striking up an irrelevant conversation with the barista just to keep from being alone with her mind—because no matter what she did, Liam wasn't far from her thoughts.

She knew she'd made the right decision to walk away, because any more time in Liam's company would have torn apart the stitches holding her heart together. She hated admitting it, even to herself, but she knew that she'd always been in love with Liam Rowen. But she needed a partner who'd be there to push her forward, not just help her up.

She couldn't be with him. And she wouldn't be returning to Denton Valley anyway. Her apartment was gone. Her graduate school enrollment canceled. Her Vector Ascent sponsor and the PR person from the Clash of the Titans had already started blowing up her phone with invitations to talk shows. They had a whole spin to the story they wanted her to champion. *Female Climber Survives a Mountain Assault and Saves Her Competitor's Life*. She even had emails from several literary agents wanting the story and promising to hire the best ghostwriters to pen the words. They were all good offers, and Jaz needed the money. Yet her soul couldn't get excited for them.

Her phone vibrated. Since she had it in privacy mode, it alerted her only for the few people in her white list—basically the climbing officials and Sebastian. Biting her lip, she shut it off without answering and headed for the hotel. She needed to think more.

The side-door keypad turned green in recognition of Jaz's room key, and she stepped into the pastel-colored corridor, trying to focus on the mountain photographs that decorated the place. Maybe she could take up nature photography on her PR circuit. Would that fill the growing hole in her chest? She tried to imagine herself with cameras in her climbing pack as she took the stairs to the second floor, found her door and stepped inside what should have been an empty room.

Except it wasn't.

Jaz couldn't tell what exactly tipped her off, but she knew at once that she wasn't alone. Her heart stuttered, then rushed into a gallop, her limbs tight and tingling with the sudden flow of strength and blood. Time seemed to slow around her, her ears picking up every creak of the floor. Every scuffle of boots. Though she'd never taken up Liam's offer of self-defense lessons, her fingers rolled into fists even as a blood-curdling scream started to make its way up her throat.

A hand clamped over her mouth.

Jaz bit into it. Tasted blood.

"Holy shit on a stick," a familiar voice hissed in pain. "I like biting and all, but this isn't exactly the right venue."

Holy shit indeed. Jaz gasped for breath over her pounding pulse.

"Promise not to scream if I let go?" said Liam.

She shook her head.

The pressure on Jaz's face disappeared anyway, the shape in the darkness stepping back from her. Liam's shape. Liam's voice.

Now that Jaz's eyes were adjusting to the dimness, she realized the hotel room wasn't altogether as dark as it seemed after first walking in from a brightly lit hallway. A few feet away, Liam ran his hand through his short-cropped hair, then sucked on his index finger, which was showing droplets of blood.

"You don't have rabies, do you?" he asked. "I hate shots."

"I'm going to murder you in your sleep," Jaz vowed, then crossed her arms over her chest. "What the hell are you doing here? And how did you get in here?"

He motioned to the window. "It's only the second floor. I didn't actually mean to scare the daylights out of you."

"No? So you were laying siege in the darkness by freakin' accident?"

"No." Liam flipped the nearest light switch. Nothing happened. He then pointed toward the little cardholder near the door. "The electricity only works when your card is inserted. I didn't really have a choice about that. You weren't answering your phone, and it's not like the front desk would have made me a key if I asked really nicely."

"That's because maybe, I don't know, I didn't invite you." Jaz stuck her room key into the trigger mechanism, and the lights obediently came to life. She crossed to the other end of the room from Liam and leaned against the wall. "What are you doing here, Liam?"

After walking over to the table, Liam pulled out one of the two chairs and sat. "Getting the next best thing to scheduling an appointment with you. You did say Trident Rescue and Security can give you a call if we need help. And we need help."

Jaz cocked a brow. "Yes, you do. But I know nothing about being a shrink."

"I'm serious. I'm offering you a job."

"Because security is such a strong point on my résumé?"

"I wouldn't trust you to run security for my neighbor's cat," Liam said bluntly. "But I'm not offering you a job in security."

Jaz crossed her arms. "Are you expanding into knitting, then? Because I can make a mean scarf."

Liam signed. "All right. Let's try this a different way." Picking up a folder she'd failed to notice before, he now slid it across the table to Jaz. "Now that Trident Rescue isn't just a hobby for a few friends, we've needed to get new personnel on board. These are the copies of safety certifications, gear schedules, and call-out reports from the new cadre of mountain search and rescue operators we brought on in the past six months. Open it and tell me what you think."

Jaz opened the manila folder. "There's nothing in here."

"Yes. So I've been told. I've also been told this is a problem."

She stared at him. Trident Rescue had been a huge part of her brother's life for years, but once Bar was born, he had to take a step back from the shifts. Apparently, so did the others, and no one had stepped in to fill the void. "I thought Aiden——"

"Aiden doesn't run rescue." Something dark entered Liam's voice. "Please don't ask why."

Jaz nodded, her mind racing all over again. The irony of being offered a job when she finally *didn't* desperately need one wasn't lost on her. "Thank you, but I've already has offers from Vector Ascent and Clash of the Titans both. Your charity is no longer required."

"Good. Because I don't put people's lives on the line for fucking charity." Liam rose and strode over to her, his shoulders spreading. "Do you want to be a talking head on TV, being paraded around like some bejeweled poodle, or do you want to climb, Jaz? You said I wanted a damsel in distress—but I think you haven't looked in a mirror lately.

"I saw you today. You *needed* to rescue Corey. You savored pushing your skills for the sake of others. And even when Roman threatened your life, you protected his. That fire and drive that lives inside you, it doesn't burn for talk shows and endorsements. It burns for making a real difference. We're the same that way, you and I. That damsel of yours, we don't want her in danger—but if she *is* in danger, we want to be there to help."

Jaz's breath caught as she stared up at him. At the utter deadly seriousness of his features that stilled and waited while the impact of his words—of the truth—found their marks. Because Liam was right. Somehow, while she thought he was looking at her as little more than a project, he'd managed to see into her soul and find her true calling. An identity that fit her inner flame the way nothing else did. And one she'd never understood before.

"You...you would really let me take charge of the search and rescue?" Jaz whispered. "Of the climbers going out into the mountains?"

He didn't blink an eye. Didn't hesitate. "Yes."

"Don't you need to ask other people first?"

"Being the owner comes with perks. Getting to hire who I want when I want is one of those."

Jaz blew out a long breath, her mind spinning. "I could build up my own cadre?" She couldn't believe she was really considering this. "Make the decisions? Plan the rescue routes?"

"Yes." Again, there was no hesitation.

She swallowed. "And what if I make a decision with which you disagree? Are you going to stride in and pull me off a case because you want to keep me safe?"

Liam tilted his head, considering the question for a few heartbeats before answering. "I have control of the company and the ultimate responsibility for everyone who works there. So yes, I'll have the power to yank you back if I think it needs to be done. But it would be no different from how I'd treat Kyan or

Aiden or anyone else if they were in the same position. Is that fair?"

That actually was fair, and everything inside Jaz tingled with a mix of hope and excitement that neither Vector's nor Titans' offers had. What Liam proposed, it was perfect for her. He was giving her the mountains. Her friends in Denton Valley. Her destiny. All she needed to do was say yes.

And then to work with Liam day in and day out. To be near him, without being with him. Because he wasn't part of the deal.

I'm not the man you need, and you're certainly not the woman I want.

A weight settled around her chest, closing her throat. "I can't do this," she whispered. "Liam, thank you. Truly. You offered me the world. But I can't accept it. I'm sorry."

Silence filled the room, loud as thunder.

Liam's jaw tightened.

Jaz turned her back to him, her eyes overfilling. "Can you please leave now?"

She could hear him shifting his feet. Stepping away. Stopping. "I love you."

Jaz froze, Liam's words startling her so much that she forgot to control the tears that now spilled onto her cheeks.

"I love you," Liam repeated into her back. "I tried not to. Hell, until I met you, I didn't think I was even capable of falling in love. But then you came into my life and changed all the rules. And then, I was so terrified that I shoved you away. It was stupid. I was stupid. I still am, aren't I?" He sucked in a breath and exhaled on a long, slow stream of air that made a swooshing sound between his teeth. "Anyway. I imagine none of that matters to you now, but I still wanted you to know the whole truth of it before you make the decision to walk out of my life."

Jaz turned slowly, shocked to find Liam's eyes glistening as he looked at her.

"What did you say?" she whispered, her heart still.

Liam lifted his face, owning his words. "I love you, Jaz Keasley. I don't just want you to work with me, I want you to *be* with me. Forever."

Jaz's stilled heart resumed its pounding, sending warmth to every part of her body. She didn't notice taking the few steps to cover the floor between them. All she knew was that one moment she was staring at his vulnerable, beautiful face, and the next, she was right beside him, her hands spread over his chest. "I love you too, Liam," she whispered. "And I want to be with you. More than anything."

He closed his eyes for a moment as a blissful peace came over his features, then lowered his face toward hers, gently brushing her lips with his own.

Jaz's lips parted, and she stood on her toes to meet his deepening kiss with her own.

42

AIDEN

"*W*hen the targets turn, you will have five seconds to draw your weapon and fire four rounds," the voice from range control announced over Aiden's headset. He shifted into his firing stance, his hand ready to snatch the Glock from his holster. In the back of his mind, ghosts of memories that were never far from his consciousness nowadays continued to play like an old movie.

He was in the woods of the Scottish Highlands, his uniform devoid of anything to connect him back to the Scottish Black Watch. It had recently rained, and there was heavy moisture in the air. The smell of wet earth and bark. He moved quietly through the darkness, high-night-vision scope showing the world in shades of black and green. He was alone.

Except he wasn't.

But by the time he figured that out, it had been too late.

Aiden's headphones crackled, the voice from the tower filling his ears again. "Is the line ready?"

Though Aiden couldn't see behind him, he knew the range safety officers were looking up and down the line and giving the tower a thumbs-up to indicate it was safe to continue. The outdoor range Liam contracted for Trident Security was stringent on safety protocols.

"The line *is* ready," the tower announced. "Shooters, watch your targets."

He was in the woods of the Scottish Highlands, his uniform devoid of anything to connect him back to the Scottish Black Watch. It had recently rained, and there was heavy moisture in the air. The smell of wet earth and—

The target turned to present itself, and Aiden's mind cleared, his focus entirely on the target silhouette. He drew his weapon. Fired into paper.

Pow pow.

Pow pow.

Done with a second to spare before the target turned away again, all the rounds hitting the center. Aiden holstered his gun and awaited the next instruction, the concentration muting the memories. There was a catharsis to the firing range. To its simple, precise mission.

Mind the target. Find the front sight. Smooth weapon draw. Smooth trigger pull. Smooth reload. Repeat.

Aiden needed the firing range's respite more than usual today, thanks to the call from his mother in Scotland. Turned out that Briar and Cassey—his twin cousins who'd moved to the States as kids—were getting out of Delta Force in a few months. Surely Aiden would be happy to host them while they figured out what to do next with their lives? Maybe he could even put in a good word with Trident Security? And wouldn't it be fun to have the boys all together?

Aiden had left the bloody continent to get away from his family. Their questions. And they somehow were managing to get their snares right back around him. Didn't the damn Delta Force have some kind of transition back to civilian life program? Didn't Briar and Cassey have anything better to do than track Aiden to Denton Valley, Colorado?

"All right, shooters. This ends our course of fire," the tower announced all too soon. "Clear your guns and holster a safe and empty weapon. Ensure your name is logged so we can record your qualification scores."

He was in the woods of the Scottish Highlands, his uniform devoid of anything to connect him back to the Scottish Black Watch. It had recently rained, and the air—

Aiden shoved the movie reel further into the depth of his mind. Forgoing marking his target, he instead grabbed a plastic bucket to get a head start on cleaning the range of brass. The sooner everything was clean of empty shells, the sooner he could shoot again. With luck, he could get his head back on straight before Liam returned from his rescue mission. The man was too observant by nature, and it was only his recent preoccupation with Jaz that had kept Aiden safe from landing squarely in Liam's sights.

"By my count, son, you've qualified at least eight times this morning alone." One of the firearms safety officers—a retired gunnery sergeant named Jim—leaned his hip against the table where Aiden was now reloading. "Something on your mind?"

"No, sir." Aiden didn't glance up from his task. "Just keeping my skills sharp. Bad guys don't care about qualification scores."

"That they don't," Jim agreed, taking off his red safety officer cap and wiping sweat off the bald spot beneath. That was a bad sign. It meant Jim was in a chatting mood. And once Jim got started, it could be difficult to escape. "You know, if you enjoy the range so much, maybe you should become an instructor. We always need good people out here."

"Thank you, sir, but I already have a job." Aiden glanced around and hid a wince. The way the range was clearing out, it would soon be only Jim and him left. That meant more conversation. More questions. "I'm afraid you're right, though. I need to get back to doing Liam's job for the wee bastard."

"Running Trident Rescue and Security from the boss's penthouse suite? A hardship, I'm sure." Jim laughed.

Aiden gave the man a noncommittal shrug. He couldn't exactly begrudge Liam the rescue trip, but Aiden was quickly discovering that, despite a knack for organization, he didn't enjoy playing boss and would happily trade it all in for the basic grunt work. He needed to be out doing things. Protecting people. Rendering explosives safe. Hell, he didn't even mind surveillance. But putting out administrative fires and smiling at idiots instead of shooting them? Liam needed to take that part back. Now.

But Liam was still in California sorting out his soul mate attempted murder, which, while a respectable reason to be out of communication, still made Aiden feel no better three hours later as he sat in Liam's office and got yelled at by Denton EMS.

"Yes, I understand that even though Trident Rescue provides services pro bono, Denton EMS still needs copies of everyone's certifications on file," Aiden said into the phone for the fifth time in as many minutes. He got up to pace across the room. "And I'm telling you, it will be handled as soon as Liam Rowen gets back. In the meantime, you can call us for help or not call us for help. But those are your two bloody choices."

He put the phone away from his ear as the dispatcher from the office of Denton Valley's central emergency services went off into another rant, then just hung up on her.

Dropping into the leather chair, Aiden massaged his temples, checked his email, and swore aloud.

It was Liam, checking in to say that Jaz was safe, but they would be taking an extra couple of days in California to deal with the fallout of Roman's attacks.

This was bad news all around. Aiden glared at the office door. It was closed. Aiden hated that, but there were too many phone calls to deal with, and the noise scraped the nerves of Liam's assistant, who sat outside the office.

Well, hearing noises in the hallway and being unable to see what was happening scraped *Aiden's* nerves. Who said that was any less important?

As if having heard his displeasure, the door started to open. Which it really shouldn't have. Aiden reached for the sidearm that he was fortunately not wearing and thus managed not to point a gun at the woman who let herself inside.

"Can I help you?" he asked, getting ahold of himself and

watching, with some misplaced satisfaction, as Liam's sister jumped in surprise.

The woman had obviously been expecting to find the office empty as much as he'd expected a lack of unannounced visitors.

Lisa, after the briefest second of disorientation, straightened herself primly. "Yes. Liam wants me to take care of family dinner today. He said I was to get some money out of petty cash?"

Aiden weighed her with his gaze, feeling her do the same to him. She had Liam's intelligent brown eyes and stubborn set of jaw, but whereas Liam carried himself with spread-shouldered openness, his sister's back was already curling again, and she emanated an almost palpable aura of perpetual discontent.

"Liam is in California," said Aiden. "I doubt he'll be home in time for family dinner."

"I never said he was invited."

"How did ye get past Mrs. Norris?"

"The secretary? She moved desks. Something about your foul language. Aren't you supposed to be some kind of *security professional?*" Lisa's tone added air quotes to the title.

"Aye."

Lisa snorted. "Figures."

Aiden knew he should leave it at that, but he spoke anyway. "How so?"

"I saw you jump at the door like some scared little girl. It doesn't seem very compatible with keeping anyone safe, does it?"

That wasn't exactly an accurate assessment of the situation, but Aiden was smart enough not to follow Lisa down the rabbit hole this time around. Plus she wasn't entirely wrong. This recently surfaced dislike of closed doors wasn't making his life any easier, and the sooner he got over it, the better. He had to get over it before the twins shoved themselves into his business.

"The money?" Lisa prompted.

Opening the second drawer of Liam's desk, Aiden took out a metal box. "How much did you need?"

"One fifty."

"For a two-person dinner?"

"It's our mom's birthday."

Aiden stopped himself from rolling his eyes. Maybe it was. More likely not. Either way, not his circus, not his monkeys. Liam could afford it and, given what he was doing now, he'd probably appreciate not having his sister on his arse.

Aiden counted out the cash and handed it to Lisa.

She snatched it from his grip. "Don't you go looking at me all judgmental like. You're as much damaged goods as I am. You know what the only difference is between us?"

"There's only one?"

"Only one that matters." Lisa's chin jutted toward Aiden's chest. "My brilliant brother hasn't caught on to you yet."

A shiver ran down Aiden's spine. "You and I are nothing alike. I assure you."

"So that thing where you nearly took my head off just for opening the door? The sleepless circles under your eyes? The way you keep checking the room over and over with your gaze?" She snorted. "You're right. Nothing like me. At least I know that I'm a fucking mess."

Aiden shut the petty cash box, the sound echoing through the office. "Have a good day, Lisa."

Instead of leaving, Lisa propped her hip against the side of the desk. Apparently, the need to dig into other people's business was another trait connecting the siblings. "So what's your story?"

"No story."

"So why are you moping around with pieces of your soul sloughing off, like flesh from an undead zombie?"

"Aren't all zombies undead by definition?"

"So what was it? Was your daddy mean to you growing up? Or was it something else?" She wiggled her brows, waited a beat, then gave up with a shrug. "Whatever. You don't gotta tell me shit. I just wanna know if my brother knows. Maybe it takes a fuckup to see another fuckup, you know?" Lisa dug into her purse, pulling out a small packet of white powder that she threw onto the desk. "Rare to see somebody who needs it more than I do, but there you go."

"Is that what I think it is?" Aiden stared at the cocaine, his gut tightening. After what he'd gone through, even the notion of a substance in his body nauseated him. He didn't even take medicine.

"Probably. Unless you're an even bigger idiot than I think. Like I said, I believe in giving to those in greater need. So, you're welcome."

Aden picked up the bag and was about to hand it back to Lisa, before realizing the stupidity of that particular action. Instead, he reopened the petty cash box and flipped the baggie in there for Liam to deal with. Right after he outright informed him that he accidently handed Lisa drug money. Squeezing his jaws together, Aiden stashed the box away in disgust. Mostly at himself. "You need help," he said quietly.

Lisa's face darkened for a moment as she seemed to teeter on the edge of fury, but then she laughed. "Sure. Why don't we go to your shrink together?"

Aiden flinched.

She snorted. "Not so easy sitting on your high horse, thinking all those loud thoughts about me when you know I can see through you, is it?"

"No. It isn't." Aiden's chest tightened, his fingers tracing the cool polished desk of Liam's table. It was hardly the first time someone had noticed the outward effects of his PTSD, but the naked brutality of Lisa's words had sliced clean through his usual defenses.

Although she had a purse with her, Lisa stuffed the cash she was still holding into the top of her bra and winked without humor. "See you around, sailor." Turning, she headed for the door.

Aiden's world slowed, each of Lisa's steps a countdown to a line of demarcation. He knew that if Liam's sister walked out that door, she wouldn't be heading back to her hotel or wherever she was staying. She would use that hundred and fifty bucks to get a hit and disappear before her family came around asking more questions. Getting into her business. Telling her how she should live her life. Because that was what Aiden would do.

Had done. Had moved to a different bloody continent.

Vaulting over the desk, Aiden caught Lisa's wrist just as she reached for the door. "Wait," he said, taking out his phone. "I'm taking you up on your offer."

Lisa's brow rose in question.

Reaching into his back pocket, Aiden pulled out his cell and dialed Dani's office number. "Hey, it's McDane," he told the psychologist by way of greeting as he put the phone in speaker mode. "Can you work two new patients into your schedule today? It's…it's a bit urgent."

"Absolutely. Do you know the names?"

Aiden captured Lisa's gaze and held it with a hard challenge as he answered. "Aiden McDane and Lisa Rowen."

43

JAZ

"*A*re you sure this is where you want your office?" Liam asked Jaz as they strolled through the Trident Rescue outpost located at the far edge of Denton Valley. "The offer of a top-floor suite downtown is still on the table."

Jaz was hardly listening. She ran her hand along the row of blue metal lockers lining the common area, the metal cool under her skin, then surveyed the rescue gear hanging in neat rows in the adjacent room. It was the best quality on the market. She also had a credit card in her pocket with enough purchasing authority to get anything she thought the Rescue needed, and her mind was already making lists, just as her hands itched to reorganize the ropes. To make the labels bigger and brighter. Under Cullen and Liam, the Rescue had been all about helping those stranded in mountains. But Jaz wanted to take it further, to help people not become victims to begin with. That started with education. Safe climbing expeditions. The right role models.

Denton High School was delighted when Jaz offered them a chance to pilot the new youth program she intended to start.

She turned around in a circle, absorbing the layout. The outpost wasn't large, but it was well loved, with a dispatch area, lockers, break and gear rooms, and a couple of small spaces for treatment and storage. Outside, the Suburban used for callout was parked in an oversized garage. Jaz intended to build a practice wall on the side of the garage to use for climbing demos and to help the kids who might be too scared to go out into mountains to get some confidence.

Realizing that Liam was still waiting for an answer, she gave him a sheepish grin. "Yes. Very sure I want to be here. No one needs mountain rescuing in downtown Denton, and I intend to personally go out on many calls."

"Why am I not surprised?" The corners of Liam's mouth twitched. The bastard had known the answer all along. He was just playing with her. Walking over to the lockers, Liam surveyed the lineup. The names Hunt, Mason, Keasley, and Rowen, the four men who'd founded the rescue, were stenciled on the first four. The names of the new men Jaz had yet to meet headed the others. Reaching into his back pocket, Liam pulled something out and pasted it to a free locker.

J. Keasley. Manager.

Warmth flooded Jaz's chest as Liam stood back to admire his handiwork. Though, with his hands in his back pockets, it was all Jaz could do to keep her mind on business and not on the way his jeans hugged his tight ass.

"Just remember you walked into this mess willingly," said Liam. "Especially when you realize that the reason no one is here right now is because four people all got scheduled for shifts tomorrow, including a new dispatcher. Speaking of you being here. I have something else for you."

Now that was too tempting. Jaz let her gaze drop to his cock. "So I noticed."

Liam laughed. "No. Not that. I mean, that too, but... Oh, never mind. Hold out your hand and close your eyes."

Jaz gave him a suspicious look, but obeyed, then felt something small and metal drop into her hand. Blinking her eyes open without waiting for his permission, she stared at a pair of keys. "What—"

Instead of answering, Liam put his hand on the middle of Jaz's back and guided her out behind the garage, where a new, fully outfitted Jeep Wrangler stood proudly on uneven ground. From the tow package in the back to a grille in the front and extra mounts for gear, it was clearly a vehicle made for work. And it was also bright pink.

Jaz's breath caught. Before she could convince air to return to her lungs, however, Liam nudged her around the truck to the other side, where an equally well-equipped—and pink—ATV stood waiting and ready, a helmet, goggles, and safety jacket laid over the seat.

"Oh my God." Jaz ran her fingers along the machines, feeling their power and Liam's confidence radiating from them. She had never gotten a more perfect gift. Not from anyone.

"I still think pink is stupid, by the way," Liam said good-naturedly. "But I figured it would keep your stuff safe from the vultures who show up to work here. Just please remember that Trident Rescue isn't a solo outfit. You have to let the guys do *something*."

Jaz grinned, trying to hide the sudden discomfort that touched her spine.

"What is it?" Liam asked.

She should have known better than to think he wouldn't notice. Liam always noticed. But how was she to explain how nerve-racking it felt for Kyan's little sister to be taking charge of a crew of former special forces operatives? What exactly was going to happen the first time she gave an instruction they didn't like? Jaz sighed, the look in Liam's eye saying he wouldn't take evasion for an answer.

"I barely come up to your shoulder," she said.

"I noticed."

"I mean," Jaz said, "that in addition to the Rescue's crew roster being a special forces who-is-who directory, everyone is going to tower over me."

"You want a stool?"

"Ugh!" Jaz threw up her hands. "What I'm saying is that I'm not sure the guys will be all that excited to take orders from me."

"No one needs to be excited. They just need to do it."

"Easy for you to say. You just assume that if you're in charge, everybody's going to listen and do what you say."

"Well, pretty much, yes." Liam perched a muscled hip on the seat of Jaz's new quad and beckoned her toward him, until she stood between his splayed knees, the scent of his clean aftershave filling her lungs. "You're an expert in ordering people around, Sprite. I have a standing weekly dinner with Patti as proof."

Jaz chuckled. All right, the part about Liam's mother was true. But with Lisa unexpectedly checked into a rehab facility in Denton Valley—thanks to some kind of backroom deal between her and Aiden—and Patti deciding to stay in the area permanently, it wasn't actually all that difficult to arrange. Plus, Jaz liked Liam's mother, and the feeling was mutual. The sailors and soldiers Trident Rescue employed? They were different animals.

Placing his hands on either side of Jaz's face, Liam lifted her gaze to meet his and ran his thumbs along her cheekbones. His shoulders were spread, his eyes intense and focused. So much so that it made heat prickle all over Jaz's skin.

Despite their time together, Liam's ability to take control with a single look—a single touch—still made Jaz melt with surprise. And pleasure.

"I've seen you work, Sprite." Liam's firm touch made her pay attention to every word. "I've watched you craft routes for world-class climbers. Seen you conquer gravity and the mountain. More importantly, I watched you handle yourself in a crisis. I've no doubt of your capability. No doubt that you're the right person for this. And once the men see, neither will they."

He grinned, releasing some tension from the air between them. "Though might I suggest you begin your acquaintance by taking the group on one of your training runs, with maybe a climb or two to set the tone?"

A chuckle escaped Jaz's chest, taking some of her anxiety with it. Liam believed in her. More than she believed in herself.

"I wouldn't put you in charge if I didn't think you were the right person for the job," he said seriously. "The *best* person for the job. Got it?"

She nodded.

"Speaking of you being in charge..." He gave her a hard look. "I would consider it a personal favor if you restrained yourself from maneuvering any more Trident employees to show up at black-tie charity events wearing running shorts."

Jaz bit her lip to contain a giggle.

Bringing her closer still, Liam covered her mouth with his, sending a blazing heat shooting all the way through her. Her toes tingled. Her back. Her sex. As the tight rod of his erection pushed against her through his zippered jeans, all Jaz could suddenly think of was the moisture now saturating her panties. The way her channel clenched in need that could be sated right here. Right now. On the hood of her brand-new Jeep. Or maybe bent over the seat of the ATV.

She pulled away, panting for breath. "You did that on purpose."

"Mmm." He nuzzled the side of her neck, his breath warm against her skin. "True. But I needed to get a bit of a tactical advantage before this next part." Reaching into his back pocket, Liam pulled out a small velvet box that was designed in the shape of a stone. Flipping it open, he held it toward her with both hands. "I love you, Jaz Keasley. And I want you in my life forever. Would you marry me?"

44

LIAM

*L*iam's heart pounded as Jaz looked at the ring, his entire body poised for her answer. He wanted her so badly. Body and soul and everything in between. The woman standing before him wasn't just a delicious force of nature in and of herself, she made him a better man. A better human. And there was nothing—nothing—on earth that he wanted more than to see Jaz happy.

Which was why the sudden tightness of her shoulders, the way she shifted her weight from foot to foot in a tell of discomfort, made his throat close.

He stepped back, giving her space. Cursing himself for pushing too hard too fast. Moving back into his apartment a couple of weeks earlier turned out to be a smoother transition than either had expected. Maybe because it was their second time around, or because they both hoped she was coming to stay. But everything about her being there, from the warmth of her in his bed to the annoyance of finding her climbing shoes discarded on the couch, felt perfect. Felt like home. At least to him.

"It's all right," Liam said, quickly closing the box. "I'm sorry, I—"

"Wait." Jaz put her hands over his, her face tight. "I didn't say no."

"But you didn't say yes," Liam said gently, his body nearly trembling to keep hold of the emotion as he put the ring away. "I don't want to pressure you into this. Into anything."

Jaz dropped her head, letting out a humorless chuckle. "But that's a problem too, isn't it?"

Liam blinked, confusion flooding his blood. Whatever Jaz meant by that, he needed to know. To understand. "Explain."

Jaz flushed the color of her new toys, her arms wrapping around her shoulders. For all her openness and excitement during intimacy, she was ironically uncomfortable *talking* about sex. It was a trait Liam usually found amusing, but not today. Not when he needed to know what gaping chasm he'd somehow missed.

"Tell me." Liam scrubbed his face, his throat tight. "Please. Just tell me."

"You need a partner you can pressure, don't you?" Jaz said finally, not meeting his eyes. "One you can...um...hurt for your pleasure. I know you've held yourself back and...and I think you would eventually come to resent me for not being able to give you that."

Of all the things Jaz could have said, this one smacked Liam upside the head with surprise. The notion was somewhere between absurd and dangerous. "Where did you get that load of horseshit?"

"From someone who has experience with you." Jaz looked up, her chin rising. That was another thing Liam loved about this woman. She didn't back away from a challenge. "And no, I'm not telling you who. Suffice to say that I know that for all our bedroom fun, you've been holding yourself back."

"Bedroom fun." Liam smirked, crossing his arms. Jaz was an enthusiastic and generous lover, and they were yet to find a room they couldn't turn into a playground of pleasure. Discovering new ways of turning her on was one of his greatest sexual pleasures, and he knew she'd enjoyed the paces he'd put her through thus far. But while he liked the erotic spankings Jaz's body roused to so deliciously, he'd never doled out true pain. Not with her, not with any partner beside a couple of masochists who'd asked him to indulge their fantasy.

His smirk faded, his face growing serious. This wasn't the time for jests or misunderstandings. "What exactly were you told?" he asked. "You can keep the *who* to yourself, but without knowing what it is I'm supposedly holding myself back from, I can hardly provide perspective."

This time, Jaz didn't look away. "When we were at the Shadow Cove, someone told me that you enjoy enforcing some of the harsher rules. That you've left scars. That isn't something—"

"I did *what?*" Liam's eyes flashed, his skin heating with sudden fury. "I ask you again, who the hell told you that?"

"Which part of 'I'm not breaking a confidence' do you find confusing?" Jaz fired back.

He grunted, accepting the blow, then spoke through clenched teeth. "I despise real hurt, Jaz. And I sure as hell wouldn't injure someone on purpose. Though I'm itching to make an exception for whoever told you that. Goddamn it." He shook his head. No wonder their one and only trip to Shadow Cove had done an about-face halfway through. "Why didn't you say anything before?"

She shrugged, and Liam could see her pulse hammering at the side of her neck. "It didn't come up. But when I saw the ring, and the real forever… What if you need things I can't give you? What happens then?"

Liam closed his hands on her hips. "Damn it, Sprite, just watching you bend over your climbing charts gets me so hard, I've had to invest in looser jeans. In fact, I've half a mind to relieve you of yours now, bend you over that ATV seat, and demonstrate my enjoyment with utter thoroughness."

The heat coming off Jaz doubled.

Liam slid his hands up her body until his palms rested on either side of her face. Of her hopeful, worried eyes. Whatever the faulty, vindictive source of her information, he could see that she needed more than words to believe in their compatibility. And more than just another tumble—on an ATV or otherwise. Jaz needed proof.

And there was only one way that Liam could think of making that happen.

Except he didn't particularly like it. But he'd been a fool to think that he could—or should—sweep that part of himself into the darkness. Whatever they decided to do going forward, he needed to show himself to Jaz as much as he asked her to show herself to him.

"There's only one way to get this settled," Liam told her. "And that's at Shadow Cove. Ground zero. I think it's time we explore the mysteries about my pleasures—and yours—that we never fully sorted out. If you trust me enough to come."

"I trust you with my life," Jaz said.

Leaning forward, Liam pressed a kiss to her forehead. "I know, Sprite. But tonight, we find out whether you trust me with your pleasure."

45

JAZ

$\mathcal{W}$alking into Shadow Cove this time was different. Scarier. More intimate. It started with the way Liam's hand splayed between Jaz's shoulder blades as he guided her inside, his presence a steady living force beside her. He wasn't bringing her for a show-and-tell. They were coming here to learn each other's truths.

Without the shield of that distant curiosity, every sound and call of pleasure now prickled over Jaz's skin. Suddenly, she wasn't sure she was worried about what she might discover about Liam, but rather of what she might learn about herself. What they both might learn.

Solana was at the front desk again, the widening of her eyes when she saw Jaz and Liam entering together as good as a confession. The girl avoided Jaz's gaze as she checked them both in and stood aside to let them pass into the main room. When Jaz threw a quick glance over her shoulder, she found Solana watching her with a sour expression.

Capturing the woman's gaze, Jaz gave her a pitiful shake of the head. *I've figured you out. And you are a sad excuse for a human.*

Solena flinched. Good. Message received.

Before Jaz could dwell further on the lying receptionist, however, they were in the main room, dim lights and upbeat music filling the space. It was near 11:00 p.m., and the Cove bustled with patrons in various states of undress and clever attire, much of which made Jaz's barely ass-covering black dress look positively modest. The dress was a last-minute present from Liam, who insisted on watching her get into it.

By the time she was done squirming into the fabric, they had nearly scrapped the rest of their evening plans.

Now, as they stood at the edge of the space, Liam's hand slid down along her spine to rest on the curve of her backside. Jaz shifted her weight. The feeling of Liam's firm, callused palm was already making her sex clench, and they hadn't taken a dozen steps inside yet. Drawing in a calming breath, Jaz took in the evening. The gentle murmur of conversation, the distinct sounds of sex and slaps of flesh rose and fell with the music. On the left side of the room, a woman with impressive acrobatics was taking full advantage of a stripper pole. Despite the admiring audience, the woman appeared to be bending and dancing and climbing for her own private enjoyment.

Meanwhile, a hot wax demonstration was taking place on the center stage, while a couple along the right wall made use of a spanking bench. The woman lying across it made mewling sounds of protest as her partner heated her bare upturned backside, but—despite the yelps—Jaz noticed the woman's ass rising eagerly to meet each spank.

Jaz looked away, hating how the way just watching that scene made moisture slither into her panties.

"See something you like?" Liam murmured into her ear, which made Jaz's face turn furnace hot. Of course he noticed. He always noticed. "I would enjoy doing that to you. And if you vex me a bit, I might add a little something between those cheeks to help focus your attention." Just in case she hadn't understood what *cheeks* he was referring to, Liam lifted the back of Jaz's dress to slide his hand into her panties and along the curve of her ass.

And then left it there.

Jaz's breath caught. Liam had threatened anal play in the bedroom, but Jaz thought she'd gotten him off the scent with feigned denial of interest. Apparently, her acting hadn't been nearly as convincing as she'd thought, and today, he wasn't pulling punches in voicing truths aloud.

"Good evening."

Jaz jumped as Dior materialized through the crowd, adjusting his suit as he nodded a greeting to them both. She waited for Liam to draw back his hand, but he kept it right where it was.

"I'm pleased to see you're back," Dior continued, as if nothing out of the ordinary was happening. "Is there anything you need?"

"No, thank you," Jaz answered breathlessly.

Liam squeezed her ass. "Actually, I wouldn't mind borrowing that riding crop of yours, if you don't mind. If you and Tiffany aren't using it just now."

Jaz swallowed.

Dior grinned and tilted his head forward in agreement. "It would be my pleasure," he said, his voice rolling with that French *r*. "If you want to get started, I'll have someone fetch it for you. It's freshly cleaned and in my locker."

With a too-casual thanks, as if he'd just asked to borrow a cup of sugar and not a riding crop turned sex toy, Liam guided Jaz to a semiprivate alcove not far from the spanking scene. By the time they came to a stop, the mix of excitement, embarrassment, and anxiety had so saturated Jaz's blood that the room seemed to sway around her.

"Look at me." Liam was suddenly in front of her, his broad shoulders taking up her entire field of view. Taking her face between his hands, Liam repeated himself, his low command sending a new shiver of desire through her. "Everything we do here is for pleasure. Yours and mine. I'll make you a bit nervous today, but I never want you to be scared. Not of me. Anything you truly want to stop, stops with a single word. You understand?"

"Yes," Jaz whispered.

Leaning forward, Liam pressed his mouth over her open lips, taking a luxurious kiss. With his tongue rolling possessively over her mouth, Jaz didn't realize that Liam had slid his hands along her bare arms until he was already holding her wrists and was raising them slowly and sensually above her head.

"What are you doing?" Jaz asked, feeling him transfer her wrists into one hand. His other, she now saw, was pulling a pink silk scarf from his pocket.

His lips brushed her ear. "Thinking some very explicit thoughts about how to best make you scream in ecstasy." As he said it, Liam efficiently wrapped the silk cloth around Jaz's wrists and tied the knot off on a metal ring dangling from the ceiling. A moment later, Liam pulled loose the knots holding the straps of her dress on her shoulders so the material floated down in a puddle around her feet. Bra and panties came next until, a few skilled movements later, Jaz stood naked before Liam and the world.

Before she could fully process how she felt about this, Liam ran his hands along her body. Her breasts. Her hips. "Did you know that sometimes when you change in the morning, I have to hop into a cold shower just to keep myself from losing it?" He trailed his fingers along her middle, then turned her to face the room as he came to stand behind her. Wrapping one hand around her waist, Liam pressed her back against him, letting her feel his erection.

"You enjoy being exposed." Liam didn't word it as a question. He knew, though she'd never told him. Never even told herself. But it was true. The thought of others' attention brushing against her bare skin, watching as Liam took charge of her body, was sending pulses of primal excitement through her with every squeeze of her heart. *Swoosh. Swoosh. Swoosh.* The discovery of how much she liked this forbidden pleasure was uncomfortable.

"It's the danger of it," Liam whispered to her, as if reading her thoughts. "You don't know what they might see exactly. You like edging danger."

Danger. Yes. Sensual, exhilarating danger. It was like skydiving with sensuality. Down to her racing pulse, to trusting Liam to take her into the abyss. *Swoosh. Swoosh. Swoosh.*

Jaz closed her eyes against the onslaught of emotion and

concentrated on the feeling of Liam's callused fingers waking her body more to his presence.

He chuckled into her ear. "One of the things I love most about your body is how honest it is. How responsive. Let me show you."

Before Jaz could fully process the meaning behind Liam's words, he dropped his hand and slid two fingers easily into her slick channel.

Jaz gasped, rising to her toes, a pang of indignation shooting through her—followed by an equally strong pang of pleasure. Her breath quickened, her channel tightening over the intrusion. Before she could get accustomed to the sensation, though, Liam pulled his hand free and showed off the sparkling wetness coating his skin.

"I think we're on the right track," he said, stepping in front of her and sucking his fingers clean. With his feet planted at shoulder width, he looked confident and in charge of the world, with his attention centered fully and undilutedly on Jaz. His mouth curved appreciatively as his hands roamed her skin again, stopping to massage her breasts and run his thumbs around her beading nipples. "One small adjustment, though."

Setting his foot between Jaz's legs, he pushed them wide apart.

Cool air brushed her sex, her reflexive attempt to close herself meeting with Liam's braced knees and a swift warning swat on her backside. The sharp sting made her cheeks clench together, a rush of heat flaring through her core as several people turned their heads at the sound.

Oh God. They saw. They all saw that. Ignoring better reason, Jaz's arousal ratcheted another notch.

Liam rested his hand on her ass again. "Shall I continue here, or will you keep your legs spread?" he asked just loudly enough for the onlookers to hear.

Unable to bring herself to answer over her pounding need, she inched her feet farther apart.

Liam hummed appreciatively, then ran two fingers skillfully between her slippery folds, tracing the hood of her quickly swelling clit. His next words came for her ears alone. "Given that you're restrained and utterly open to me, I think we can both agree that whatever I do next is by my choice. *This* is what brings me pleasure, Sprite. Not anything else you might have heard. *This.*"

Taking Jaz's breast into his mouth, Liam sucked on the nipple until the sensitive skin tightened to a peak, then repeated the treatment on the other side. Down below, his hand stroked her folds in maddening harmony to the insistent suckles above. Forward and back, forward and back, until her hips thrust toward him greedily, her toes so tightly curled inside her sandals that her thighs shook.

Jaz's pulse pounded. She pulled against the unyielding restraint, her emotions spinning at the intoxicating focus of Liam's attention. At his touch. At the mix of desire and frustration. "All right," she breathed. "I believe you. Okay. You can stop."

"Oh no. Not even close. I want you to be sure. And we still have that riding crop to try." Liam teased Jaz's hood to emphasize his last words, his finger oh so casually flicking over her clit again as his teeth closed lightly over a tender nipple.

The tiny sting of pain morphed into a scalding pleasure that washed through her like a storm whose force drowned out that tiny judgmental voice insisting how *wrong* everything about this naked, exposed enjoyment was.

Releasing her nipple, Liam soothed it with little laps of his tongue that started to drop lower and lower along her Jaz's flesh. Once Liam was on one knee, he gripped the insides of her wet thighs. With his strong hands keeping her utterly open, he swirled his tongue over her clit.

A cry of rising frustration escaped Jaz's chest, her engorged clit pulsating so hard that she couldn't stand the pressure. And yet, with Liam's restraint, she couldn't escape it either. Could do nothing but feel. Shutting her eyes tightly, she clung to the scarf binding her wrists, her fingers wrapping about the cloth.

Lap. Lap. Lap.

She panted, reaching for the approaching abyss. Sweat trickled down her temples. Along her naked flesh. Then Liam's tongue caressed the whole length of her sex before he took her clit tightly between his teeth.

And sucked.

Every muscle in Jaz's body tightened. Waves of pleasure so intense they hurt raced through her, the climax coming again and again with unapologetic fury. Her legs buckled and gave out until only Liam's hold kept her upright, holding her tight through the exquisite spasms.

Heartbeats passed as Jaz sagged in his arms, breathing in his clean scent. By the time he slowly let her take her own weight again, she felt a drunken satisfaction settle over her.

"That was…" She didn't know what she wanted to say and frowned at the sudden difficulty in choosing words. "That was…um…"

"The beginning," Liam said, taking Jaz's sentence in a different direction as he picked up the riding crop Dior must have delivered. "Brace yourself, Sprite."

Before Jaz could protest, Liam adjusted her stance so her backside was jutting out. A fact that she should care about but did not. Especially not when he started tapping the flat part of the crop all along her skin, rousing her nerves. Sliding it along the slippery wetness between her folds. Slapping the wet leather against her vulnerable ass until her whole body reawakened and turned taut.

Just as the mounting need, punctuated with forceful waves of hot pleasure, approached the pinnacle, Liam suddenly stopped. Tossing aside the crop, he came to stand in front of her, his gaze studying her intently. Like her own breath, his was quick with arousal, and the bulge at the front of his jeans twitched visibly.

"It's up to you how we finish," Liam said. Reaching up, he pulled open the silk scarf binding Jaz's hands. The knot slipped, the silk unraveling to the floor as he traced a thumb along her cheek, a slight tremble to his hand. "Up to you *whether* we finish."

Liam's cockiness was gone now, and Jaz knew that even as he'd taken her on a journey, he'd gone on one himself as well. That it took all his willpower to now hand over the reins. Though Jaz was the one without clothes, at this moment it was Liam who was the more naked of the two as he stood in judgment before her. And they both knew it. Because this was about so much more than sex.

"You've let me bring you here. Let me show you my games in

action. Let me take charge of your body and your pleasure." Liam's strained whisper filled the air between them. "The Cove doesn't matter to me. What matters—the only thing that matters—is whether you still think that I have any desire to hurt you." He dropped his hands to his sides and raised his chin, visibly bracing himself for whatever verdict she'd deliver.

In answer, Jaz stepped forward without hesitation and opened Liam's zipper.

His cock sprang out so forcefully that the bit of moisture beading on its tip flew through the air.

Liam exhaled audibly. "Thank fucking God."

"God can wait his turn," said Jaz. "It's me who needs fucking now."

Liam grinned and pulled a condom from his back pocket. He sheathed himself quickly before hoisting Jaz onto his hips and taking her against the wall. After the teasing play, the feel of his cock filling her channel was ecstasy. The missing piece that made her whole.

Despite the strain of need on his beautiful, strong face, Liam didn't rush their coupling. He thrust deeply, perfectly, in the rhythm of their bodies. Each time the large head of his shaft slid along her channel, Jaz felt a jolt of sensation zapping through her nerves. Little shocks of pure pleasure, punctuated by the thump of his sac against her skin.

Thrust. Thrust. Thrust.

Jaz dug her fingers into Liam's shoulders, everything inside her coiling tighter and tighter. The arousal climbing higher and higher. Until it was impossible to hold off from falling into the gaping abyss. She screamed as her climax seized her, every fiber in her body tightening at once. Agonizing waves of pleasure rippled from her sex, raking across her back and legs until even her toes felt the unyielding rush of release.

She heard Liam cry her name as he climaxed right along with her, the pair of them tumbling together into oblivion.

EPILOGUE. LIAM

*L*iam paused just outside the newly furnished training room at the Rescue and unobtrusively watched his tiny fiancée demonstrate a complex set of knots to an attentive audience of three former special forces operatives. The sprite was in her element, talking enthusiastically about rope bends and bites. The way she presented the class made it impossible to be anything less than mesmerized.

Liam scowled, an absurd possessiveness rushing over him. The three men had better contain their *mesmerization* to the knots and ropes, and away from Jaz. He shook his head at himself. It was utterly illogical to expect the men not to look at their teacher. It was just hard to imagine anyone watching Jaz lead a group and not fall in love with her. Hell, Liam had already passed the class—she'd made him take it, CEO of Trident or not—and was tempted to step farther into the shadows and watch her demonstrate all over again just to see her face animated with excitement and passion.

Also, time was currently of the essence, and Jaz would eviscerate him if they missed the arrival of Eli and Dani's second baby. From the way Aiden had described things—he'd been in the middle of a therapy session with Dani when she went into labor—things were progressing quickly.

Liam knocked.

Jaz glanced his way, her face lighting as she fingered the engagement ring on her finger. Liam had it commissioned to look like a climbing knot with a diamond in the middle, and it suited her perfectly. Six months ago, if anyone had said that Kyan's little sister would be anything but pissed at an interruption from Liam, he'd have laughed in their face. It was different now. Somehow, she found him deserving of her.

"Excuse me for a moment," Jaz told the class and headed for the door.

The three men rose in unison.

Jaz blushed a shade of burgundy. "I'm not... You guys really don't need to, you know...do that."

The men continued to stand at attention, their eyes forward—though Liam could see the small twitches at the corners of their mouths as they worked to conceal their grins. As Liam had predicted, the men—being trained special forces operators—had quickly recognized Jaz's competence. Likewise—again, being special forces operators—they couldn't let someone they liked go without a bit of friendly teasing and had ferreted out the sprite's weak point in a matter of weeks.

Now, whenever she ran a class or meeting, the men pulled out full military courtesies. And it never failed to make Jaz blush. Especially when someone else was watching.

Unable to leave them standing there, Jaz turned about. "Listen, why don't you guys go and practice with the anchor setup? We've got the new gear that just came in for testing, and you can tell me if you like the feel."

"Ma'am, yes, ma'am," the three intoned in unison.

Jaz groaned.

Liam laughed.

"Not funny." Striding over, she poked her finger into the middle of his chest.

"No, of course not. Well…maybe just a little amusing."

Jaz growled softly, which was, of course, way too much to resist. Leaning forward, Liam captured her bottom lip between his teeth and took a long luxurious kiss, losing himself in Jaz's sweetness—right up until the phone in his pocket started to vibrate, reminding him of exactly why he'd come to interrupt her class.

"Dani is in labor," he told her, pulling away.

Jaz looked disoriented for a second, then her eyes widened as she grabbed the tops of Liam's arms. "Now? Already? Why didn't you tell me sooner? Ivy said second babies come quickly." Her earlier blushing forgotten, Jaz stuck her head into the classroom long enough to rattle off instructions, then whizzed past Liam into the car. "You know the aggressive driving they taught you in army school? You better start using it."

"You mean defensive driving and the navy?" Liam started up the car.

"I don't care what you call it, but I'll kill you if we're late."

By the time they reached Denton Memorial, everyone else of their makeshift family was already there, including Bumblebee, who lay with his head on his paws and kept a careful eye on his toddling charge, Bar.

"They let you bring a dog in here?" Liam asked.

"Cullen pretty much owning the hospital has its advantages," said Eli, obliging little Ella's demand to be taken off his shoulders and passed to Liam's. "Not that it stopped Dani from ordering me out of the room."

"What? Why?" Liam swung the giggling girl around as he frowned at his friend. Unlike Liam could ever hope to be, Eli was an amazing father.

"I believe the woman's exact words were 'Get out of here, you bloody annoying Brit, and don't come back until you have your head glued on straight,'" Aiden put in helpfully.

Stepping up, Patti patted Eli's muscled arm. "Eli was maybe just a little too enthusiastic with his concern and encouragement."

With Lisa in rehab in Colorado, Liam's mother had decided

against returning to Ann Arbor and was busily making up for Liam's lost childhood years by adopting all his friends. Making matters worse, instead of discouraging it, Liam's bastard friends had adopted Patti right back. Hell, the assholes even seemed to enjoy having her around, which just figured. Though so far as Liam was aware, not even Patti knew what deal Lisa and Aiden had worked out.

Patti glanced at the closed door to the delivery room. "I think you're safe to make another approach, though. Just remember, she's right and you're wrong. About everything. If she says the sky is purple, you agree. If she's sure the baby has three legs—"

"I say that I've already ordered special shoes." Squaring his shoulders, Eli marched to the door.

Patti smiled at the man's departing back, then glanced back at Liam. "You better be taking notes for when it's your turn."

"Ma…" Liam stepped away, focusing his attention on the little girl on his shoulders to avoid the conversation. Jaz was a bright woman, and she knew Liam too well to want to have children with him. They hadn't said it in so many words, but Liam had made it clear that the choice as to when—and whether—to have children was entirely up to her. One didn't need a psychology degree to know which way that was going to swing.

But that was all right. For reasons unknown, Ella had taken a liking to him, and Liam would be content to be an uncle.

"Do you know where Ivy and Jaz went?" Kyan asked, walking up to him. Behind Kyan, Bar followed along with a decent imitation of his father's confident gait, the image spoiled only slightly by the thumb in the boy's mouth. "And for the record, I still can't believe you're going to be my brother-in-law. I really thought my sister had better taste."

Liam snorted. "Honestly, so did I." He was only half joking. The more time he spent with Jaz, the more disbelieving he became of his own good fortune. "Are they with Dani?"

Kyan shook his head. "I saw whispering, widened eyes, and then they disappeared down the hall. Sky is now running interference for anyone who tries to head that way. I don't know what's going on, but it's making me nervous."

"Can Cullen make Sky talk?"

Kyan raised a brow.

"Right. Stupid question." Liam turned to watch Sky, who was indeed standing nonchalantly in the middle of the hallway. As he watched, the woman pulled out her phone and read something on it, then called Patti over.

Patti looked at the screen, gasped, and turned her back to Liam and Kyan.

"We need to recon," said Liam and swung Ella off his shoulders. Getting down on one knee before the little girl, he re-pigged a loose pigtail and gave the child a serious look. "Listen here, kid. Auntie Sky and Nana Patti are playing keep away. I need you to go, be cute, and find out what they're whispering about. You copy?"

"You *copy?*" said Kyan. "How is she supposed to understand that?"

"Copy that, base command!" Ella retorted. "En route." She paused long enough to stick her tongue out at Kyan and then scampered off, skipping along the checkered tiles.

Kyan whistled.

"Eli has been bringing her to the gym," Liam explained. "We have an understanding." What had started as a favor to a friend had turned into a routine Liam had found himself looking forward to. All logic to the contrary, he discovered he truly enjoyed having a child around. He only hoped the practice wouldn't end now the pregnancy was over.

The girl returned just as Ivy and Jaz herself reappeared in the waiting area.

"Well?" Liam asked Ella.

"Two."

"Two what?"

She shrugged. "Dunno. Just two." She held up her fingers to demonstrate how big a number, lest Liam misunderstood.

Kyan snorted. "Good going there, Commander."

The sudden unmistakable sound of a crying baby echoed from the delivery room, making Liam's throat tighten. Though he was happy for Eli and Dani, he suddenly wished that call was for him. That a little person might enter into the world and trust Liam to lead him through it, the way Liam's own father never had.

He felt Jaz slide her hand into his and swallowed hard. He didn't want to pressure her. Not that she'd give in to something she didn't believe was right.

"It's a boy," Eli announced, peeking out of the delivery room, a tiny bundle in his arms. Joy radiated from the large SEAL, his trained muscles cradling the little child with a practiced gentleness that Liam envied. "None of you vultures get to hold him for another twenty minutes, but you can start queueing up."

"You should get in the queue," Jaz said into Liam's ear. "You need the practice."

"Mmm?" Liam forced his attention away from the door, his mind finally catching up to Jaz's words. "Oh, I don't think Dani is going to let him bring the baby to the gym for a few months at least."

"Right. Um…" She put her hands into her pockets. "I wasn't talking about Eli and Dani."

"I don't follow." He glanced down at Ella, whose lower lip was starting to signal a coming discontent with the turn of events, and picked the girl up quickly. "Do you have any idea what Aunt Jaz is talking about?"

"Two," Ella announced sagely.

"That's exactly right," said Liam, eliciting a grin from the child —and a frown from Jaz.

"Wait, you know it's two?" said Jaz.

"I know it's two. I just don't happen to know what we're counting. Hopefully not apocalypses."

"Well, it depends how you look at things," Jaz said, biting her lip. "In this case, we're counting children. I'm pregnant. With twins."

Liam froze, everything inside him stuttering to an emergency halt before starting up again with a vengeance. "You...you stopped taking birth control?"

Jaz frowned, a worried glance fluttering over her smooth skin. "Yes, of course. I mean you *did* say that you were ready whenever I was, didn't you?"

"I did." He just never thought she'd take him up on it. But she did. She trusted him. A lump formed in Liam's throat, and suddenly, it was hard to swallow. Hard to talk. "So this, um, this wasn't an accident?"

Jaz backed up. "No. Liam... Is this not—"

"It's perfect." He stepped toward her, his breath finally making it into his lungs. "It's more than perfect." Joy, pure liquid joy, rushed through Liam's veins and made his eyes sting. Through blurry vision, he adjusted Ella on his hip and leaned down to cover Jaz's mouth with his. "You're perfect," he whispered against her lips.

You've finished Liam's book, but there are more Tridents to get to know. If you enjoyed this book, you may also like the other stories in the TRIDENT RESCUE Series.

ENEMY ZONE
Cullen and Sky

ENEMY CONTACT
Eli and Dani

ENEMY LINES
Kyan and Ivy

If you are reading this in ebook version, continue on for a FREE preview of ENEMY ZONE.

I know all about guys like Cullen Hunt.
Gorgeous. Wealthy. Powerful.
I just fled New York to escape one.

AVAILABLE HERE IN KINDLE UNLIMITED.

Young Adult Fantasy Novels

TIDES

FIRST COMMAND (Audiobook available)

AIR AND ASH (Audiobook available)

WAR AND WIND (Audiobook available)

SEA AND SAND (Audiobook available)

SCOUT

TRACING SHADOWS (Audiobook available)

UNRAVELING DARKNESS (Audiobook available)

TILDOR

THE CADET OF TILDOR

SIGN UP FOR NEW RELEASE NOTIFICATIONS at https://links.
alexlidell.com/News

ABOUT THE AUTHOR

Alex Lidell is an Amazon KU All Star Top 50 Author Awards winner (July, 2018). Her debut novel, THE CADET OF TILDOR (Penguin, 2013) was an Amazon Breakout Novel Awards finalist. Her Reverse Harem romances, POWER OF FIVE and MISTAKE OF MAGIC, both received Amazon KU Top 100 awards for individual titles.

Alex is an avid horseback rider, a (bad) hockey player, and an ice-cream addict. Born in Russia, Alex learned English in elementary school, where a thoughtful librarian placed a copy of Tamora Pierce's ALANNA in Alex's hands. In addition to becoming the first English book Alex read for fun, ALANNA started Alex's life long love for books. Alex lives in Washington, DC.

Join Alex's newsletter for news, special offers and sneak peeks: https://links.alexlidell.com/News

Find out more on Alex's website: www.alexlidell.com

SIGN UP FOR NEWS AND RELEASE NOTIFICATIONS

Connect with Alex!
www.alexlidell.com
alex@alexlidell.com

Printed in Great Britain
by Amazon